George Moritz Ebers

Homo Sum

A Novel

George Moritz Ebers

Homo Sum
A Novel

ISBN/EAN: 9783337349554

Printed in Europe, USA, Canada, Australia, Japan

Cover: Foto ©Andreas Hilbeck / pixelio.de

More available books at **www.hansebooks.com**

HOMO SUM.

A NOVEL.

BY

GEORGE EBERS.

NEW YORK:
GEORGE MUNRO, PUBLISHER,
17 TO 27 VANDEWATER STREET.

GEORGE EBERS'S WORKS

CONTAINED IN THE SEASIDE LIBRARY (POCKET EDITION):

PREFACE.

In the course of my labors preparatory to writing a history of the Sinaitic peninsula, the study of the first centuries of Christianity for a long time claimed my attention; and in the mass of martyrology, of ascetic writings, and of histories of saints and monks, which it was necessary to work through and sift for my strictly limited object, I came upon a narrative (in Cotelerius Ecclesiæ Grecæ Monumenta) which seemed to me peculiar and touching notwithstanding its improbability. Sinai and the oasis of Pharan which lies at its foot were the scene of action.

When, in my journey through Arabia Petræa, I saw the caves of the anchorites of Sinai with my own eyes and trod their soil with my own feet, that story recurred to my mind, and did not cease to haunt me while I traveled on further in the desert.

A soul's problem of the most exceptional type seemed to me to be offered by the simple course of this little history.

An anchorite, falsely accused instead of another, takes his punishment of expulsion on himself without exculpating himself, and his innocence becomes known only through the confession of the real culprit.

There was a peculiar fascination in imagining what the emotions of a soul might be which could lead to such apathy, to such an annihilation of all sensibility; and while the very deeds and thoughts of the strange cave-dweller grew more and more vivid in my mind, the figure of Paulus took form, as it were as an example, and soon a crowd of ideas gathered round it, growing at last to a distinct entity, which excited and urged me on till I ventured to give it artistic expression in the form of a narrative. I was prompted to elaborate this subject—which had long been shaping itself to perfect conception in my mind as ripe material for a romance—by my readings in Coptic monkish annals, to which I was led by Abel's Coptic studies; and I afterward received a further stimulus from the small but weighty essay by H. Weingarten on the origin of monasticism, in which I still study the early centuries of Christianity, especially in Egypt.

This is not the place in which to indicate the points on which I feel myself obliged to differ from Weingarten. My acute fellow-laborer at Breslau clears away much which does not deserve to remain, but in many parts of his book he seems to me to sweep with too hard a broom.

Easy as it would have been to lay the date of my story in the beginning of the fortieth year of the fourth century instead of the thirtieth, I have forborne from doing so because I feel able to prove with certainty that at the time which I have chosen there were not only heathen recluses in the temples of Serapis but also Christian anchorites; I fully agree with him that the beginnings of organized Christian monasticism can in no case be dated earlier than the year 350.

The Paulus of my story must not be confounded with the "first hermit," Paulus of Thebes, whom Weingarten has with good reason struck out of the category of historical personages. He, with all the figures in this narrative, is a purely fictitious person, the vehicle for an idea, neither more nor less. I selected no particular model for my hero, and I claim for him no attribute but that of his having been possible at the period; least of all did I think of Saint Anthony, who is now deprived even of his distinguished biographer Athanasius, and who is represented as a man of very sound judgment, but of so scant an education that he was master only of Egyptian.

The dogmatic controversies which were already kindled at the time of my story I have, on careful consideration, avoided mentioning. The dwellers on Sinai and in the oasis took an eager part in them at a later date.

That Mount Sinai to which I desire to transport the reader

must not be confounded with the mountain which lies at a long day's journey to the south of it. It is this that has borne the name, at any rate since the time of Justinian; the celebrated convent of the Transfiguration lies at its foot, and it has been commonly accepted as the Sinai of Scripture. In the description of my journey through Arabia Petræa I have endeavored to bring fresh proof of the view, first introduced by Lepsius, that the giant-mountain, now called Serbal, must be regarded as the mount on which the law was given; and was indeed so regarded before the time of Justinian—and not the Sinai of the monks.

As regards the stone house of the senator Petrus, with its windows opening on the street—contrary to eastern custom—I may remark, in anticipation of well-founded doubts, that to this day wonderfully well-preserved, fire-proof walls stand in the oasis of Paran, the remains of a pretty large number of similar buildings.

But these and such external details hold a quite secondary place in this study of a soul. While in my earlier romances the scholar was compelled to make concessions to the poet and the poet to the scholar, in this one I have not attempted to instruct, nor sought to clothe the outcome of my studies in forms of flesh and blood; I have aimed at absolutely nothing but to give artistic expression to the vivid realization of an idea that had deeply stirred my soul. The simple figures whose inmost being I have endeavored to reveal to the reader fill the canvas of a picture where, in the dark background, rolls the flowing ocean of the world's history.

The Latin title was suggested to me by an often used motto which exactly agrees with the fundamental view to which I have been led by my meditations on the mind and being of man; even of those men who deem that they have climbed the very highest steps of that stair which leads into the heavens.

In the "Heautontimorumenos of Terence," Chremes answers his neighbor Menedemus (Act I., Sc. I., v. 25):

"Homo sum; humani nil a me alienum puto," which Donner translates literally:

"I am human; nothing that is human can I regard as alien to me."

But Cicero and Seneca already used this line as a proverb, and in a sense which far transcends that which it would seem to convey in context with the passage whence it is taken; and as I coincide with them, I have transferred it to the title-page of this book with this meaning:

"I am a man; and I feel that I am above all else a man."

LEIPZIG, *November* 11, 1887.

GEORG EBERS.

HOMO SUM.

PART I.

CHAPTER I.

Rocks—naked, hard, red-brown rocks all round; not a bush, not a blade, not a clinging moss such as elsewhere nature has lightly flung on the rocky surface of the heights, as if a breath of her creative life had softly touched the barren stone. Nothing but smooth granite, and above it a sky as bare of cloud as the rocks are of shrubs and herbs.

And yet in every cave of the mountain wall there moves a human life; two small gray birds, too, float softly in the pure, light air of the desert that glows in the noonday sun, and then they vanish behind a range of cliffs, which shuts in the deep gorge as though it were a wall built by man.

There it is pleasant enough, for a spring bedews the stony soil; and there, as wherever any moisture touches the desert, aromatic plants thrive, and umbrageous bushes grow. When Osiris embraced the goddess of the desert—so runs the Egyptian myth—he left his green wreath on her couch.

But at the time and in the sphere where our history moves the old legends are no longer known or are ignored. We must carry the reader back to the beginning of the thirtieth year of the fourth century after the birth of the Saviour, and away to the mountains of Sinai, on whose sacred ground solitary anchorites have for some few years been dwelling—men weary of the world, and vowed to penitence, but as yet without connection or rule among themselves.

Near the spring in the little ravine of which we have spoken grows a many-branched feathery palm, but it does not shelter it from the piercing rays of the sun of those latitudes; it seems only to protect the roots of the tree itself; still the feathered boughs are strong enough to support a small threadbare blue cloth, which projects like a pent-house, screening the face of a girl who lies dreaming, stretched at full length on the glowing stones, while a few yellowish mountain goats spring from stone to stone in search of pasture as gayly as though they found the midday heat pleasant and exhilarating. From time to time

the girl seizes the herdsman's crook that lies beside her, and
calls the goats with a hissing cry that is audible at a consider-
able distance.   A young kid comes dancing up to her.   Few
beasts can give expression to their feelings of delight; but
young goats can.

The girl puts out her bare slim foot, and playfully pushes
back the little kid who attacks her in fun, pushes it again and
again each time it skips forward, and in so doing the shepherdess bends her toes as gracefully as if she wished some looker-on
to admire their slender form.   Once more the kid springs forward, and this time with its head down.   Its brow touches the
sole of her foot, but as it rubs its little hooked nose tenderly
against the girl's foot, she pushes it back so violently that the
little beast starts away, and ceases its game with loud bleating.

It was just as if the girl had been waiting for the right moment to hit the kid sharply; for the kick was a hard one—
almost a cruel one.   The blue cloth hid the face of the maiden,
but her eyes must surely have sparkled brightly when she so
roughly stopped the game.   For a minute she remained motionless; but the cloth, which had fallen low over her face,
waved gently to and fro, moved by her fluttering breath.   She
was listening with eager attention, with passionate expectation;
her convulsively clinched toes betrayed her.

Then a noise became audible; it came from the direction of
the rough stair of unhewn blocks, which led from the steep
wall of the ravine down to the spring.   A shudder of terror
passed through the tender and not yet fully developed limbs
of the shepherdess; still she did not move; the gray birds which
were now sitting on a thorn-bush near her flew up, but they
had merely heard a noise, and could not distinguish who it was
that it announced.

The shepherdess's ear was sharper than theirs.   She heard
that a man was approaching, and well knew that one only
trod with such a step.   She put out her hand for a stone that
lay near her, and flung it into the spring so that the waters immediately became troubled; then she turned on her side, and
lay as if asleep with her head on her arm.   The heavy steps
became more and more distinctly audible.

A tall youth was descending the rocky stair; by his dress he
was seen to be one of the anchorites of Sinai, for he wore nothing but a shirt-shaped garment of coarse linen, which he
seemed to have outgrown, and raw leather sandals, which were
tied on to his feet with fibrous palm bast.

No slave could be more poorly clothed by his owner, and yet
no one would have taken him for a bondman, for he walked

erect and self-possessed. He could not be more than twenty
years of age; that was evident in the young soft hair on his
upper lip, chin, and cheeks; but in his large blue eyes there
shone no light of youth, only discontent, and his lips were
firmly closed as if in defiance.

He now stood still, and pushed back from his forehead the
superabundant and unkempt brown hair that flowed round his
head like a lion's mane; then he approached the well, and as
he stooped to draw the water in the large dried gourd shell
which he held, he observed first that the spring was muddy,
and then perceived the goats, and at last their sleeping mistress.

He impatiently set down the vessel and called the girl loudly, but she did not move till he touched her somewhat roughly
with his foot. Then she sprung up as if stung by an asp, and
two eyes as black as night flashed at him out of her dark young
face; the delicate nostrils of her aquiline nose quivered, and
her white teeth gleamed as she cried:

"Am I a dog that you wake me in this fashion?"

He colored, pointed sullenly to the well and said, sharply:
"Your cattle have troubled the water again; I shall have to
wait here till it is clear and I can draw some."

"The day is long," answered the 'shepherdess; and while she
rose she pushed, as if by chance, another stone into the water.

Her triumphant, flashing glance as she looked down into the
troubled spring did not escape the young man, and he exclaimed, angrily:

"He is right! You are a venomous snake—a demon of
hell."

She raised herself and made a face at him, as if she wished
to show him that she really was some horrible fiend; the unusual sharpness of her mobile and youthful features gave her a
particular facility for doing so. And she fully attained her
end, for he drew back with a look of horror, stretched out his
arms to repel her, and exclaimed, as he saw her uncontrollable
laughter:

"Back, demon, back! In the name of the Lord! I ask
thee, who art thou?"

"I am Miriam—who else should I be?" she answered,
haughtily.

He had expected a different reply; her vivacity annoyed him,
and he said, angrily: "Whatever your name is you are a fiend,
and I will ask Paulus to forbid you to water your beasts at our
well."

"You might run to your nurse, and complain of me to her

if you had one," she answered, pouting her lips contemptuously at him.

He colored; she went on boldly, and with eager play of gesture.

"You ought to be a man, for you are strong and big, but you let yourself to be kept like a child or a miserable girl; your only business is to hunt for roots and berries, and fetch water in that wretched thing there. I have learned to do that ever since I was as big as that!" and she indicated a contemptibly little measure, with the outstretched pointed fingers of her two hands, which were not less expressively mobile than her features. "Phoh! you are stronger and taller than all the Amalekite lads down there, but you never try to measure yourself with them in shooting with a bow and arrows or in throwing a spear!"

"If I only dared as much as I wish!" he interrupted, and flaming scarlet mounted to his face, "I would be a match for ten of those lean rascals."

"I believe you," replied the girl, and her eager glance measured the youth's broad breast and muscular arms with an expression of pride. "I believe you, but why do you not dare? Are you the slave of that man up there?"

"He is my father, and besides—"

"What besides?" she cried, waving her hand as if to wave away a bat. "If no bird ever flew away from the nest there would be a pretty swarm in it. Look at my kids there—as long as they need their mother they run about after her, but as soon as they can find their food alone they seek it wherever they can find it, and I can tell you the yearlings there have quite forgotten whether they sucked the yellow dam or the brown one. And what great things does your father do for you?"

"Silence!" interrupted the youth, with excited indignation. "The Evil One speaks through thee. Get thee from me, for I dare not hear that which I dare not utter."

"Dare, dare, dare!" she sneered. "What do you dare, then? not even to listen!"

"At any rate not to what you have to say, you goblin!" he exclaimed, vehemently. "Your voice is hateful to me, and if I meet you again by the well I will drive you away with stones."

While he spoke thus she stared speechless at him, the blood had left her lips, and she clinched her small hands. He was about to pass her to fetch some water, but she stepped into his path, and held him spell-bound with the fixed gaze of her eyes.

A cold chill ran through him when she asked him, with trembling lips and a smothered voice: "What harm have I done you?"

"Leave me!" said he, and he raised his hand to push her away from the water.

"You shall not touch me," she cried, beside herself. "What harm have I done you?"

"You know nothing of God," he answered, "and he who is not of God is of the devil."

"You do not say that of yourself," answered she, and her voice recovered its tone of light mockery. "What they let you believe pulls the wires of your tongue just as a hand pulls the strings of a puppet. Who told you that I was of the devil?"

"Why should I conceal it from you?" he answered, proudly. "Our pious Paulus warned me against you, and I will thank him for it. 'The Evil One,' he says, 'looks out of your eyes,' and he is right, a thousand times right. When you look at me I feel as if I could tread everything that is holy under foot; only last night again I dreamed I was whirling in a dance with you—"

At these words all gravity and spite vanished from Miriam's eyes; she clapped her hands and cried: "If it had only been the fact and not a dream! Only do not be frightened again, you fool! Do you know, then, what it is when the pipes sound, and the lutes tinkle, and our feet fly round in circles as if they had wings?"

"The wings of Satan," Hermas interrupted, sternly. "You are a demon, a hardened heathen."

"So says our pious Paulus," laughed the girl.

"So say I too," cried the young man. "Who ever saw you in the assemblies of the just? Do you pray? Do you ever praise the Lord and our Saviour?"

"And what should I praise them for?" asked Miriam. "Because I am regarded as a foul fiend by the most pious among you, perhaps?"

"But it is because you are a sinner that Heaven denies you its blessing."

"No—no, a thousand times no!" cried Miriam. "No god has ever troubled himself about me. And if I am not good, why should I be when nothing but evil ever has fallen to my share? Do you know who I am and how I became so? I was wicked, perhaps, when both my parents were slain in their pilgrimage hither? Why, I was then no more than six years old, and what is a child of that age! But I still very well remem-

ber that there were many camels grazing near our house, and
horses, too, that belonged to us, and that on a hand that often
caressed me—it was my mother's hand—a large jewel shone.
I had a black slave, too, that obeyed me; when she and I did
not agree I used to hang on to her gray woolly hair and beat
her. Who knows what may have become of her? I did not
love her, but if I had her now, how kind I would be to her.
And now for twelve years I myself have eaten the bread of
servitude, and have kept Senator Petrus's goats, and if I ventured to show myself at a festival among the free maidens, they
would turn me out and pull the wreath out of my hair. And
am I to be thankful? What for, I wonder? And pious?
What god has taken any care of me? Call me an evil demon
—call me so! But if Petrus and your Paulus there say that
He who is up above us and who let me grow up to such a lot
is good, they tell a lie. God is cruel, and it is just like Him
to put it into your heart to throw stones and scare me away
from your well."

With these words she burst out into bitter sobs, and her
features worked with various and passionate distortion.

Hermas felt compassion for the weeping Miriam. He had
met her a hundred times and she had shown herself now
haughty, now discontented, now exacting, and now wrathful,
but never before soft or sad. To-day, for the first time, she
had opened her heart to him; the tears which disfigured her
countenance gave her character a value which it had never before had in his eyes, and when he saw her weak and unhappy
he felt ashamed of his hardness. He went up to her kindly
and said:

"You need not cry; come to the well again always, I will
not prevent you."

His deep voice sounded soft and kind as he spoke, but she
sobbed more passionately than before, almost convulsively, and
she tried to speak but she could not. Trembling in every
slender limb, shaken with grief, and overwhelmed with sorrow, the slight shepherdess stood before him, and he felt as if
he must help her. His passionate pity cut him to the heart
and fettered his by no means ready tongue.

As he could find no word of comfort, he took the water-
gourd in his left hand and laid his right, in which he had
hitherto held it, gently on her shoulder. She started, but
she let him do it; he felt her warm breath; he would have
drawn back, but he felt as if he could not; he hardly knew
whether she were crying or laughing while she let his hand rest
on her black waving hair.

She did not move. At last she raised her head, her eyes flashed into his, and at the same instant he felt two slender arms clasped round his neck. He felt as if a sea were roaring in his ears, and fire blazing in his eyes. A nameless anguish seized him; he tore himself violently free, and with a loud cry, as if all the spirits of hell were after him, he fled up the steps that led from the well, and heeded not that his water-jar was shattered into a thousand pieces against the rocky wall.

She stood looking after him as if spell-bound. Then she struck her slender hand against her forehead, threw herself down by the spring again and stared into space; there she lay motionless, only her mouth continued to twitch.

When the shadow of the palm-tree grew longer she sprung up, called her goats and looked up, listening, to the rock-steps by which he had vanished; the twilight is short in the neighborhood of the tropics, and she knew that she would be overtaken by the darkness on the stony and fissured road down the valley if she lingered any longer. She feared the terrors of the night, the spirits and demons, and a thousand vague dangers whose nature she could not have explained even to herself; and yet she did not stir from the spot nor cease listening and waiting for his return till the sun had disappeared behind the sacred mountain, and the glow in the west had paled.

All around was as still as death; she could hear herself breathe, and as the evening chill fell she shuddered with cold.

She now heard a loud noise above her head. A flock of wild mountain goats, accustomed to come at this hour to quench their thirst at the spring, came nearer and nearer, but drew back as they detected the presence of a human being. Only the leader of the herd remained standing on the brink of the ravine, and she knew that he was only awaiting her departure to lead the others down to drink. Following a kindly impulse, she was on the point of leaving to make way for the animals, when she suddenly recollected Hermas's threat to drive her from the well, and she angrily picked up a stone and flung it at the buck, which started and hastily fled. The whole herd followed him. Miriam listened to them as they scuttered away, and then, with her head sunk, she led her flock home, feeling her way in the darkness with her bare feet.

CHAPTER II.

HIGH above the ravine where the spring was lay a level plateau of moderate extent, and behind it rose a fissured cliff of bare, red-brown porphyry. A vein of diorite of iron hard-

ness lay at its foot like a green ribbon, and below this there
opened a small round cavern, hollowed and arched by the cun-
ning hand of nature. In former times wild beasts, panthers
or wolves, had made it their home; it now served as a dwelling
for young Hermas and his father.

Many similar caves were to be found in the holy mountain,
and other anchorites had taken possession of the larger ones
among them.

That of Stephanus was exceptionally high and deep, and yet
the space was but small which divided the two beds of dried
mountain herbs where, on one, slept the father, and on the
other the son.

It was long past midnight, but neither the younger nor the
elder cave-dweller seemed to be sleeping. Hermas groaned
aloud and threw himself vehemently from one side to the other
without any consideration for the old man who, tormented
with pain and weakness, sorely needed sleep. Stephanus meanwhile denied himself the relief of turning over or of sighing,
when he thought he perceived that his more vigorous son had
found rest.

"What could have robbed him of his rest, the boy who
usually slept so soundly, and was so hard to waken?"

"Whence comes it," thought Shephanus, "that the young
and strong sleep so soundly and so much, and the old, who
need rest, and even the sick, sleep so lightly and so little? Is
it that wakefulness may prolong the little term of life, of
which they dread the end? How is it that man clings so
fondly to this miserable existence, and would fain slink away,
and hide himself when the angel calls and the golden gates
open before him? We are like Saul, the Hebrew, who hid himself when they came to him with the crown! My wound burns
painfully; if I only had a drink of water. If the poor child
were not so sound asleep I might ask him for the jar."

Stephanus listened to his son and would not wake him when
he heard his heavy and regular breathing. He curled himself
up shivering under the sheep-skin which covered only half his
body, for the icy night-wind now blew through the opening of
the cave, which by day was as hot as an oven.

Some long minutes wore away; at last he thought he perceived that Hermas had raised himself. Yes, the sleeper must
have wakened, for he began to speak and to call on the name
of God.

The old man turned to his son and began, softly: "Do you
hear me, my boy?"

"I can not sleep," answered the youth.

"Then give me something to drink," asked Stephanus, "my wound burns intolerably."

Hermas rose at once, and reached the water-jar to the sufferer.

"Thanks, thanks, my child," said the old man, feeling for the neck of the jar. But he could not find it, and exclaimed, with surprise:

"How damp and cold it is—this is clay, and our jar was a gourd."

"I have broken it," interrupted Hermas, "and Paulus lent me his."

"Well, well," said Stephanus, anxious for drink; he gave the jar back to his son, and waited till he had stretched himself again on his couch. Then he asked, anxiously:

"You were out a long time this evening, the gourd is broken, and you groaned in your sleep. Whom did you meet?"

"A demon of hell," answerd Hermas. "And now the fiend pursues me into our cave, and torments me in a variety of shapes."

"Drive it out then, and pray," said the old man, gravely. "Unclean spirits flee at the name of God."

"I have called upon Him," sighed Hermas, "but in vain; I see women with ruddy lips and flowing hair, and white marble figures with rounded limbs and flashing eyes beckon to me again and again."

"Then take the scourge," ordered the father, "and so win peace."

Hermas once more obediently rose, and went out into the air with the scourge; the narrow limits of the cave did not admit of his swinging it with all the strength of his arms.

Very soon Stephanus heard the whistle of the leathern thongs through the stillness of the night, their hard blows on the springy muscles of the man, and his son's painful groaning.

At each blow the old man shrunk as if it had fallen on himself. At last he cried, as loud as he was able: "Enough—that is enough."

Hermas came back into the cave, his father called him to his couch, and desired him to join with him in prayer.

After the "Amen" he stroked the lad's abundant hair and said: "Since you went to Alexandria you have been quite another being. I would I had withstood Bishop Agapitus, and forbidden you the journey. Soon, I know, my Saviour will call me to Himself, and no one will keep you here; then the tempter will come to you, and all the splendors of the great

city, which after all only shine like rotten wood, like shining
snakes and poisonous purple berries—"

"I do not care for them," interrupted Hermas; "the noisy
place bewildered and frightened me. Never, never will I
tread the spot again."

"So you have always said," replied Stephanus, "and yet
the journey quite altered you. How often before that I used
to think when I heard you laugh that the sound must surely
please our Father in Heaven. And now? You used to be
like a singing bird, and now you go about silent, you look sour
and morose, and evil thoughts trouble your sleep."

"That is my loss," answered Hermas. "Pray let go of
my hand; the night will soon be past, and you have the whole
livelong day to lecture me in."

Stephanus sighed, and Hermas returned to his couch. .

Sleep avoided them both, and each knew that the other was
awake, and would willingly have spoken to him, but dissatis-
faction and defiance closed the son's lips, and the father was
silent because he could not find exactly the heart-searching
words that he was seeking.

At last it was morning, a twilight glimmer struck through
the opening of the cave, and it grew lighter and lighter in the
gloomy vault; the boy awoke and rose yawning. When he
saw his father lying with his eyes open, he asked, indifferently:
"Shall I stay here or go to morning worship?"

"Let us pray here together," begged the father. "Who
knows how long it may yet be granted to us to do so. I am
not far from the day that no evening ever closes. Kneel down
here, and let me kiss the image of the Crucified."

Hermas did as his father desired him, and as they were end-
ing their song of praise, a third voice joined in the "Amen."

"Paulus!" cried the old man. "The Lord be praised! pray
look to my wound then. The arrow-head seeks to work some
way out, and it burns fearfully."

The new-comer, an anchorite, who for all clothing wore a
shirt-shaped coat of brown undress linen, and a sheep-skin, examined the wound carefully, and laid some herbs on it, mur-
muring meanwhile some pious texts.

"That is much easier," sighed the old man. "The Lord
has mercy on me for your goodness' sake."

"My goodness? I am a vessel of wrath," replied Paulus,
with a deep, rich, sonorous voice, and his peculiarly kind blue
eyes were raised to heaven as if to attest how greatly men were
deceived in him. Then he pushed the bushy grizzled hair,

which hung in disorder over his neck and face, out of his eyes, and said, cheerfully:

"No man is more than man, and many men are less. In the ark there were many beasts, but only one Noah."

"You are the Noah of our little ark," replied Stephanus.

"Then this great lout here is the elephant," laughed Paulus.

"You are no smaller than he," replied Stephanus.

"It is a pity this stone roof is so low, else we might have measured ourselves," said Paulus. "Ay! if Hermas and I were as pious and pure as we are tall and strong, we should both have the key of Paradise in our pockets. You were scourging yourself this night, boy; I heard the blows. It is well; if the sinful flesh revolts, thus we may subdue it."

"He groaned heavily and could not sleep," said Stephanus.

"Ay, did he indeed!" cried Paulus to the youth, and held his powerful arms out toward him with clinched fists; but the threatening voice was loud rather than terrible, and wild as the exceptionally big man looked in his sheep-skin, there was such irresistible kindliness in his gaze and in his voice that no one could have believed that his wrath was in earnest.

"Friends of hell had met him," said Stephanus, in excuse for his son, "and I should not have closed an eye even without his groaning; it is the fifth night."

"But in the sixth," said Paulus, "sleep is absolutely necessary. Put on your sheep-skin, Hermas; you must go down to the oasis to the senator Petrus, and fetch a good sleeping-draught for our sick man from him or from Dame Dorothea, the deaconess. Just look! the youngster has really thought of his father's breakfast—one's own stomach is a good reminder. Only put the bread and the water down here by the couch; while you are gone I will fetch some fresh—now, come with me."

"Wait a minute, wait," cried Stephanus. "Bring a new jar with you from the town, my son. You lent us yours yesterday, Paulus, and I must—"

"I should soon have forgotten it," interrupted the other. "I have to thank the careless fellow, for I have now for the first time discovered the right way to drink, as long as one is well and able. I would not have the jar back for a measure of gold; water has no relish unless you drink it out of the hollow of your hand! The shard is yours. I should be warring against my own welfare if I required it back. God be praised! the craftiest thief can now rob me of nothing save my sheep-skin."

Stephanus would have thanked him, but he took Hermas by the hand, and led him out into the open.

For some time the two men walked in silence over the clefts and bowlders up the mountain side. When they had reached a plateau, which lay on the road that led from the sea over the mountain into the oasis, he turned to the youth, and said:

"If we always considered all the results of our actions there would be no sins committed."

Hermas looked at him inquiringly, and Paulus went on:

"If it had occurred to you to think how sorely your poor father needed sleep, you would have lain still this night."

"I could not," said the youth sullenly. "And you know very well that I scourged myself hardly enough."

"That was quite right, for you deserved a flogging for a misconducted boy."

Hermas looked defiantly at his reproving friend, the flaming color mounting to his cheek, for he remembered the shepherdess's words that he might go and complain to his nurse, and he cried out angrily:

"I will not let any one speak to me so; I am no longer a child."

"Not even your father's?" asked Paulus, and he looked at the boy with such an astonished and inquiring air that Hermas turned away his eyes in confusion.

"It is not right, at any rate, to trouble the last remnant of life of that very man who longs to live for your sake only."

"I should have been very willing to lie still, for I love my father as well as any one else."

"You do not beat him," replied Paulus, "you carry him bread and water, and do not drink up the wine yourself which the bishop sends him home for the Lord's Supper; that is something certainly, but not enough by a long way."

"I am no saint!"

"Nor I neither," exclaimed Paulus; "I am full of sin and weakness. But I know what the love is which is taught us by the Saviour, and that you, too, may know. He suffered on the cross for you and for me, and for all the poor and the vile. Love is at once the easiest and the most difficult of attainments. It requires sacrifice. And you? How long is it now since you last showed your father a cheerful countenance?"

"I can not be a hypocrite."

"Nor need you, but you must love. Certainly it is not by what his hand does but by what his heart cheerfully offers, and by what he forces himself to give up that a man proves his love."

"And is it no sacrifice that I waste all my youth here?" asked the boy.

Paulus stepped back from him a little way, shook his matted head, and said: "Is that it? You are thinking of Alexandria! Ay! no doubt life runs away much quicker there than on our solitary mountain. You do not fancy the tawny shepherd girl, but perhaps some pretty pink and white Greek maiden down there has looked into your eyes?"

"Let me alone about the women," answered Hermas, with genuine annoyance. "There are other things to look at there."

The youth's eyes sparkled as he spoke, and Paulus asked, not without interest: "Indeed?"

"You know Alexandria better than I," answered Hermas, evasively. "You were born there, and they say you had been a rich young man."

"Do they say so?" said Paulus. "Perhaps they are right; but you must know that I am glad that nothing any longer belongs to me of all the vanities that I possessed, and I thank my Saviour that I can now turn my back on the turmoil of men. What was it that seemed to you so particularly tempting in all that whirl?"

Hermas hesitated. He feared to speak, and yet something urged and drove him to say out all that was stirring his soul. If any one of all those grave men who despised the world and among whom he had grown up, could ever understand him, he knew well that it would be . Paulus; Paulus whose rough beard he had pulled when he was little, on whose shoulders he had often sat, and who had proved to him a thousand times how truly he loved him. It is true the Alexandrian was the severest of them all, but he was harsh only to himself. Hermas must once for all unburden his heart, and with sudden decision he asked the anchorite:

"Did you often visit the baths?"

"Often? I only wonder that I did not melt away and fall to pieces in the warm water like a wheaten loaf."

"Why do you laugh at that which makes men beautiful?" cried Hermas, hastily. "Why may Christians even visit the baths in Alexandria, while we up here, you and my father and all anchorites, only use water to quench our thirst. You compel me to live like one of you, and I do not like being a dirty beast."

"None can see us but the Most High," answered Paulus, "and for Him we cleanse and beautify our souls."

"But the Lord gave us our body too," interrupted Hermas.

"It is written that man is the image of God. And we! I appeared to myself as repulsive as a hideous ape when at the great baths by the Gate of the Sun I saw the youths and men with beautifully arranged and scented hair and smooth limbs that shone with cleanliness and purification. And as they went past, and I looked at my mangy sheep-fell, and thought of my wild mane and my arms and feet, which are no worse formed or weaker than theirs were, I turned hot and cold, and I felt as if some bitter drink were choking me. I should have liked to howl out with shame and envy and vexation. I will not be like a monster!"

Hermas ground his teeth as he spoke the last words, and Paulus looked uneasily at him as he went on:

"My body is God's as much as my soul is, and what is allowed to the Christians in the city—"

"That we nevertheless may not do," Paulus interrupted gravely. "He who has once devoted himself to Heaven must detach himself wholly from the charm of life, and break one tie after another that binds him to the dust. I, too, once upon a time have anointed this body, and smoothed this rough hair, and rejoiced sincerely over my mirror; but I say to you, Hermas—and, by my dear Saviour, I say it only because I feel it, deep in my heart I feel it—to pray is better than to bathe, and I, poor wretch, have been favored with hours in which my spirit has struggled free, and has been permitted to share as an honored guest in the festal joys of heaven!"

While he spoke his wide open eyes had turned toward heaven and had acquired a wondrous brightness.

For a short time the two stood opposite each other silent and motionless; at last the anchorite pushed the hair from off his brow, which was now for the first time visible. It was well-formed, though somewhat narrow, and its clear fairness formed a sharp contrast to his sunburned face.

"Boy," he said with a deep breath, "you know not what joys you would sacrifice for the sake of worthless things. Long ere the Lord calls the pious man to heaven, the pious has brought heaven down to earth in himself."

Hermas well understood what the anchorite meant, for his father often for hours at a time gazed up into heaven in prayer, neither seeing nor hearing what was going on around him, and was wont to relate to his son, when he awoke from his ecstatic vision, that he had seen the Lord or heard the angel choir.

He himself had never succeeded in bringing himself into such a state, although Stephanus had often compelled him to remain on his knees praying with him for many interminable hours. It often happened that the old man's feeble flame of life had threatened to become altogether extinct after these deeply soul-stirring exercises, and Hermas would gladly have forbidden him giving himself up to such hurtful emotions, for he loved his father; but they were looked upon as special manifestations of grace, and how should a son dare to express his aversion to such peculiarly sacred acts? But to Paulus, and in his present mood, he found courage to speak out.

"I have sure hope of Paradise," he said, "but it will be first opened to us after death. The Christian should be patient; why can you not wait for heaven till the Saviour calls you, instead of desiring to enjoy its pleasures here on earth? This first and that after! Why should God have bestowed on us the gifts of the flesh if not that we may use them? Beauty and strength are not empty trifles, and none but a fool gives noble gifts to another only in order to throw them away."

Paulus gazed in astonishment at the youth, who up to this moment had always unresistingly obeyed his father and him, and he shook his head as he answered:

"So think the children of this world who stand far from the Most High. In the image of God are we made no doubt, but what child would kiss the image of his father when the father offers him his own living lips?"

Paulus had meant to say "mother" instead of "father," but he remembered in time that Hermas had early lost the happiness of caressing a mother, and had hastily amended the phrase. He was one of those to whom it is so painful to hurt another that they never touch a wounded soul unless to heal it, divining the seat of even the most hidden pain.

He was accustomed to speak but little, but now he went on eagerly:

"By so much as God is far above our miserable selves, by so much is the contemplation of Him worthier of the Christian than that of his own person. Oh! who is indeed so happy as to have wholly lost that self and to be perfectly absorbed in God! But it pursues us, and when the soul fondly thinks itself already blended in union with the Most High it cries out, 'Here am I!' and drags our nobler part down again into the dust. It is bad enough that we must hinder the flight of the soul, and are forced to nourish and strengthen the perishable part of our being with bread and water and slothful sleep, to the injury of the immortal part, however much we may fast and watch. And shall we indulge the flesh, to the detriment of the spirit, by granting it any of its demands that can be easily denied? Only he who despises and sacrifices his wretched self can, when he has lost his baser self, by the Redeemer's grace, find himself again in God."

Hermas had listened patiently to the anchorite, but he now shook his head, and said:

"I can not understand either you or my father. So long as I walk on this earth I am I and no other. After death, no doubt, but not till then, will a new and eternal life begin."

"Not so," cried Paulus, hastily, interrupting him. "That other and higher life of which you speak does not begin only after death for him who while yet he lives does not cease from dying, from mortifying the flesh, and from subduing its lusts, from casting from him the world and his baser self, and from seeking the Lord. It has been vouchsafed to many even in the midst of life to be born again to a higher existence. Look at me, the basest of the base. I am not two but one, and yet am I in the sight of the Lord as certainly another man than I was before grace found me, as this young shoot, which has grown from the roots of an overthrown palm-tree is another tree than the rotten trunk. I was a heathen and enjoyed every pleasure of the earth to the utmost; then I became a Christian; the grace of the Lord fell upon me, and I was born again, and became a child again, but this time—the Reedeemer be praised!—the child of the Lord. In the midst of life I died, I rose again, I found the joys of heaven. I had been Menander, and like unto Saul I became Paulus. All that Menander loved—baths, feasts, theaters, horses and chariots, games in the arena, anointed limbs, roses and garlands, purple garments, wine and the love of women—lie behind me like some foul bog out of which a traveler has struggled with difficulty. Not a vein of the old man survives in the new, and a new life has begun for me, midway to the grave; nor for me only, but for all pious men. For you, too, the hour will sound, in which you will die too—"

"If only I, like you, had been a Menander," cried Hermas, sharply interrupting the speaker. "How is it possible to cast away that which I never possessed? In order to die one first must live. This wretched life seems to me contemptible, and I am weary of running after you like a calf after a cow. I am free-born and of noble race; my father himself has told me so, and I am certainly no feebler in body than the citizens' sons in the town with whom I went from the baths to the wrestling-school."

"Did you go the Palæstra?" asked Paulus, in surprise.

"To the wrestling-school of Timagetus," cried Hermas, coloring. "From outside the gate I watched the games of the

youths as they wrestled and threw heavy disks at a mark.
My eyes almost sprung out of my head at the sight, and I
could have cried out aloud with envy and vexation at having
to stand there in my ragged sheep-skin excluded from all competition. If Pachomius had not just then come up, by the
Lord I must have sprung into the arena, and have challenged
the strongest of them all to wrestle with me, and I could have
thrown the disk much further than the scented puppy who
won the victory and was crowned."

"You may thank Pachomius," said Paulus, laughing, "for
having hindered you, for you would have earned nothing in
the arena but mockery and disgrace. You are strong enough,
certainly, but the art of the discobolus must be learned like
any other. Hercules himself would be beaten at that game
without practice, and if he did not know the right way to
handle the disk."

"It would not have been the first time I had thrown one,"
cried the boy. "See what I can do!" With these words he
stooped and raised one of the flat stones, which lay piled up
to secure the pathway; extending his arm with all his strength,
he flung the granite disk over the precipice away into the abyss.

"There you see," cried Paulus, who had watched the throw
carefully and not without some anxious excitement. "However strong your arm may be, any novice could throw further
than you if only he knew the art of holding the discus. It is
not so—not so; it must cut through the air like a knife with
its sharp edge. Look how you hold your hand—you throw like
a woman! The wrist straight, and now your left foot behind,
and your knee bent! see, how clumsy you are! Here, give me
the stone. You take the discus so, then you bend your body,
and press down your knees like the arc of a bow, so that every
sinew in your body helps to speed the shot when you let go.
Ay—that is better, but it is not quite right yet. First heave
the discus with your arm stretched out, then fix your eye on
the mark; now swing it out high behind you—stop! once
more! your arm must be more strongly strained before you
throw. That might pass, but you ought to be able to hit the
palm - tree yonder. Give me your discus and that stone.
There, the unequal corners hinder its flight—now pay attention!" Paulus spoke with growing eagerness, and now he
grasped the flat stone, as he might have done many years since
when no youth in Alexandria had been his match in throwing
the discus.

He bent his knees, stretched out his body, gave play to his
wrist, extended his arm to the utmost, and hurled the stone

into space, while the clinched toes of his right foot deeply
dinted the soil.

But it fell to the ground before reaching the palm, which
Paulus had indicated as the mark.

"Wait!" cried Hermas. "Let me try now to hit the tree."

His stone whistled through the air, but it did not even reach
the mound into which the palm-tree had struck root.

Paulus shook his head disapprovingly, and in his turn seized
a flat stone; and now an eager contest began. At every throw
Hermas's stone flew further, for he copied his teacher's action
and grasp with increasing skill, while the older man's arm
began to tire. At last Hermas for the second time hit the
palm-tree, while Paulus had failed to reach even the mound
with his last fling.

The pleasure of the contest took stronger possession of the
anchorite; he flung his raiment from him, and seizing another
stone he cried out—as though he were standing once more in
the wrestling-school among his old companions, all shining with
their anointment:

"By the silver-bowed Apollo, and the arrow-speeding Arte-
mis, I will hit the palm-tree."

The missile sung through the air, his body sprung back, and
he stretched out his left arm to save his tottering balance;
there was a crash, the tree quivered under the blow, and
Hermas shouted, joyfully:

"Wonderful! wonderful! that was indeed a throw. The
old Menander is not dead! Farewell—to-morrow we will try
again."

With these words Hermas quitted the anchorite, and hastened
with wide leaps down the hill in the oasis.

Paulus started at the words like a sleep-walker who is suddenly wakened by hearing his name called. He looked about
him in bewilderment, as if he had to find his way in some
strange world. Drops of sweat stood on his brow, and with
sudden shame he snatched up his garments that were lying on
the ground, and covered his naked limbs.

For some time he stood gazing after Hermas, then he clasped
his brow in deep anguish, and large tears ran down upon his
beard.

"What have I said?" he muttered to himself. "That
every vein of the old man in me was extirpated? Fool! vain
madman that I am. They named me Paulus, and I am in
truth Saul, ay, and worse than Saul!"

With these words he threw himself on his knees, pressing
his forehead against the hard rock, and began to pray. He

felt as if he had been flung from a height on to spears and lances, as if his heart and soul were bleeding, and while he remained there, dissolved in grief and prayer, accusing and condemning himself, he felt not the burning of the sun as it mounted in the sky, heeded not the flight of time, nor heard the approach of a party of pilgrims, who, under the guidance of Bishop Agapitus, were visiting the holy places. The palmers saw him at prayer, heard his sobs, and, marveling at his piety, at a sign from their pastor they knelt down behind him.

When Paulus at last rose he perceived with surprise and alarm the witnesses of his devotions, and approached Agapitus to kiss his robe. But the bishop said:

" Not so; he that is most pious is the greatest among us. My friends, let us bow down before this saintly man!"

The pilgrims obeyed his command. Paulus hid his face in his hands and sobbed out:

." Wretch, wretch that I am!"

And the pilgrims lauded his humility and followed their leader, who left the spot.

CHAPTER III.

HERMAS had hastened onward without delay. He had already reached the last bend of the path he had followed down the ravine, and he saw at his feet the long narrow valley and the gleaming waters of the stream, which here fertilized the soil of the desert. He looked down on lofty palms and tamarisk shrubs innumerable, among which rose the houses of the inhabitants, surrounded by their little gardens and small, carefully irrigated fields; already he could hear the crowing of a cock and the hospitable barking of a dog, sounds which came to him like a welcome from the midst of that life for which he yearned, accustomed as he was to be surrounded day and night by the deep and lonely stillness of the rocky heights.

He stayed his steps, and his eyes followed the thin column of smoke, which floated tremulously up in the clear light of the ever mounting sun from the numerous hearths that lay below him.

" They are cooking breakfast now," thought he, " the wives for their husbands, the mothers for their children, and there, where that dark smoke rises, very likely a splendid feast is being prepared for guests; but I am nowhere at home, and no one will invite me in."

The contest with Paulus had excited and cheered him, but
the sight of the city filled his young heart with renewed bitterness, and his lips trembled as he looked down on his sheep-
skin and his unwashed limbs. With hasty resolve he turned
his back on the oasis and hurried up the mountain. By the
side of the brooklet that he knew of he threw off his coarse
garment, let the cool water flow over his body, washed himself carefully and with much enjoyment, stroked down his
thick hair with his fingers, and then hurried down again into
the valley.

The gorge through which he had descended debouched by a
hillock that rose from the valley plain; a small newly built
church leaned against its eastern declivity, and it was fortified
on all sides by walls and dikes, behind which the citizens
found shelter when they were threatened by the Saracen robbers of the oasis. This hill passed for a particularly sacred
spot. Moses was supposed to have prayed on its summit during the battle with the Amalekites, while his arms were held
up by Aaron and Hur.

But there were other notable spots in the neighborhood of
the oasis. There, further to the north, was the rock whence
Moses had struck the water; there, higher up and more to the
south-east, was the hill where the Lord had spoken to the law-
giver face to face, and where he had seen the burning bush;
there again was the spring where he had met the daughters of
Jethro, Zippora and Ledja, so called in the legend. Pious
pilgrims came to these holy places in great numbers, and
among them many natives of the peninsula, particularly
Nabateans, who had previously visited the holy mountain in
order to sacrifice on its summit to their gods, the sun, moon,
and planets. At the outlet, toward the north, stood a castle,
which ever since the Syrian Prefect, Cornelius Palma, had sub-
dued Arabia Petræa in the time of Trajan, had been held by a
Roman garrison for the protection of the blooming city of the
desert against the incursions of the marauding Saracens and
Blemmyes.

But the citizens of Pharan themselves had taken measures
for the security of their property. On the topmost cliffs of
the jagged crown of the giant mountain—the most favorable
spots for a look-out far and wide—they placed sentinels, who
day and night scanned the distance, so as to give a warning-
signal in case of approaching danger. Each house resembled
a citadel, for it was built of strong masonry, and the younger
men were all well exercised bowmen. The more distinguished
families dwelt near the church-hill, and there, too, stood the

houses of the bishop Agapitus, and of the city councilors of Pharan.

Among these the senator Petrus enjoyed the greatest respect, partly by reason of his solid abilities, and of his possessions in quarries, garden ground, date-palms, and cattle; partly in consequence of the rare qualities of his wife, the deaconess Dorothea, the granddaughter of the long-deceased and venerable Bishop Chæremon, who had fled hither with his wife during the persecution of the Christians under Decius, and who had converted many of the Pharanites to the knowledge of the Redeemer.

The house of Petrus was of strong and well-joined stone, and the palm-garden adjoining was carefully tended. Twenty slaves, many camels, and even two horses belonged to him, and the centurion in command of the Imperial garrison, the Gaul Phœbicius, and his wife Sirona, lived as lodgers under his roof; not quite to the satisfaction of the councilor, for the Centurion was no Christian, but a worshiper of Mithras, in whose mysteries the wild Gaul had risen to the grade of a " Lion," whence his people, and with them the Pharanites in general, were wont to speak of him as " the Lion."

His predecessor had been an officer of much lower rank but a believing Christian, whom Petrus had himself requested to live in his house, and when, about a year since, the Lion Phœbicius had taken the place of the pious Pankratius, the senator could not refuse him the quarters, which had · become a right.

Hermas went shyly and timidly toward the court of Petrus' house, and his embarrassment increased when he found himself in the hall of the stately stone-house, which he had entered without let or hinderance, and did not know which way to turn. There was no one there to direct him, and he dared not go up the stairs which led to the upper story, although it seemed that Petrus must be there. Yes, there was no doubt, for he heard talking overhead and clearly distinguished the senator's deep voice. Hermas advanced, and set his foot on the first step of the stairs; but he had scarcely begun to go up with some decision, and feeling ashamed of his bashfulness, when he heard a door fly open just above him, and from it there poured a flood of fresh laughing children's voices, like a pent up stream when the miller opens the sluice gate.

He glanced upward in surprise, but there was no time for consideration, for the shouting troop of released little ones had already reached the stairs. In front of all hastened a beautiful young woman with golden hair; she was laughing gayly, and held a gaudily dressed doll high above her head. She came backward toward the steps turning her fair face beaming with fun and delight toward the children, who, full of their eager longing, half demanding, half begging, half laughing, half crying, shouted in confusion, "Let us be, Sirona," "Do not take it away again, Sirona," "Do stay here, Sirona," again and again, "Sirona—Sirona."

A lovely six-year-old maiden stretched up as far as she could to reach the round white arm that held the plaything; with her left hand, which was free, she gayly pushed away three smaller children, who tried to cling to her knees, and exclaimed, still stepping backward, "No, no; you shall not have it till it has a new gown; it shall be as long and as gay as the emperor's robe. Let me go, Cæcilia, or you will fall down as naughty Nikon did the other day."

By this time she had reached the steps; she turned suddenly, and with outstretched arms she stopped the way of the narrow stair on which Hermas was standing, gazing open-mouthed at the merry scene above his head. Just as Sirona was preparing to run down, she perceived him and started; but when she saw that the anchorite from pure embarrassment could find no words in which to answer her question as to what he wanted, she laughed heartily again and called out:

"Come up, we shall not hurt you—shall we children?"

Meanwhile Hermas had found courage enough to give utterance to his wish to speak with the senator, and the young woman, who looked with complacency on his strong and youthful frame, offered to conduct him to him.

Petrus had been talking to his grown-up elder sons; they were tall men, but their father was even taller than they, and of unusual breadth of shoulder.

While the young men were speaking he stroked his short gay beard and looked down at the ground in somber gravity, as it might have seemed to the careless observer; but any one who looked closer might quickly perceive that not seldom a pleased smile, though not less often a somewhat bitter one, played upon the lips of the prudent and judicious man. He was one of those who can play with their children like a young mother, take the sorrows of another as much to heart as if they were their own, and yet who look so gloomy, and allow themselves to make such sharp speeches that only those who are on terms of perfect confidence with them, cease to misunderstand them and fear them. There was something fretting the soul of this man, who nevertheless possessed all that could contribute to human happiness. His was a thankful

nature, and yet he was conscious that he might have been
destined to something greater than fate had permitted him to
achieve or to be. He had remained a stone-cutter, but his
sons had both completed their education in good schools in
Alexandria. The elder, Antonius, who already had a house of
his own and a wife and children, was an architect and artist-
mechanic; the younger, Polykarp, was a gifted young sculptor. The noble,church of the oasis city had been built under
the direction of the elder; Polykarp, who had only come home
a month since, was preparing to establish and carry on works
of great extent in his father's quarries, for he had received a
commission to decorate the new court of the Sebasteion or
Cæsareum, as it was called—a grand pile in Alexandria—with
twenty granite lions. More than thirty artists had competed
with him for this work, but the prize was unanimously ad-
judged to his models by qualified judges. The architect whose
function it was to construct the colonnades and pavement of
the court was his friend, and had agreed to procure the blocks
of granite, the flags and the columns which he required from
Petrus's quarries, and not, as had formerly been the custom,
from those of Syene by the first Cataract.

Antonius and Polykarp were now standing with their father
before a large table, explaining to him a plan which they had
worked out together and traced on the thin wax surface of a
wooden tablet. The young architect's proposal was to bridge
over a deep but narrow gorge, which the beasts of burden were
obliged to avoid by making a wide circuit, and so to make a
new way from the quarries to the sea, which should be shorter
by a third than the old one. The cost of this structure would
soon be recouped by the saving in labor, and with perfect certainty, if only the transport-ships were laden at Clysma with a
profitable return freight of Alexandrian manufactures, instead
of returning empty, as they had hitherto done. Petrus, who
could shine as a speaker in the council meetings, in private life
spoke but little. At each of his son's new projects he raised
his eyes to the speaker's face, as if to see whether the young
man had not lost his wits, while his mouth, only half hidden
by his gray beard, smiled approvingly.

When Antonius began to unfold his plan for remedying the
inconvenience of the ravine that impeded the way, the senator
muttered: "Only get feathers to grow on the slaves, and turn
the black ones into ravens and the white ones into gulls, and
then they might fly across. What do not people learn in the
metropolis!"

When he heard the word "bridge" he stared at the young

2

artist. "The only question," said he, "is whether Heaven
will lend us a rainbow." But when Polykarp proposed to get
some cedar trunks from Syria, through his friend in Alexandria,
and when his elder son explained his drawings of the arch with
which he promised to span the gorge and make it strong and
safe, he followed their words with attention; at the same time
he knit his eyebrows as gloomily and looked as stern as if he
were listening to some narrative of crime. Still, he let them
speak on to the end, and though at first he only muttered
that it was mere "fancy-work" or, "Ay, indeed, if I were the
emperor," he afterward asked clear and precise questions, to
which he received positive and well considered answers. Antonius proved by figures that the profit on the delivery of
material for the Cæsareum only would cover more than three-
quarters of the outlay. Then Polykarp began to speak, and
declared that the granite of the Holy Mountain was finer in
color and in larger blocks than that from Syene.

"We work cheaper here than at the Cataract," interrupted
Antonius. "And the transport of the blocks will not come
too dear when we have the bridge and command the road to
the sea, and avail ourselves of the canal of Trajan, which
joins the Nile to the Red Sea, and which in a few months will
again be navigable."

"And if my lions are a success," added Polykarp, "and if
Zenodotus is satisfied with our stone and our work, it may
easily happen that we outstrip Syene in competition, and that
some of the enormous orders that now flow from Constantine's
new residence to the quarries at Syene may find their way to
us."

"Polykarp is not oversanguine," continued Antonius,
"for the emperor is beautifying and adding to Byzantium
with eager haste. Whoever erects a new house has a yearly
allowance of corn, and in order to attract folks of our stamp—
of whom he can not get enough—he promises entire exemption
from taxation to all sculptors, architects, and even to skilled
laborers. If we finish the blocks and pillars here exactly to
the designs, they will take up no superfluous room in the ships,
and no one will be able to deliver them so cheaply as we."

"No, nor so good," cried Polykarp, "for you yourself are
an artist, father, and understand stone-work as well as any
man. I never saw a finer or more equally colored granite
than the block you picked out for my first lion. I am finish-
ing it here on the spot, and I fancy it will make a show. Certainly it will be difficult to take a foremost place among the

noble works of the most splendid period of art, which already
filled the Cæsareum, but I will do my best.''
"The lions will be admirable," cried Antonius, with a
glance of pride at his brother. " Nothing like them has been
done by any one these ten years, and I know the Alexandrians.
If the master's work is praised that is made out of granite
from the Holy Mountain, all the world will have granite from
thence and from nowhere else. It all depends on whether the
transport of the stone to the sea can be made less difficult and
costly."
"Let us try it, then," said Petrus, who during his sons' talk
had walked up and down before them in silence. "Let us try
the building of the bridge, in the name of the Lord. We will
work out the road if the municipality will declare themselves
ready to bear half the cost; not otherwise, and I tell you
frankly, you have both grown most able men."
The younger son grasped his father's hand and pressed it with
warm affection to his lips. Petrus hastily stroked his brown
locks, then he offered his strong right arm to his eldest-born,
and said:
"We must increase the number of our slaves. Call your
mother, Polykarp."
The youth obeyed with cheerful alacrity, and when Dame
Dorothea—who was sitting at the loom with her daughter
Marthana and some of her female slaves—saw him rush into
the women's room with a glowing face, she rose with youthful
briskness in spite of her stout and dignified figure, and called
out to her son:
" He has approved of your plans?"
" Bridge and all, mother—everything," cried the young
man. "Finer granite for my lions than my father has
picked out for me is nowhere to be found, and how glad I
am for Antonius! only we must have patience about the roadway. He wants to speak to you at once."
Dorothea signed to her son to moderate his ecstasy, for he
had seized her hand and was pulling her away with him; but
the tears that stood in her kind eyes testified how deeply she
sympathized in her favorite's excitement.
"Patience, patience, I am coming directly," cried she,
drawing away her hand in order to arrange her dress and her
gray hair, which was abundant and carefully dressed, and
formed a meet setting for her still pleasing and unwrinkled
face.
" I knew it would be so; when you have a reasonable thing
to propose to your father, he will listen to you and agree with

you without any intervention; women should not mix themselves up with men's work. Youth draws a strong bow and often shoots beyond the mark. It would be a pretty thing if out of foolish affection for you I were to try to play the siren that should insnare the steersman of the house—your father—with flattering words. You laugh at the gray-haired siren? But love overlooks the ravages of years and has a good memory for all that once was pleasing. Besides, men have not always wax in their ears when they should have. Come now to your father."

Dorothea went out past Polykarp and her daughter. The former held his sister back by the hand and asked:

"Was not Sirona with you?"

The sculptor tried to appear quite indifferent, but he blushed as he spoke; Marthana observed this and replied, not without a roguish glance:

"She did show us her pretty face; but important business called her away."

"Sirona?" asked Polykarp, incredulously.

"Certainly, why not!" answered Marthana, laughing. "She had to sew a new gown for the children's doll."

"Why do you mock at her kindness?" said Polykarp, reproachfully.

"How sensitive you are!" said Marthana, softly. "Sirona is as kind and sweet as an angel; but you had better look at her rather less, for she is not one of us, and repulsive as the choleric centurion is to me—"

She said no more, for Dame Dorothea, having reached the door of the sitting-room, looked round for her children.

Petrus received his wife with no less gravity than was usual with him, but there was an arch sparkle in his half-closed eyes as he asked:

"You scarcely know what is going on, I suppose?"

"You are madmen, who would fain take Heaven by storm," she answered, gayly.

"If the undertaking fails," said Petrus, pointing to his sons, "those young ones will feel the loss longer than we shall."

"But it will succeed," cried Dorothea. "An old commander and young soldiers can win any battle." She held out her small, plump hand with frank briskness to her husband; he clasped it cheerily and said:

"I think I can carry the project for the road through the senate. To build our bridge we must also procure helping hands, and for that we need your aid, Dorothea. Our slaves will not suffice."

"Wait," cried the lady, eagerly; she went to the window and called: "Jethro, Jethro!"

The person thus addressed, the old house-steward, appeared, and Dorothea began to discuss with him as to which of the inhabitants of the oasis might be disposed to let them have some able-bodied men, and whether it might not be possble to employ one or another of the house-slaves at the building.

All that she said was judicious and precise, and showed that she herself superintended her household in every detail, and was accustomed to command with complete freedom.

"That tall Anubis, then, is really indispensable in the stable?" she asked, in conclusion. The steward, who up to this moment had spoken shortly and intelligently, hesitated to answer; at the same time he looked up at Petrus, who, sunk in the contemplation of the plan, had his back to him; his glance, and a deprecating movement, expressed very clearly that he had something to tell, but feared to speak in the presence of his master. Dame Dorothea was quick of comprehension, and she quite understood Jethro's meaning; it was for that very reason that she said, with more of surprise than displeasure:

"What does the man mean with his winks? What I may hear Petrus may hear too."

The senator turned, and looked at the steward from head to foot with so dark a glance that he drew back and began to speak quickly. But he was interrupted by the children's clamors on the stairs and by Sirona, who brought Hermas to the senator, and said, laughing:

"I found this great fellow on the stairs; he was seeking you."

Petrus looked at the youth, not very kindly, and asked:

"Who are you? what is your business?"

Hermas struggled in vain for speech; the presence of so many human beings, of whom three were women, filled him with the utmost confusion. His fingers twisted the woolly curls on his sheep-skin, and his lips moved but gave no sound; at last he succeeded in stammering out: "I am the son of old Stephanus, who was wounded in the last raid of the Saracens. My father has hardly slept these five nights, and now Paulus has sent me to you—the pious Paulus of Alexandria—but you know—and so I—"

"I see, I see," said Petrus, with encouraging kindness. "You want some medicine for the old man. See, Dorothea,

what a fine young fellow he is grown; this is the little man
that the Antiochian took with him up the mountain."

Hermas colored and drew himself up; then he observed
with great satisfaction that he was taller than the senator's
sons, who were of about the same age as he, and for whom he
had a stronger feeling, allied to aversion and fear, than even
for their stern father. · Polykarp measured him with a glance,
and said aloud to Sirona, with whom he had exchanged a
greeting, and off whom he had never once taken his eyes since
she had come in:

"If we could get twenty slaves with such shoulders as those
we should get on well. There is work to be done here, you
big fellow—"

"My name is not ' fellow,' but Hermas," said the anchorite,
and the veins of his forehead began to swell.

Polykarp felt that his father's visitor was something more
than his poor clothing would seem to indicate, and that he had
hurt his feelings. He had certainly seen some old anchorites,
who led a contemplative and penitential life up on the sacred
mountain, but it had never occurred to him that a strong
youth could belong to the brotherhood of hermits. So he said
to him, kindly:

"Hermas—is that your name? We all use our hands here,
and labor is no disgrace; what is your handicraft?"

This question roused the young anchorite to the highest excitement, and Dame Dorothea, who perceived what was passing in his mind, said, with quick decision:

"He nurses his sick father. That is what you do, my son,
is it not? Petrus will not refuse you his help."

"Certainly not," the senator added; "I will accompany
you by and by to see him. You must know, my children,
that this youth's father was a great lord, who gave up rich
possessions in order to forget the world, where he had gone
through bitter experiences, and to serve God in his own way,
which we ought to respect though it is not our own. Sit down
there, my son. First we must finish some important business,
and then I will go with you."

"We live high up on the mountain," stammered Hermas.

"Then the air will be all the purer," replied the senator.
"But stay—perhaps the old man is alone—no? The good
Paulus, you say, is with him? Then he is in good hands, and
you may wait."

For a moment Petrus stood considering, then he beckoned
to his sons, and said: "Antonius, go at once and see about
some slaves—you, Polykarp, find some strong beasts of burden.

You are generally rather easy with your money, and in this case it is worth while to buy the dearest. The sooner you return well supplied the better. Action must not halt behind decision, but follow it quickly and sharply, as the sound follows the blow. You, Marthana,' mix some of the brown fever-potion, and prepare some bandages; you have the key."

"I will help her," cried Sirona, who was glad to prove herself useful, and who was sincerely sorry for the sick old hermit; besides, Hermas seemed to her like a discovery of her own, for whom she involuntarily felt more consideration since she had learned that he was the son of a man of rank.

While the young women were busy at the medicine cupboard Antonius and Polykarp left the room.

The latter had already crossed the threshold, when he turned once more and cast a long look at Sirona. Then, with a hasty movement, he went on, closed the door, and with a heavy sigh descended the stairs.

As soon as his sons were gone Petrus returned to the steward again.

"What is wrong with the slave Anubis?" he asked.

"He is—wounded, hurt," answered Jethro, "and for the next few days will be useless. The goat-girl Miriam—the wild cat—cut his forehead with her reaping-hook."

"Why did I not hear of this sooner?" cried Dorothea, reprovingly. "What have you done to the girl?"

"We have shut her up in the hay-loft," answered Jethro, "and there she is raging and storming." The mistress shook her head disapprovingly. "The girl will not be improved by that treatment," she said. "Go and bring her to me."

As soon as the attendant had left the room she exclaimed, turning to her husband: "One may well be perplexed about these poor creatures when one sees how they behave to each other. I have seen it a thousand times! No judgment is so hard as that dealt by a slave to slaves!"

Jethro and a woman now led Miriam into the room. The girl's hands were bound with thick cords, and dry grass clung to her dress and rough black hair. A dark fire glowed in her eyes, and the muscles of her face moved incessantly, as if she had St. Vitus's dance. When Dorothea looked at her she drew herself up defiantly and looked round the room, as if to estimate the strength of her enemies.

She then perceived Hermas; the blood left her lips, with a violent effort she tore her slender hands out of the loops that confined them, covering her face with them, and fled to the door. But Jethro put himself in her way, and seized her shoulder with a strong grasp. Miriam shrieked aloud, and the senator's daughter, who had set down the medicines she had had in her hand, and had watched the girl's movements with much sympathy, hastened toward her. She pushed away the old man's hand, and said: "Do not be frightened, Miriam. Whatever you may have done, my father can forgive you."

Her voice had a tone of sisterly affection, and the shepherdess followed Marthana unresistingly to the table, on which the plans for the bridge were lying, and stood there by her side.

For a minute all were silent; at last Dame Dorothea went up to Miriam, and asked: "What did they do to you, my poor child, that you could so forget yourself?"

Miriam could not understand what was happening to her; she had been prepared for scoldings and blows, nay, for bonds and imprisonment, and now these gentle words and kind looks! Her defiant spirit was quelled, her eyes met the friendly eyes of her mistress, and she said, in a low voice:

"He had followed me for such a long time, and wanted to ask you for me as his wife; but I can not bear him—I hate him, as I do all your slaves." At these words her eyes sparkled wildly again, and with her old fire she went on: "I wish I had only hit him with a stick instead of a sickle; but I took what first came to hand to defend myself. When a man touches me—I can not bear it, it is horrible, dreadful! Yesterday I came home later than usual with the beasts, and by the time I had milked the goats, and was going to bed, every one in the house was asleep. Then Anubis met me, and began chattering about love; I repelled him, but he seized me, and held me with his hand here on my head and wanted to kiss me; then my blood rose, I caught hold of my reaping-hook that hung by my side, and it was not till I saw him roaring on the ground that I saw I had done wrong. How it happened I really can not tell—something seemed to rise up in me—something—I don't know what to call it. It drives me on as the wind drives the leaves that lie on the road, and I can not help it. The best thing you can do is to let me die, for then you would be safe once for all from my wickedness, and all would be over and done with."

"How can you speak so?" interrupted Marthana. "You are wild and ungovernable, but not wicked."

"Only ask him!" cried the girl, pointing with flashing eyes to Hermas, who, on his part, looked down at the floor in confusion. The senator exchanged a hasty glance with his wife; they were accustomed to understand each other without speech, and Dorothea said:

"He who feels that he is not what he ought to be, is already on the high-road to amendment. We let you keep the goats because you were always running after the flocks, and never can rest in the house. You are up on the mountain before morning prayer, and never come home till after supper is over, and no one takes any thought for the better part of you. Half of your guilt recoils upon us, and we have no right to punish you. You need not be so astonished; every one sometimes does wrong. Petrus and I are human beings like you, neither more nor less; but we are Christians, and it is our duty to look after the souls which God has intrusted to our care, be they our children or our slaves. You must go no more up the mountain, but shall stay with us in the house. I shall willingly forgive your hasty deed if Petrus does not think it necessary to punish you."

The senator gravely shook his head in sign of agreement, and Dorothea turned to inquire of Jethro:

"Is Anubis badly wounded, and does he need any care?"

"He is lying in a fever and wanders in his talk," was the answer. "Old Praxinoa is cooling his wound with water."

"Then Miriam can take her place and try to remedy the mischief which she was the cause of," said Dorothea. "Half of your guilt will be atoned for, girl, if Anubis recovers under your care. I will come presently with Marthana, and show you how to make a bandage." The shepherdess cast down her eyes, and passively allowed herself to be conducted to the wounded man.

Meanwhile Marthana had prepared the brown mixture. Petrus had his staff and felt hat brought to him, gave Hermas the medicine and desired him to follow him.

Sirona looked after the couple as they went. "What a pity for such a fine lad!" she exclaimed. "A purple coat would suit him better than that wretched sheep-skin."

The mistress shrugged her shoulders, and signing to her daughter, said:

."Come to work, Marthana, the sun is already high. How the days fly! the older one grows the quicker the hours hurry away."

"I must be very young, then," said the centurion's wife, "for in this wilderness time seems to me to creep along frightfully slow. One day is the same as another, and I often feel as if life were standing perfectly still, and my heart pulses with it. What should I be without your house and the children!—always the same mountain, the same palm-trees, the same faces—"

"But the mountain is glorious, the trees are beautiful!" answered Dorothea. "And if we love the people with whom we are in daily intercourse, even here we may be contented and happy. At least we ourselves are, so far as the difficulties of life allow. I have often told you what you want is work."

"Work! but for whom?" asked Sirona. "If indeed I had children like you! Even in Rome I was not happy—far from it; and yet there was plenty to do and to think about. Here a procession, there a theater; but here! And for whom should I dress even? My jewels grow dull in my chest, and the moths eat my best clothes. I am making doll's clothes now of my colored cloak for your little ones. If some demon were to transform me into a hedge-hog or a gray owl, it would be all the same to me."

"Do not be so sinful," said Dorothea, gravely, but looking with kindly admiration at the golden hair and lovely sweet face of the young woman. "It ought to be a pleasure to you to dress yourself for your husband."

"For him!" said Sirona. "He never looks at me, or if he does it is only to abuse me. The only wonder to me is that I can still be merry at all; nor am I, except in your house, and not there even but when I forget him altogether."

"I will not hear such things said—not another word," interrupted Dorothea, severely. "Take the linen and the cooling lotion, Marthana; we will go and bind up Anubis's wound."

CHAPTER IV.

PETRUS went up the mountain side with Hermas. The old man followed the youth, who showed him the way, and as he raised his eyes from time to time, he glanced with admiration at his guide's broad shoulders and elastic limbs. The road grew broader when it reached a little mountain plateau, and from thence the two men walked on side by side, but for some time without speaking, till the senator asked: "How long now has your father lived up on the mountain?"

"Many years," answered Hermas. "But I do not know how many—and it is all one. No one inquires about time up here among us."

"You have been with your father ever since he came?" he asked.

"He never lets me out of his sight," replied Hermas. "I have been only twice into the oasis, even to go to the church."

"Then you have been to no school?"

"To what school should I go! My father has taught me to read the Gospels and I could write, but I have nearly forgotten how. Of what use would it be to me? We live like praying beasts."

Deep bitterness sounded in the last words, and Petrus could see into the troubled spirit of his companion, overflowing as it was with weary disgust, and he perceived how the active powers of youth revolted in aversion against the slothful waste of life to which he was condemned. He was grieved for the boy, and he was not one of those who pass by those in peril without helping them. Then he thought of his own sons, who had grown up in the exercise and fulfillment of serious duties, and he owned to himself that the fine young fellow by his side was in no way their inferior, and needed nothing but to be guided aright. He thoughtfully looked first at the youth and then on the ground, and muttered unintelligible words into his gray beard as they walked along. Suddenly he drew himself up and nodded decisively; he would make an attempt to save Hermas; and, faithful to his own nature, action trod on the heels of resolve. Where the little level ended the road divided; one path continued to lead upward, the other deviated to the valley and ended at the quarries. Petrus was for taking the latter, but Hermas cried out: "That is not the way to our cave; you must follow me."

"Follow thou mé!" replied the senator, and the words were spoken with a tone and expression that left no doubt in the youth's mind as to their double meaning. "The day is yet before us, and we will see what my laborers are doing. Do you know the spot where they quarry the stone?"

"How should I not know it?" said Hermas, passing the senator to lead the way. "I know every path from our mountain to the oasis and to the sea. A panther had its lair in the ravine behind your quarries."

"So we have learned," said Petrus. "The thievish beasts have slaughtered two young camels, and the people can neither catch them in their toils nor run them down with dogs."

"They will leave you in peace now," said the boy, laughing. "I brought down the male from the rock up there with an arrow, and I found the mother in a hollow with her young ones. I had a harder job with her; my knife is so bad, and the copper blade bent with the blow; I had to strangle the gaudy devil with my hands, and she tore my shoulder and bit my arm. Look! there are the scars. But thank God, my wounds heal quicker than my father's. Paulus says I am like an earth-worm; when it is cut in two the two halves say good-

bye to each other, and crawl off sound and gay, one one way,
and the other another way. The young panthers were so
funny and helpless I would not kill them, but I did them up
in my sheep-skin and brought them to my father. He
laughed at the little beggars, and then a Nabatæan took them
to be sold at Clysma to a merchant from Rome. There and at
Byzantium there is a demand for all kinds of living beasts of
prey. I got some money for them, and for the skins of the
old ones, and kept it to pay for my journey when I went with
the others to Alexandria to ask the blessing of the new
Patriarch."

"You went to the metropolis?" asked Petrus. "You saw
the great structures that secure the coast from the inroads of
the sea, the tall Pharos with the far-shining fire, the strong
bridges, the churches, the palaces and temples with their
obelisks, pillars, and beautiful paved courts? Did it never
enter your mind to think that it would be a proud thing to
construct such buildings?"

Hermas shook his head. "Certainly I would rather live in
an airy house with colonnades than in our dingy cavern, but
building would never be in my way. What a long time it
takes to put one stone on another! I am not patient, and
when I leave my father I will do something that shall win me
fame. But there are the quarries—" Petrus did not let his
companion finish his sentence, but interrupted him with all
the warmth of youth, exclaiming:

"And do you mean to say that fame can not be won by the
arts of building? Look there at the blocks and flags, here at
the pillars of hard stone. These are all to be sent to Aila,
and there my son Antonius, the elder of the two that you saw
just now, is going to build a house of God, with strong walls
and pillars, much larger and handsomer than the church in
the oasis, and that is his work, too. He is not much older
than you are, and already he is famous among the people far
and wide. Out of those blocks down there my younger son
Polykarp will hew noble lions, which are destined to decorate
the finest building in the capital itself. When you and I and
all that are now living shall have been long since forgotten,
still it will be said: These are the work of the Master Polykarp,
the son of Petrus, the Pharanite. What he can do is certainly
a thing peculiar to himself. No one who is not one of the
chosen and gifted ones can say, 'I will learn to do that.' But
you have a sound understanding, strong hands and open eyes,
and who can tell what else there is hidden in you? If you
could begin to learn soon it would not yet be too late to make

a worthy master of you, but of course he who would rise so high must not be afraid of work. Is your mind set upon fame? That is quite right, and I am very glad of it; but you must know that he who would gather that rare fruit must water it, as a noble heathen once said, with the sweat of his brow. Without trouble and labor and struggles there can be no victory, and men rarely earn fame without fighting for victory."

The old man's vehemence was contagious; the lad's spirit was roused, and he exclaimed, warmly:

"What do you say—that I am afraid of struggles and trouble?- I am ready to stake everything, even my life, only to win fame. But to measure stone, to batter defenseless blocks with a mallet and chisel, or to join the squares with accurate pains—that does not tempt me. I should like to win the wreath in the Palæstra by flinging the strongest to the ground, or surpass all others as a warrior in battle; my father was a slodier, too, and he may talk as much as he will of 'peace,' and nothing but 'peace,' all the same in his dreams he speaks of bloody strife and burning wounds. If you only cure him I will stay no longer on this lonely mountain, even if I must steal away in secret. For what did God give me these arms, if not to use them?"

Petrus made no answer to these words, which came in a stormy flood from Hermas's lips, but he stroked his gray beard, and thought to himself: "The young of the eagle does not catch flies. I shall never win over this soldier's son to our peaceful handicraft, but he shall not remain on the mountain among these queer sluggards, for there he is being ruined, and yet he is not of a common sort."

When he had given a few orders to the overseer of his workmen, he followed the young man to see his suffering father.

It was now some hours since Hermas and Paulus had left the wounded anchorite, and he still lay alone in his cave. The sun, as it rose higher and higher, blazed down upon the rocks, which began to radiate their heat, and the hermit's dwelling was suffocatingly hot. The pain of the poor man's wound increased, his fever was greater, and he was very thirsty. There stood the jug which Paulus had given him, but it was long since empty, and neither Paulus nor Hermas had come back. He listened anxiously to the sounds in the distance, and fancied at first that he heard the Alexandrian's footstep, and then that he heard loud words and suppressed groans coming from his cave. Stephanus tried to call out, but he himself could hardly hear the feeble sound, which, with his wounded breast and parched mouth, he succeeded in uttering. Then he fain would have prayed, but fearful mental anguish disturbed his devotion. All the horrors of desertion came upon him, and he who had lived a life overflowing with action and enjoyment, with disenchantment and satiety, who now in solitude carried on an incessant spiritual struggle for the highest goal—this man felt himself as disconsolate and lonely as a bewildered child that has lost its mother.

He lay on his bed of pain softly crying, and when he observed by the shadow of the rock that the sun had passed its noonday height, indignation and bitter feeling were added to pain, thirst, and weariness. He doubled his fists and muttered words which sounded like soldiers' oaths, and with them the name now of Paulus, now of his son. At last anguish gained the upper-hand of his anger, and it seemed to him as though he were living over again the most miserable hour of his life, an hour now long since past and gone.

He thought he was returning from a noisy banquet in the palace of the Cæsars. His slaves had taken the garlands of roses and poplar leaves from his brow and breast, and robed him in his night-dress; now, with a silver lamp in his hand he was approaching his bedroom, and he smiled, for his young wife was awaiting him, the mother of his Hermas. She was fair, and he loved her well, and he had brought home witty sayings to repeat to her from the table of the emperor. He, if any one, had a right to smile. Now he was in the anteroom, in which two slave-women were accustomed to keep watch; he found only one, and she was sleeping and breathing deeply; he still smiled as he threw the light upon her face—how stupid she looked with her mouth open! An alabaster lamp shed a dim light in the bedroom. Softly and still smiling he went up to Glycera's ivory couch, and held up his lamp, and stared at the empty and undisturbed bed—and the smile faded from his lips. The smile of that evening came back to him no more through all the long years, for Glycera had betrayed him, and left him—him and her child. All this had happened twenty years since, and to-day all that he had then felt had returned to him, and he saw his wife's empty couch with his " mind's eye " as plainly as he had then seen it, and he felt as lonely and as miserable as in that night. But now a shadow appeared before the opening of the cave, and he breathed a deep sigh as he felt himself released from the hideous vision, for he had recognized Paulus, who came up and knelt down beside him.

" Water, water!" Stephanus implored in a low voice, and
Paulus, who was cut to the heart by the moaning of the old
man, which he had not heard till he entered the cave, seized
the pitcher. He looked into it, and, finding it quite dry, he
rushed down to the spring as if he were running for a wager,
filled it to the brim and brought it to the lips of the sick man,
who gulped the grateful drink down with deep draughts, and
at last exclaimed, with a sigh of relief: " That is better; why
were you so long away? I was so thirsty!' Paulus, who had
fallen again on his knees by the old man, pressed his brow
against the couch, and made no reply. Stephanus gazed in
astonishment at his companion, but perceiving that he was
weeping passionately he asked no further questions. Perfect
stillness reigned in the cave for about an hour; at last Paulus
raised his face, and said: " Forgive me, Stephanus. I forgot
your necessity in prayer and scourging, in order to recover the
peace of mind I had trifled away—no heathen would have
done such a thing!" The sick man stroked his friend's arm
affectionately; but Paulus murmured: " Egoism, miserable
egoism guides and governs us. Which of us ever thinks of
the needs of others? And we—we who profess to walk in the
way of the Lamb!"

He sighed deeply, and leaned his head on the sick man's
breast, who lovingly stroked his rough hair, and it was thus
that the senator found him when he entered the cave with
Hermas.

The idle way of life of the anchorites was wholly repulsive
to his views of the task for men and for Christians, but he
succored those whom he could, and made no inquiries about
the condition of the sufferer. The pathetic union in which he
found the two men touched his heart, and, turning to Paulus,
he said, kindly:

" I can leave you in perfect comfort, for you seem to me to
have a faithful nurse."

The Alexandrian reddened; he shook his head, and replied:
" I? I thought of no one but myself, and left him to suffer
and thirst in neglect, but now I will not quit him—no, indeed,
I will not, and by God's help and yours, he shall recover."

Petrus gave him a friendly nod, for he did not believe in
the anchorite's self-accusation, though he did in his good-will;
and before he left the cave he desired Hermas to come to him
early on the following day to give him news of his father's
state. He wished not only to cure Stephanus, but to continue
his relations with the youth, who had excited his interest in

the highest degree, and he had resolved to help him to escape from the inactive life which was weighing upon him.

Paulus declined to share the simple supper that the father and son were eating, but expressed his intention of remaining with the sick man. He desired Hermas to pass the night in his dwelling, as the scanty limits of the cave left but narrow room for the lad.

A new life had this day dawned upon the young man; all the grievances and desires which had filled his soul ever since his journey to Alexandria, crowding together in dull confusion, had taken form and color, and he knew now that he could not remain an anchorite, but must try his over-abundant strength in real life.

"My father," thought he, "was a warrior, and lived in a palace before he retired into our dingy cave; Paulus was Menander, and to this day has not forgotten how to throw the discus; I am young, strong, and free-born as they were, and Petrus says I might have been a fine man. I will not hew and chisel stones like his sons, but Cæsar needs soldiers, and among all the Amalekites, nay, among the Romans in the oasis, I saw none with whom I might not match myself."

While thus he thought he stretched his limbs and struck his hands on his broad breast, and when he was asleep he dreamed of the wrestling-school, and of a purple robe that Paulus held out to him, of a wreath of poplar leaves that rested on his scented curls, and of the beautiful woman who had met him on the stairs of the senator's house.

CHAPTER V.

THANKS to the senator's potion, Stephanus soon fell asleep. Paulus sat near him and did not stir; he held his breath, and painfully suppressed even an impulse to cough, so as not to disturb the sick man's light slumbers.

An hour after midnight the old man awoke, and after he had lain meditating for some time with his eyes open, he said, thoughtfully:

"You called yourself and us all egotistic, and I certainly am so. I have often said so to myself; not for the first time to-day, but for weeks past, since Hermas came back from Alexandria and seems to have forgotten how to laugh. He is not happy, and when I ask myself what is to become of him when I am dead, and if he turns from the Lord and seeks the pleasures of the world, the heart sickens. I meant it for the best when I brought him with me up to the Holy Mountain,

but that was not the only motive—it seemed to me too hard to
part altogether from the child. My God! the young of brutes
are secure of their mother's faithful love, and his never asked
for him when she fled from my house with her seducer. I
thought he should at least not lose his father, and that if he
grew up far away from the world he would be spared all the
sorrow that it had so profusely heaped upon me. I would
have brought him up fit for Heaven, and yet through a life
devoid of suffering. And now—and now? If he is miserable
it will be through me, and added to all my other troubles
comes this grief.".

"You have sought out the way for him," interrupted
Paulus, "and the rest will be sure to come; he loves you and
will certainly not leave you so long as you are suffering."

"·Certainly not?" asked the man, sadly. "And what
weapons has he to fight through life with?"

"You gave him the Saviour for a guide; that is enough,"
said Paulus, soothingly. "There is no smooth road from
earth to Heaven, and none can win salvation for another."

Stephanus was silent for a long time, then he said:

"It is not even allowed to a father to earn the wretched experience of life for his son, or to a teacher for his pupil. We
may point out the goal, but the way thither is by a different
road for each of us."

"And we may thank God for that," cried Paulus. "For
Hermas has been started on the road which you and I had first
to find for ourselves."

"You and I," repeated the sick man, thoughtfully. "Yes,
each of us has sought his own way, but has inquired only which
was his own way, and has never concerned himself about that
of the other. Self! self! How many years we have dwelt close
together, and I have never felt impelled to ask you what you
could recall to mind about your youth, and how you were led
to grace. I learned by accident that you were an Alexandrian,
and had been a heathen, and had suffered much for the faith,
and with that I was satisfied. Indeed, you do not seem very
ready to speak of those long past days. Our neighbor should
be as dear to us as ourself, and who is nearer to me than you?
Ay, self and selfishness! There are many gulfs on the road
toward God."

"I have not much to tell," said Paulus. "But a man
never forgets what he once has been. We may cast the old
man from us, and believe we have shaken ourselves free, when
lo! it is there again and greets us as an old acquaintance. If

a frog only once comes down from his tree he hops back into the pond again."

"It is true, memory can never die!" cried the sick man. "I can not sleep any more; tell me about your early life and how you became a Christian. When two men have journeyed by the same road, and the moment of parting is at hand, they are fain to ask each other's name and where they came from."

Paulus gazed for some time into space, and then he began: "The companions of my youth called me Menander, the son of Herophilus. Besides that, I know for certain very little of my youth, for as I have already told you, I have long since ceased to allow myself to think of the world. He who abandons a thing, but clings to the idea of the thing, continues—"

"That sounds like Plato," said Stephanus, with a smile.

"All that heathen farrago comes back to me to-day," cried Paulus. "I used to know it well, and I have often thought that his face must have resembled that of the Saviour."

"But only as a beautiful song might resemble the voice of an angel," said Stephanus, somewhat dryly. "He who plunges into the depths of philosophic systems—"

"That never was quite my case," said Paulus. "I did indeed go through the whole educational course; grammar, rhetoric, dialectic, and music—"

"And arithmetic, geometry, and astronomy," added Stephanus.

"Those were left to the learned many years since," continued Paulus, "and I was never very eager for learning. In the school of rhetoric I remained far behind my fellows, and if Plato was dear to me I owe it to Pædonomus of Athens, a worthy man whom my father engaged to teach us."

"They say he had been a great merchant," interrupted Stephanus. "Can it be that you were the son of that rich Herophilus, whose business in Antioch was conducted by the worthy Jew Urbib?"

"Yes, indeed," replied Paulus, looking down at the ground in some confusion. "Our mode of life was almost royal, and the multitude of our slaves quite sinful. When I look back on all the vain trifles that my father had to care for, I feel quite giddy. Twenty sea-going ships in the harbor of Eunostus, and eighty Nile boats on Lake Mareotis belonged to him. His profits on the manufacture of papyrus might have maintained a city full of poor. But we needed our revenue for other things. Our Cyrænian horses stood in marble stalls, and the great hall, in which my father's friends were wont to meet, was like a temple. But you see how the world takes

possession of us when we begin to think about it! Rather let
us leave the past in peace. You want me to tell you more of
myself? Well, my childhood passed like that of a thousand
other rich citizens' sons, only my mother, indeed, was exceptionally beautiful and sweet, and of angelic goodness."

"Every child thinks his own mother the best of mothers,"
murmured the sick man.

"Mine certainly was the best to me," cried Paulus. "And
yet she was a heathen. When my father hurt me with severe
words of blame, she always had a kind word and loving glance
for me. There was little enough, indeed, to praise in me.
Learning was utterly distasteful to me, and even if I had done
better at school, it would hardly have counted for much to
my credit, for my brother Apollonius, who was about a year
younger than I, learned all the most difficult things as if they
were mere child's play, and in dialectic exercises there soon
was no rhetorician in Alexandria who could compete with him.
No system was unknown to him, and though no one ever knew
of his troubling himself particularly to study, he nevertheless
was master of many departments of learning. There were but
two things in which I could beat him—in music and in all
athletic exercises; while he was studying and disputing I was
winning garlands in the palæstra. But at that time the best
master of rhetoric and argument was the best man, and my
father, who himself could shine in the senate as an ardent and
elegant orator, looked upon me as a half idiotic ne'er-do-well,
until one day a learned client of our house presented him with
a pebble on which was carved an epigram to this effect: 'He
who would see the noblest gifts of the Greek race should visit
the house of Herophilus, for there he might admire strength
and vigor of body in Menander, and the same qualities of mind
in Apollonius.' These lines, which were written in the form
of a lute, passed from mouth to mouth, and gratified my
father's ambition; from that time he had words of praise for
me when my quadriga won the race in the Hippodrome, or
when I came home crowned from the wrestling-ring or the
singing-match. My whole life was spent in the baths and the
palæstra, or in gay feasting."

"I know it all," exclaimed Stephanus, interrupting him,
"and the memory of it all often disturbs me. Did you find it
easy to banish these images from your mind?"

"At first I had a hard fight," sighed Paulus. "But for
some time now, since I have passed my fortieth year, the
temptations of the world torment me less often. Only I must

keep out of the way of the carriers who bring fish from the
fishing towns on the sea, and from Raithu to the oasis."

Stephanus looked inquiringly at the speaker, and Paulus
went on:

"Yes, it is very strange. I may see men or women—the
sea yonder or the mountain here, without ever thinking of
Alexandria, but only of sacred things; but when the savor of
fish rises up to my nostrils I see the market and fish-stalls and
the oysters—"

"Those of Kanopus are famous," interrupted Stephanus;
"they make little pastics there—" Paulus passed the back of
his hand over his bearded lips, exclaiming: "At the shop of
the fat cook—Philemon—in the street of Herakleotis."

But he broke off, and cried, with an impulse of shame: "It
were better that I should cease telling of my past life. The
day does not dawn yet, and you must try to sleep."

"I can not sleep," sighed Stephanus; "if you love me go
on with your story."

"But do not interrupt me again, then," said Paulus, and
he went on:

"With all this gay life I was not happy—by no means.
When I was alone sometimes, and no longer sitting in the
crowd of merry boon companions and complaisant wenches,
emptying the wine-cup and crowned with poplar, I often felt
as if I were walking on the brink of a dark abyss—as if everything in myself and around me were utterly hollow and
empty. I could stand gazing for hours at the sea, and as the
waves rose only to sink again and vanish, I often reflected that
I was like them, and that the future of my frivolous present
must be a mere empty nothing. Our gods were of little account with us. My mother sacrificed now in one temple, and
now in another, according to the needs of the moment; my
father took part in the high festivals, but he laughed at the
belief of the multitude, and my brother talked of the
'Primæval Unity,' and dealt with all sorts of demons and
magic formulas. He accepted the doctrine of Iamblichus,
Ablavius, and the other Neoplatonic philosophers, which to
my poor understanding seemed either superhumanly profound
or else debasingly foolish; nevertheless my memory retains
many of his sayings, which I have learned to understand here
in my loneliness. It is vain to seek reason outside ourselves;
the highest to which we can attain is for reason to behold itself in us! As often as the world sinks into nothingness in
my soul, and I live in God only, and have Him, and comprehend him, and feel Him only—then that doctrine recurs to

me. How all these fools sought and listened everywhere for the truth which was being proclaimed in their very ears! There were Christians everywhere about me, and at that time they had no need to conceal themselves, but I had nothing to do with them. Twice only did they cross my path; once I was not a little annoyed when, on the Hippodrome, a Christian's horses, which had been blessed by a Nazarite, beat mine; and on another occasion it seemed strange to me when I myself received the blessing of an old Christian dock-laborer, having pulled his son out of the water.

" Years went on; my parents died. My mother's last glance was directed at me, for I had always been her favorite child. They said, too, that I was like her, I and my sister Arsinoe, who, soon after my father's death, married the Prefect Pompey. At the division of the property I gave up to my brother the manufactories and the management of the business, nay, even the house in the city, though, as the elder brother, I had a right to it, and I took in exchange the land near the Kanopic gate, and filled the stables there with splendid horses, and the lofts with not less noble wine. This I needed, because I gave up the days to baths and contests in the arena, and the nights to feasting, sometimes at my own house, sometimes at a friend's, and sometimes in the taverns of Kanopus, where the fairest Greek girls seasoned the feasts with singing and dancing. What have these details of the vainest worldly pleasure to do with my conversion? you will ask. But listen awhile. When Saul went forth to seek his father's asses he found a crown. One day we had gone out in our gilded boats, and the Lesbian girl Archidike had made ready a feast for us in her house,.a feast such as could scarcely be offered even in Rome.

" Since the taking of our city by Diocletian, after the insurrection of Achilleus, the Imperial troops who came to Alexandria behaved insolently enough. Between some of my friends and certain of the young officers of Roman patrician families there had been a good deal of rough banter for some months past, as to their horses, women—I know not what; and it happened that we met these very gentry at the house of Archidike. Sharp speeches were made, which the soldiers replied to after their fashion, and at last they came to insulting words and then to loud threats. The Romans left the house of entertainment before we did. Crowned with garlands, singing, and utterly careless, we followed soon after them, and had almost reached the quay when a noisy troop rushed out of a side street and fell upon us with naked weapons. The moon was high in the heavens, and I could recognize some of our adversaries. I threw myself on a tall tribune, throttled him, and, as he fell, I fell with him in the dust; I am but dimly conscious of what followed, for sword-strokes were showered upon me, and all grew black before my eyes. I only know what I thought then, face to face with death."

"Well?" asked Stephanus.

"I thought," said Paulus, reddening, "of my fighting-quails at Alexandria, and whether they had had any water. Then my dull heavy unconciousness increased; for weeks I lay in that state, for I was hacked like sausage meat; I had twelve wounds, not counting the slighter ones, and any one else would have died of any one of them. You have often wondered at my scars."

"And whom did the Lord choose, then, to be the means of your salvation?"

"When I recovered my senses," continued Paulus, "I was lying in a large, clean room behind a curtain of light material; I could not raise myself; but, just as if I had been sleeping so many minutes instead of days, I thought again directly of my quails. In their last fight my best cock had severely handled handsome Nikander's, and yet he wanted to dispute the stakes with me, but I would assert my rights! At least the quails should fight again, and if Nikander should refuse I would force him to fight me with his fists in the Palæstra, and give him a blue reminder of his debt on the eye. My hands were still weak, and yet I clinched them as I thought of the vexatious affair. 'I will punish him,' I muttered to myself. Then I heard the door of the room open, and I saw three men respectfully approaching a fourth. He greeted them with dignity, but yet with friendliness, and rolled up a scroll which he had been reading. I would have called out, but I could not open my parched lips, and yet I saw and heard all that was going on around me in the room. It all seemed strange enough to me then; even the man's mode of greeting was unusual. I soon perceived that he who sat in the chair was a judge, and that the others had come as complainants; they were all three old and poor, but some good men had left them the use and interest of a piece of land. During seed-time one of them, a fine old man with long white hair, had been ill, and he had not been able to help in the harvest either; 'and now they want to withhold his portion of the corn,' thought I; but it was quite otherwise. The two men who were in health had taken a third part of the produce to the house of the sick man, and he obstinately refused to accept the corn because he had helped neither to sow nor to reap it, and he demanded of

the judge that he should signify to the other two that he had
no right to receive goods which he had not earned. The judge
had so far kept silence. But he now raised his sagacious and
kindly face and asked the old man: ' Did you pray for your
companions and for the increase of their labors?'

" ' I did,' replied the other.

" ' Then by your intercession you helped them,' the judge
decided, ' and the third part of the produce is yours, and you
must keep it.'

" The old man bowed, the three men shook hands, and in a
few minutes the judge was alone in the room again. I did not
know what had come over me; the complaint of the men and
the decision of the judge seemed to me senseless, and yet both
the one and the other touched my heart. I went to sleep
again, and when I awoke refreshed the next morning, the judge
came up to me and gave me medicine, not only for my body,
but also for my soul, which certainly was not less in need of
it than my poor wounded limbs."

" Who was the judge?" asked Stephanus.

" Eusebius, the Presbyter of Kanopus. Some Christians
had found me half dead on the road, and had carried me into
his house, for the widow Theodora, his sister, was the deaconess of the town. The two had nursed me as if I were their
dearest brother. It was not till I grew stronger that they
showed me the cross and the crown of thorns of Him who for
my sake also had taken upon Him such far more cruel suffering than mine, and they taught me to love His wounds, and
to bear my own with submission. In the dry wood of despair
soon budded green shoots of hope, and instead of annihilation
at the end of this life they showed me heaven and all its joys.
I became a new man, and before me there lay in the future an
eternal and blessed existence; after this life I now learned to
look forward to eternity. The gates of heaven were wide
open before me, and I was baptized at Kanopus. In Alexandria they had mourned for me as dead, and my sister Arsinoe, as heiress to my property, had already moved into my
country-house with her husband, the prefect. I willingly left
her there, and now lived again in the city, in order to support
the brethren, as the persecutions had begun again. This was
easy for me, as through my brother-in-law I could visit all the
prisons. At last I was obliged to confess the faith, and I
suffered much on the rack and in the porphyry quarries; but
every pain was dear to me, for it seemed to bring me nearer
to the goal of my longings, and if I find aught to complain of
up here on the holy mountain, it is only that the Lord deems

me unworthy to suffer harder things, when His beloved and only Son took such bitter torments on himself for me and for every wretched sinner."

"Ah! saintly man!" murmured Stephanus, devoutly kissing Paulus's sheep-skin; but Paulus pulled it from him, exclaiming, hastily:

"Cease, pray cease—he who approaches me with honors now in this life throws a rock in my way to the life of the blessed. Now I will go to the spring and fetch you some fresh water."

When Paulus returned with the water-jar he found Hermas, who had come to wish his father good-morning before he went down to the oasis to fetch some new medicine from the senator.

CHAPTER VI.

Sirona was sitting at the open window of her bedroom, having her hair arranged by a black woman that her husband had bought in Rome. She sighed, while the slave lightly touched the shining tresses here and there with perfumed oil which she had poured into the palm of her hand; then she firmly grasped the long thick waving mass of golden hair and was parting it to make a plait, when Sirona stopped her, saying: "Give me the mirror."

For some minutes she looked with a melancholy gaze at the image in the polished metal, then she sighed again; she picked up the little greyhound that lay at her feet, and placing it in her lap, showed the animal its image in the mirror.

"There, poor Iambe," she said; "if we two, inside these four walls, want to see anything like a pleasing sight we must look at ourselves."

Then she went on, turning to the slave: "How the poor little beast trembles! I believe it longs to be back again at Arelas, and is afraid we shall linger too long under this burning sky. Give me my sandals."

The black woman reached her mistress two little slippers with gilt ornaments on the slight straps, but Sirona flung her hair off her face with the back of her hand, exclaiming: "The old ones, not these. Wooden shoes even would do here."

And with these words she pointed to the court-yard under the window, which was in fact as ill-contrived as though gilt sandals had never yet trodden it. It was surrounded by buildings; on one side was a wall with a gate-way, and on the other buildings which formed a sharply bent horseshoe.

Opposite the wing in which Sirona and her husband had

found a home stood the much higher house of Petrus, and both
had attached to them, in the background of the court-yard,
sheds constructed of rough reddish-brown stones, and covered
with a thatch of palm branches; in these agricultural imple-
ments were stored, and the senator's slaves lived. In front
lay a heap of black charcoal, which was made on the spot by
burning the wood of the thorny sajal—a species of acacia; and
there, too, lay a goodly row of well-smoothed mill-stones,
which were shaped in the quarry and exported to Egypt. At
this early hour the whole unlovely domain lay in deep shadow,
and was crowded with fowls and pigeons. Sirona's window
alone was touched by the morning sun. If she could have
known what a charm the golden light shed over her figure, on
her rose and white face, and her shining hair, she would have
welcomed the day-star instead of complaining that it had too
early waked her from sleep—her best comfort in her solitude.

Besides a few adjoining rooms, she was mistress of a larger
room, the dwelling-room, which looked out upon the street.

She shaded her eyes with her hand, exclaiming: "Oh! the
wearisome sun. It looks at us the first thing in the morning
through the window, as if the day were not long enough. The
beds must be put in the front room, I insist upon it."

The slave shook her head, and stammered an answer:
"Phœbicius will not have it so."

Sirona's eyes flashed angrily, and her voice, which was particularly sweet, trembled slightly as she asked: "What is
wrong with him again?"

"He says," replied the slave, "that the senator's son,
Polykarp, goes oftener past your window than altogether
pleases him, and it seems to him that you occupy yourself
more than is necessary with his little brothers and sisters, and
the other children up there."

"Is he still in there?" asked Sirona, with glowing cheeks,
and she pointed threateningly to the dwelling-room.

"The master is out," stuttered the old woman. "He
went out before sunrise. You are not to wait for breakfast;
he will not return till late."

The Gaulish lady made no answer, but her head fell, and
the deepest melancholy overspread her features.

The greyhound seemed to feel for the troubles of his mistress, for he fawned upon her, as if to kiss her. The solitary
woman pressed the little creature, which had come with her
from her home, closely to her bosom; for an unwonted sense
of wretchedness weighed upon her heart, and she felt as lonely,
friendless, and abandoned as if she were driving alone—alone

—over a wide and shoreless sea. She shuddered, as if she were cold—for she thought of her husband, the man who here in the desert should have been all in all to her, but whose presence filled her with aversion, whose indifference had ceased to wound her, and whose tenderness she feared far more than his wild irritability—she had never loved him.

She had grown up free from care among a number of brothers and sisters. Her father had been the chief accountant of the decurions' college in his native town; and he had lived opposite the circus, where, being of a stern temper, he had never permitted his daughters to look on at the games; but he could not prevent their seeing the crowd streaming into the amphitheater, or hearing their shouts of delight, and their eager cries of approbation.

Sirona thus grew up in the presence of other people's pleasure, and in a constantly revived and never satisfied longing to share it; she had, indeed, no time for unnecessary occupations, for her mother died before she was fully grown up, and she was compelled to take charge of the eight younger children. This she did in all fidelity, but in her hours of leisure she loved to listen to the stories told her by the wives of officials who had seen and could praise the splendors of Rome the golden.

She knew that she was fair, for she need only go outside the house to hear it said; but though she longed to see the capital, it was not for the sake of being admired, but because there was there so much that was splendid to see and to admire. So, when the Centurion Phœbicius, the commandant of the garrison of her native town, was transferred to Rome, and when he desired to take the seventeen-years-old girl with him to the Imperial City as his wife—she was more than forty years younger than he—she followed him full of hope and eager anticipation.

Not long after their marriage she started for Rome by sea from Massilia, accompanied by an old relative; and he went by land at the head of his cohorts.

She reached their destination long before her husband, and without waiting for him, but constantly in the society of her old duenna, she gave herself up with the freedom and eagerness of her fresh youth to the delights of seeing and admiring.

It did not escape her, while she did so, that she attracted all eyes wherever she went, and however much this flattered and pleased her at first, it spoiled many of her pleasures when the Romans, young and old, began to follow and court her. At last Phœbicius arrived, and when he found his house crowded

with his wife's admirers he behaved to Sirona as though she
had long since betrayed his honor.

Nevertheless, he dragged her from pleasure to pleasure, and
from one spectacle to another, for it gratified him to show
himself in public with his beautiful young wife. She certainly
was not free from frivolity, but she had learned early from her
strict father, as being the guide of her younger sisters, to distinguish clearly right from wrong, and the pure from the unclean; and she soon discovered that the joys of the capital,
which had seemed at first to be gay flowers with bright colors,
and redolent with intoxicating perfume, bloomed on the surface of a foul bog.

She at first had contemplated all that was beautiful and pleasant with characteristic delight; but her husband took pleasure
only in things which revolted her as being common and
abominable. He watched her every glance, and yet he pointed
nothing out to her but what was hurtful to the feelings of a
pure woman. Pleasure became her torment, for the sweetest
wine is repulsive when it has been tasted by impure lips.
After every feast and spectacle he loaded her with outrageous
reproaches, and when at last, weary of such treatment, she
refused to quit the house, he obliged her, nevertheless, to accompany him as often as the Legate Quintillus desired it.
The legate was his superior officer, and he sent her every day
some present of flowers.

Up to this time she had borne with him, and had tried to
excuse him, and to think herself answerable for much of what
she endured. But at last—about ten months after her marriage—something occurred between her and Phœbicius—something which stood like a wall of brass between him and her;
and as this something had led to his banishment to the remote
oasis, and to his degradation to the rank of captain of a miserable maniple, instead of his obtaining his hoped-for promotion,
he began to torment her systematically while she tried to protect herself by icy coldness; so that at last it came to this, that
the husband, for whom she felt nothing but contempt, had no
more influence on her life than some physical pain which a
sick man is doomed to endure all through his existence.

In his presence she was silent, defiant and repellent, but as
soon as he quitted her, her innate warm-hearted kindliness
and child-like merriment woke up to new life, and their fairest
blossoms opened out in the senator's house among the little
troop who amply repaid her love with theirs.

Phœbicius belonged to the worshipers of Mithras, and he
often fasted in his honor to the point of exhaustion; while on

the other hand he frequently drank with his boon companions
at the feasts of the god till he was in a state of insensibility.

Here even, in Mount Sinai, he had prepared a grotto for the
feast of Mithras, had gathered together a few companions in
his faith, and when it happened that he remained out all day
and all night, and came home paler even than usual, she well
knew where he had been. .

Just now she .vividly pictured to herself the person of this
man, with his eyes that now were dull with sleep and now
glowed with rage, and she asked herself whether it were indeed
possible that of her own free will she had chosen to become his
wife. Her bosom heaved with quicker breathing as she remembered the ignominy he had subjected her to in Rome, and
she clinched her small hands. At this instant the little dog
sprung from her lap and flew barking to the window-sill; she
was easily startled, and she drew on her morning-gown, which
had slipped from her white shoulders; then she fastened the
straps of her sandals, and went to look down into the court-
yard.

A smile played upon her lips as she perceived young Hermas, who had already been for some time leaning motionless
against the wall of the house opposite, and devouring with his
gaze the figure of the beautiful young woman. She had a
facile and volatile nature. Like the eye which retains no im-
pression of the disabling darkness so soon as the rays of light
have fallen on it, no gloom of suffering touched her so deeply
that the lightest breath of a new pleasure could not blow her
troubles to the winds. Many rivers are quite different in color
at their source and at their mouth, and so it was often with
her tears; she began to weep for sorrow, and then found it
difficult to dry her eyes for sheer overflow of mirth. It would
have been so easy for Phœbicius to make her lot a fair one!
for she had a most susceptible heart, and was grateful for the
smallest proofs of love. But between him and her every bond
was broken.

The form and face of Hermas took her fancy; she thought
he looked of noble birth in spite of his poor clothing, and when
she observed that his cheeks were glowing, and that the hand
in which he held the medicine vial trembled, she understood
that he was watching her, and that the sight of her had stirred
his youthful blood. A woman—still more, a woman who is
pleased to please—forgives any sin that is committed for her
beauty's sake, and Sirona's voice had a friendly ring in it as
she bade Hermas good-morning and asked him how his father
was, and whether the senator's medicine had been of service,

The youth's answers were short and confused, but his looks betrayed that he would fain have said quite other things than those which his indocile tongue allowed him to reiterate timidly.

"Dame Dorothea was telling me last evening," she said kindly, "that Petrus had every hope of your father's recovery, but that he is still very weak. Perhaps some good wine would be of service to him—not to-day but to-morrow or the day after. Only come to me if you need it; we have some old Falernian in the loft, and white Mareotis wine, which is particularly good and wholesome."

Hermas thanked her, and as she still urged him to apply to her in all confidence, he took courage and succeeded in stammering rather than saying: "You are as good as you are beautiful."

The words were hardly spoken when the topmost stone of an elaborately constructed pile near the slaves' house fell down with a loud clatter. Sirona started and drew back from the window, the greyhound set up a loud barking, and Hermas struck his forehead with his hand as if he were roused from a dream.

In a few instants he had knocked at the senator's door; hardly had he entered the house when Miriam's slight form passed across behind the pile of stones, and vanished swiftly and silently into the slaves' quarters. These were by this time deserted by their inhabitants, who were busy in the field, the house, or the quarries; they consisted of a few ill-lighted rooms with bare, unfinished walls.

The shepherdess went into the smallest, where, on a bed of palm-sticks, lay the slave that she had wounded, and who turned over as with a hasty hand she promptly laid a fresh but ill-folded bandage all askew on the deep wound in his head. As soon as this task was fulfilled she left the room again, placed herself behind the half-open door which led into the court-yard, and, pressing her brow against the stone door-post, looked first at the senator's house and then at Sirona's window, while her breath came faster and faster.

A new and violent emotion was stirring her young soul; not many minutes since she had squatted peacefully on the ground by the side of the wounded man, with her head resting on her hand and thinking of her goats on the mountain. Then she had heard a slight sound in the court, which any one else would not have noticed; but she not only perceived it, but knew with perfect certainty with whom it originated. She could never fail to recognize Hermas's footstep, and it had an

irresistible effect upon her.   She raised her head quickly from
her hand and her elbow from the knee on which it was resting,
sprung to her feet and went out into the yard.   She was hidden by the mill-stones, but she could see Hermas lost in ad
miration.   She followed the direction of his eyes and saw the
same image which had fascinated his gaze—Sirona's lovely
form, flooded with sunlight.   She looked as if formed out of
snow, and roses, and gold, like the angel at the sepulcher in
the new picture in the church.   Yes, just like the angel, and
the thought flew through her mind how brown and black she
was herself, and that he had called her a she-devil.   A sense of
deep pain came over her; she felt as though paralyzed in body
and soul; but soon she shook off the spell, and her heart began
to beat violently; she had to bite her lip hard with her white
teeth to keep herself from crying out with rage and anguish.

How she wished she could swing herself up to the window on
which Hermas's gaze was fixed, and clutch Sirona's golden hair
and tear her down to the ground, and suck the very blood
from her red lips like a vampire, till she lay at her feet as pale
as the corpse of a man dead of thirst in the desert.   Then she
saw the light mantle slip from Sirona's shoulders, and observed
Hermas start and press his hand to his heart.

Then another impulse seized her.   It was to call to her and
warn her of his presence; for even women who hate each other
hold out the hand of fellowship in the spirit when the sanctity
of woman's modesty is threatened with danger.   She blushed
for Sirona, and had actually opened her lips to call when the
greyhound barked and the dialogue began.   Not a word escaped her sharp ears, and when she told Sirona that she was as
good as she was beautiful she felt seized with giddiness; then
the topmost stone, by which she had tried to steady herself,
lost its balance, its fall interrupted their conversation, and
Miriam-returned to the sick man.

Now she was standing at the door, waiting for Hermas.
Long, long did she wait; at last he appeared with Dorothea,
and she could see that he glanced up again at Sirona; but a
spiteful smile passed over her lips, for the window was empty
and the fair form that he had hoped to see again had vanished.

Sirona was now sitting at her loom in the front room,
whither she had been tempted by the sound of approaching
hoofs.   Polykarp had ridden by on his father's fine horse, had
greeted her as he passed, and had dropped a rose on the roadway.   Half an hour later the old black slave came to Sirona,
who was throwing the shuttle through the warp with a skillful
hand.

"Mistress!" cried the negress with a hideous grin; the lonely woman paused in her work, and as she looked up inquiringly the old woman gave her a rose. Sirona took the flower, blew away the road-side dust that had clung to it, rearranged the tumbled delicate petals with her finger-tips, and said, while she seemed to give the best part of her attention to this occupation:

"For the future let roses lie when you find them. You know Phœbicius, and if any one sees it, it will be talked about."

The black woman turned away, shrugging her shoulders; but Sirona thought: "Polykarp is a handsome and charming man, and has finer and more expressive eyes than any other here, if he were not always talking of his plans, and drawings, and figures, and mere stupid grave things that I do not care for!"

CHAPTER VII.

THE next day, after the sun had passed the meridian and it was beginning to grow cool, Hermas and Paulus yielded to Stephanus's wish; as he began to feel stronger, and carried him out into the air. The anchorites sat near each other on a low block of stone, which Hermas had made into a soft couch for his father by heaping up a high pile of fresh herbs. They looked after the youth, who had taken his bow and arrows, as he went up the mountain to hunt a wild goat; for Petrus had prescribed a strengthening diet for the sick man. Not a word was spoken by either of them till the hunter had disappeared. Then Stephanus said:

"How much he has altered since I have been ill. It is not so very long since I last saw him by the broad light of day, and he seems meantime to have grown from a boy into a man. How self-possessed his gait is."

Paulus, looking down at the ground, muttered some words of assent. He remembered the discus-throwing and thought to himself: "The Palæstra certainly sticks in his mind, and he has been bathing, too; and yesterday, when he came up from the oasis, he strode in like a young athlete."

That friendship only is indeed genuine when two friends, without speaking a word to each other, can nevertheless find happiness in being together. Stephanus and Paulus were silent, and yet a tacit intercourse subsisted between them as they sat gazing toward the west, where the sun was near its setting.

Far below them gleamed the narrow, dark blue-green streak of the Red Sea, bounded by the bare mountains of the coast, which shone in a shimmer of golden light. Close beside them rose the toothed crown of the great mountain which, as soon as the day-star had sunk behind it, appeared edged with a ribbon of glowing rubies. The flaming glow flooded the western horizon, filmy veils of mist floated across the hilly coast-line, the silver clouds against the pure sky changed their hue to the tender blush of a newly opened rose, and the undulating shore floated in the translucent violet of the amethyst. There not a breath of air was stirring, not a sound broke the solemn stillness of the evening. Not till the sea was taking a darker and still darker hue, till the glow on the mountain peaks and in the west had begun to die away, and the night to spread its shades over the heights and hollows, did Stephanus unclasp his folded hands and softly speak his companion's name. Paulus started and said, speaking like a man who is aroused from a dream and who is suddenly conscious of having heard some one speak: "You are right; it is growing dark and cool, and you must go back into the cave."

· Stephanus offered no opposition and let himself be led back to his bed; while Paulus was spreading the sheep-skin over the sick man he sighed deeply.

"What disturbs your soul?" asked the older man.

"It is—it was—what good can it do me!" cried Paulus, in strong excitement. "There we sat, witnesses of the most glorious marvels of the Most High, and I, in shameless idolatry, seemed to see before me the chariot of Helios with its glorious winged horses, snorting fire as they went, and Helios himself in the guise of Hermas with gleaming golden hair, and the dancing houris, and the golden gates of the night. Accursed rabble of demons—"

At this point the anchorite was interrupted, for Hermas entered the cave, and laying a young steinbock that he had killed before the two men, exclaimed: "A fine fellow, and he cost me no more than one arrow. I will light a fire at once and roast the best pieces. There are plenty of bucks still on our mountain, and I know where to find them."

In about an hour father and son were eating the pieces of meat, which had been cooked on a spit. Paulus declined to sup with them, for after he had scourged himself in despair and remorse for the throwing of the discus, he had vowed a strict fast.

"And now," cried Hermas, when his father declared himself satisfied, after seeming to relish greatly the strong meat from which he had so long abstained, "and now the best is to come! In this flask I have some strengthening wine, and when it is empty it will be filled afresh."

Stephanus took the wooden beaker that his son offered him, drank a little, and then said, while he smacked his tongue to relish the after-taste of the noble juice:

"That is something choice!—Syrian wine! only taste it, Paulus."

Paulus took the beaker in his hand, inhaled the fragrance of the golden fluid, and then murmured, but without putting it to his lips:

"This is not Syrian; it is Egyptian, I know it well. I should take it to be Mareotis."

"So Sirona called it," cried Hermas, "and you know it by the mere smell! She said it was particularly good for the sick."

"That it is," Paulus agreed; but Stephanus asked, in surprise:

"Sirona? who is she?"

The cave was but dimly lighted by the fire that had been made at the opening, so that the two anchorites could not perceive that Hermas reddened all over as he replied: "Sirona? The Gaulish woman Sirona? Do you not know her? She is the wife of a centurion down in the oasis."

"How do you come to know her?" asked his father.

"She lives in Petrus's house," replied the lad, "and as she had heard of your wound—"

"Take her my thanks when you go there to-morrow morning," said Stephanus. "To her and her husband, too. Is he a Gaul?"

"I believe so—nay, certainly," answered Hermas; "they call him the lion, and he is no doubt a Gaul."

When the lad had left the cave the old man laid himself down to rest, and Paulus kept watch by him on his son's bed. But Stephanus could not sleep, and when his friend approached him to give him some medicine he said: "The wife of a Gaul has done me a kindness, and yet the wine would have pleased me better if it had not come from a Gaul."

Paulus looked at him inquiringly, and though total darkness reigned in the cave Stephanus felt his gaze, and said:

"I owe no man a grudge and I love my neighbor. Great injuries have been done me, but I have forgiven—from the bottom of my heart forgiven. Only one man lives to whom I wish evil, and he is a Gaul."

3

"Forgive him, too," said Paulus, "and do not let evil thoughts disturb your sleep."

"I am not tired," said the sick man, "and if you had gone through such things as I have it would trouble your rest at night, too."

"I know, I know," said Paulus, soothingly. "It was a Gaul that persuaded your wretched wife into quitting your house and her child."

"And I loved, oh! how I loved Glycera!" groaned the old man. "She lived like a princess, and I fulfilled her every wish before it was uttered. She herself had said a hundred times that I was too kind and too yielding, and that there was nothing left for her to wish. Then the Gaul came to our house, a man as acrid as sour wine, but with a fluent tongue and sparkling eyes. How he entangled Glycera I know not, nor do I want to know; he shall atone for it in hell. For the poor lost woman I pray day and night. A spell was on her and she left her heart behind in my house, for her child was there—and she loved Hermas so fondly; indeed, she was deeply devoted to me. Think what the spell must be that can annihilate a mother's love! Wretch, hapless wretch that I am! Did you ever love a woman, Paulus?"

"You ought to be asleep," said Paulus, in a warning tone. "Who ever lived nearly half a century without feeling love! Now I will not speak another word, and you must take this drink that Petrus has sent for you." The senator's medicine was potent, for the sick man fell asleep and did not wake till broad day lighted up the cave.

Paulus was still sitting on his bed, and after they had prayed together he gave him the jar which Hermas had filled with fresh water before going down to the oasis.

"I feel quite strong," said the old man. "The medicine is good; I have slept well and dreamed sweetly; but you look pale and as if you had not slept."

"I," said Paulus—"I lay down there on the bed. Now let me go out in the air for a moment." With these words he went out of the cave.

As soon as he was out of sight of Stephanus he drew a deep breath, stretched out his limbs and rubbed his burning eyes; he felt as if there was sand gathered under their lids, for he had forbidden them to close for three days and nights. At the same time he was consumed by a violent thirst, for neither food nor drink had touched his lips for the same length of time. His hands were beginning to tremble, but the weakness and pain that he experienced filled him with silent joy, and he would willingly have retired into his cave and have indulged, not for the first time, in the ecstatic pain of hanging on the cross and bleeding from five wounds in imitation of the Saviour.

But Stephanus was calling him, and without hesitation he returned to him and replied to his questions; indeed it was easier to him to speak than to listen, for in his ears there was a roaring, moaning, singing, and piping, and he felt as if drunk with strong wine.

"If only Hermas does not forget to thank the Gaul!" exclaimed Stephanus.

"Thank—ay, we should always be thankful!" replied his companion, closing his eyes.

"I dreamed of Glycera," the old man began again. "You said yesterday that love had stirred your heart, too, and yet you never were married. You are silent? Answer me something."

"I—who called me?" murmured Paulus, staring at the questioner with a fixed gaze.

Stephanus was startled to see that his companion trembled in every limb; he raised himself and held out to him the flask with Sirona's wine, which the other, incapable of controlling himself, snatched eagerly from his hand and emptied with frantic thirst. The fiery liquor revived his failing strength, brought the color to his cheeks, and lent a strange luster to his eyes. "How much good that has done me!" he cried, with a deep sigh and pressing his hands on his breast.

Stephanus was perfectly reassured and repeated his question, but he almost repented of his curiosity, for his friend's voice had an utterly strange ring in it as he answered:

"No, I was never married—never, but I have loved for all that, and I will tell you the story from beginning to end; but you must not interrupt me, no, not once. I am in a strange mood—perhaps it is the wine. I had not drunk any for so long; I had fasted since—since—but it does not matter. Be silent, quite silent, and let me tell my story."

Paulus sat down on Hermas's bed; he threw himself far back, leaned the back of his head against the rocky wall of the cavern through whose door-way the daylight poured, and began thus, while he gazed fixedly into vacancy:

"What she was like?—who can describe her? She was tall and large like Hera, and yet not proud, and her noble Greek face was lovely rather than handsome.

"She could no longer have been very young, but she had eyes like those of a gentle child. I never knew her other than very pale; her narrow forehead shone like ivory under her soft brown hair; her beautiful hands were as white as her forehead

—hands that moved as if they themselves were living and in-spired creatures with a soul and language of their own. When she folded them devotedly together it seemed as if they were putting up a mute prayer. She was pliant in form as a young palm-tree when it bends, and withal she had a noble dignity even on the occasion when I first saw her.

" It was in a hideous spot, the revolting prison-hall of Rhya-kotis. She wore only a threadbare robe that had once been costly, and a foul old woman followed her about—as a greedy rat might pursue an imprisoned dove—and loaded her with abusive language. . She answered not a word, but large heavy tears flowed slowly over her pale cheeks and down on to her hands, which she kept crossed on her bosom. Grief and anguish spoke from her eyes, but no vehement passion de-formed the regularity of her features. She knew how to en-dure even ignominy with grace; and what words the raging old woman poured out upon her!

" I had long since been baptized, and all the prisons were open to me, the rich Menander, the brother-in-law of the pre-fect—those prisons in which under Maximin so many Chris-tians were destined to be turned from the true faith.

" But she did not belong to us. Her eye met mine, and I signed my forehead with the cross, but she did not respond to the sacred sign. The guards led away the old woman, and she drew back into a dark corner, sat down, and covered her face with her hands. A wondrous sympathy for the hapless woman had taken possession of my soul; I felt as if she be-longed to me, and I to her, and I believed in her, even when the turnkey had told me in coarse language that she had lived with a Roman at the old woman's, and had defrauded her of a large sum of money. The next day I went again to the prison, for her sake and my own; there I found her again in the same corner that she had shrunk into the day before; by her side stood her prison fare untouched—a jar of water and a piece of bread.

" As I went up to her, I saw how she broke a small bit off the thin cake for herself, and then called a little Christian boy who had come into the prison with his mother, and gave him the remainder. The child thanked her prettily, and she drew him to her and kissed him with passionate tenderness, though he was sickly and ugly.

" ' No one who can love children so well is wholly lost,' said I to myself, and I offered to help her as far as lay in my power.

" She looked at me not without distrust, and said that noth-ing had happened to her but what she deserved, and she would bear it. Before I could inquire of her any further, we were interrupted by the Christian prisoners, who crowded round the worthy Ammonius, who was exhorting and comforting them with edifying discourse. She listened attentively to the old man, and on the following day I found her in conversation with the mother of the boy to whom she had given her bread.

"One morning I had gone there with some fruit to offer as a treat to the prisoners, and particularly to her. She took an apple, and said, rising as she spoke, 'I would now ask another favor of you. You are a Christian, send me a priest, that he may baptize me, if he does not think me unworthy, for I am burdened with sins so heavily as no other woman can be.' Her large, sweet, child-like eyes filled again with big silent tears, and I spoke to her from my heart, and showed her as well as I could the grace of the Redeemer. Shortly after Ammonius secretly baptized her, and she begged to be given the name of Magdalen, and so it was, and after that she took me wholly into her confidence.

"She had left her husband and her child for the sake of a diabolical seducer, whom she had followed to Alexandria, and who there had abandoned her. Alone and friendless, in want and guilt, she remained behind with a hard-hearted and covetous hostess, who had brought her before the judge, and so into prison. What an abyss of the deepest anguish of soul I could discover in this woman, who was worthy of a better lot! What is highest and best in a woman? Her love, her mother's heart, her honor; and Magdalen had squandered and ruined all these by her own guilt. The blow of overwhelming fate may be easily borne, but woe to him whose life is ruined by his own sin! She was a sinner; she felt it with anguish of repentance, and she steadily refused my offers to purchase her freedom.

"She was greedy of punishment, as a man in a fever is greedy of the bitter potion which cools his blood. And, by the crucified Lord! I have found more noble humanity among sinners than in many just men in priestly garb. Through the presence of Magdalen, the prison recovered its sanctity in my eyes. Before this I had frequently quitted it full of deep contempt, for among the imprisoned Christians there were too often lazy vagabonds, who had loudly confessed the Saviour only to be fed by the gifts of the brethren; there I had seen accursed criminals, who hoped by a martyr's death to win back the redemption that they had forfeited; there I had heard the woful cries of the faint-hearted, who feared death as much as they feared treason to the Most High. There were things to be seen there that might harrow the soul, but also examples of the sublimest greatness. Men have I seen there, ay, and women, who went to their death in calm and silent bliss, and whose end was, indeed, noble—more noble than that of the much-lauded Codrus or Decius Mus.

" Among all the prisoners there was neither man nor woman who was more calmly self-possessed, more devoutly resigned, than Magdalen. The words, ' There is more joy in Heaven over one sinner that repenteth than over ninety-and-nine that need no repentance,' strengthened her greatly, and she re-pented—yea and verily, she did. And for my part, God is my witness that not an impulse as from man to woman drew me to her, and yet I could not leave her, and I passed the day at her side, and at night she haunted my soul, and it would have seemed to me fairer than all in life besides to have been allowed to die with her.

" It was at the time of the fourth decree of persecution, a few months before the promulgation of the first edict of tolera-tion.

" He that sacrifices, it is said, shall go unpunished, and he that refuses shall by some means or other be brought to it, but those who continue stiff-necked shall suffer death. For a long time much consideration had been shown to the prisoners, but now they were alarmed by having the edict read to them anew. Many hid themselves groaning and lamenting, others prayed aloud, and most awaited what might happen with pale lips and painful breathing.

" Magdalen remained perfectly calm. The names of the Christian prisoners were called out, and the Imperial soldiers led them all together to one spot. Neither my name nor hers was called, for I did not belong to the prisoners, and she had not been apprehended for the faith's sake. The officer was rolling up his list when Magdalen rose and stepped modestly forward, saying, with quiet dignity, ' I, too, am a Christian.'

" If there be an angel who wears the form and features of man, his face must resemble hers, as she looked in that hour. The Roman, a worthy man, looked at her with a benevolent but searching gaze. ' I do not find your name here,' he said, aloud, shaking his head and pointing to the roll; and he added, in a lower voice, ' Nor do I intend to find it.'

" She went closer up to him, and said out loud, ' Grant me my place among the believers, and write down that Magdalen, the Christian, refuses to sacrifice.'

" My soul was deeply moved, and with joyful eagerness I

cried out, ' Put down my name, too, and write that Menander, the son of Herophilus, also refuses.' The Roman did his duty.

"Time has not blotted out from my memory a single moment of that day. There stood the altar, and near it the heathen priest on one side, and on the other the emperor's officer. We were taken up two by two; Magdalen and I were the last. One word now—one little word—would give us life and freedom, another the rack and death. Out of thirty of us only four had found courage to refuse to sacrifice, but the feeble-hearted broke out into lamentations, and beat their foreheads, and prayed that the Lord might strengthen the courage of the others. An unutterably pure and lofty joy filled my soul, and I felt as if we were out of the body floating on ambient clouds. Softly and calmly we refused to sacrifice, thanked the Imperial official, who warned us kindly, and in the same hour and place we fell into the hands of the torturers. She gazed only up to heaven, and I only at her, but in the midst of the most frightful torments I saw before me the Saviour beckoning to me, surrounded by angels that soared on soft airs, whose presence filled my eyes with the purest light, and my ears with heavenly music. She bore the utmost torture without flinching, only once she called out the name of her son Hermas; then I turned to look at her, and saw her gazing up to heaven with wide open eyes and trembling lips— living, but already with the Lord—on the rack, and yet in bliss. My stronger body clung to the earth; she found deliverance at the first blow of the torturer.

"I myself closed her eyes, the sweetest eyes in which heaven was ever mirrored; I drew a ring from her dear, white, blood-stained hand, and here under the rough sheepskin I have it yet; and I pray, I pray, I pray—oh! my heart! My God if it might be—if this is the end—"

Paulus put his hand to his head and sunk exhausted on the bed in a deep swoon. The sick man had followed his story with breathless interest. Some time since he had risen from his bed, and, unobserved by his companion, had sunk on his knees; he now dragged himself, all hot and trembling, to the side of the senseless man, tore the sheep's-fell from his breast, and with hasty movement sought the ring; he found it, and fixing on it passionate eyes as though he would melt it with their fire, he pressed it again and again to his lips, to his heart, to his lips again; buried his face in his hands and wept bitterly.

It was not till Hermas returned from the oasis that Stephanus thought of his exhausted and fainting friend, and with his son's assistance restored him to consciousness. Paulus did not refuse to take some food and drink, and in the cool of the evening, when he was refreshed and invigorated, he sat again by the side of Stephanus, and understood from the old man that Magdalen was certainly his wife.

"Now I know," said Paulus, pointing to Hermas, "how it is that from the first I felt such a love for the lad there."

The old man softly pressed his hand, for he felt himself tied to his friend by a new and tender bond, and it was with silent ecstasy that he received the assurance that the wife he had always loved, the mother of his child, had died a Christian and a martyr, and had found before him the road to heaven.

The old man slept as peacefully as a child the following night, and when, next morning, messengers came from Raithu to propose to Paulus that he should leave the Holy Mountain and go with them to become their elder and ruler, Stephanus said:

"Follow this high call with all confidence, for you deserve it. I really no longer have need of you, for I shall get well now without any further nursing."

But Paulus, far more disturbed than rejoiced, begged of the messengers a delay of seven days for reflection, and after wandering restlessly from one holy spot to another, at last went down into the oasis, there to pray in the church.

CHAPTER VIII.

It was a delicious refreshing evening; the full moon rose calmly in the dark blue vault of the night sky, and poured a flood of light down on the cool earth. But its rays did not give a strong enough light to pierce the misty veil that hung over the giant mass of the Holy Mountain; the city of the oasis on the contrary was fully illuminated; the broad roadway of the high street looked to the wanderer who descended from the height above like a shining path of white marble, and the freshly plastered walls of the new church gleamed as white as in the light of day. The shadows of the houses and palm-trees lay like dark strips of carpet across the road, which was nearly empty in spite of the evening coolness, which usually tempted the citizens out into the air.

The voices of men and women sounded out through the open windows of the church; then the door opened and the Pharanite Christians, who had been partaking of the Supper—the bread and the cup passed from hand to hand—came out into the moonlight. The elders and deacons, the readers and singers, the acolytes and the assembled priesthood of the place followed the bishop Agapitus, and the laymen came behind Obedianus, the head man of the oasis, and the senator Petrus; with Petrus came his wife, his grown-up children and numerous slaves.

The church was empty when the door-keeper, who was extinguishing the lights, observed a man in a dark corner of an antechamber through which a spring of water softly plashed and trickled, and which was intended for penitents. The man was prostrate on the ground and absorbed in prayer, and he did not raise himself till the porter called him and threw the light of his little lamp full in his face.

He began to address him with hard words, but when he recognized in the belated worshiper the anchorite Paulus of Alexandria he changed his key, and said, in a soft and almost submissive tone of entreaty:

"You have surely prayed enough, pious man. The congregation have left the church, and I must close it on account of our beautiful new vessels and the heathen robbers. I know that the brethren of Raithu have chosen you to be their elder, and that this high honor was announced to you by their messengers, for they came to see our church, too, and greatly admired it. Are you going at once to settle with them, or shall you keep the high feast with us?"

"That you shall hear to-morrow," answered Paulus, who had risen from his knees and was leaning against a pillar of the narrow, bare, penitential chamber. "In this house dwells One of whom I would fain take counsel, and I beg of you to leave me here alone. If you will you can lock the door and fetch me out later, before you go to rest for the night."

"That can not be," said the man, considering, "for my wife is ill, and my house is a long way from here, at the end of the town by the little gate, and I must take the key this very evening to the senator Petrus, because his son, the architect Antonius, wants to begin the building of the new altar the first thing to-morrow morning. The workmen are to be here by sunrise, and if—"

"Show me the key," interrupted Paulus. "To what untold blessing may this little instrument close or open the issues! Do you know, man, that I think there is a way for us both out of the difficulty! You go to your sick wife, and I will take the key to the senator so soon as I have finished my devotions."

The door-keeper considered for a few minutes, and then acceded to the request of the future presbyter of Raithu, while at the same time he begged him not to linger too late

As he went by the senator's house he smelled the savor of

roast meat; he was a poor man and thought to himself: "They fast in there just when it pleases them, but as for us, we fast when it pleases us least."

The good smell, which provoked this lament, rose from a roast sheep, which was being prepared as a feast-supper for the senator and the assembed members of his household; even the slaves shared in the late evening meal.

Petrus and Dame Dorothea sat in the Greek fashion, side by side in a half-reclining position on a simple couch, and before them stood a table which no one shared with them, but close to which was the seat for the grown-up children of the house. The slaves squatted on the ground nearer to the door, and crowded into two circles, each surrounding a steaming dish, out of which they helped themselves to the brown stew of lentils with the palm of the hand. A round, gray-looking cake of bread lay near each, and was not to be broken till the steward Jethro had cut and apportioned the sheep. The juicy pieces of the back and thighs of the animal were offered to Petrus and his family to choose from, but the carver laid a slice for each slave on his cake—a larger for the men and a smaller for the women. Many looked with envy on the more succulent piece that had fallen to a neighbor's share, but not even those that had fared worse dared to complain, 'for a slave was allowed to speak only when his master addressed him, and Petrus forbid even his children to discuss their food, whether to praise it or to find fault.

In the midst of the underlings sat Miriam; she never eat much, and all meat was repulsive to her, so she pushed the cut from the ribs that was given to her over to an old garden-woman, who sat opposite, and who had often given her a fruit or a little honey, for Miriam loved sweet things. Petrus spoke not a word to-day to his slaves, and very little even to his family; Dorothea marked the deep lines between his grave eyes, not without anxiety, and noted how he pinched his lips, when, forgetful of the food before him, he sat lost in meditation.

The meal was ended, but still he did not move, nor did he observe the inquiring glances which were turned on him by many eyes. No one dared to rise before the master gave the signal.

Miriam followed all his movements with more impatience than any of the others who were present; she rocked restlessly backward and forward, crumbled the bread that she had left with her slender fingers, and her breath now came fast and faster, and now seemed to stop entirely. She had heard the court-yard gate open, and had recognized Hermas's step.

"He wants to speak to the master; in a moment he will come in and find me among these—" thought she, and she involuntarily stroked her hand over her rough hair to smooth it, and threw a glance at the other slaves, in which hatred and contempt were equally marked.

But Hermas came not. Not for an instant did she think that her ear had deceived her—was he waiting now at the door for the conclusion of the meal? Was his late visit intended for the Gaulish lady, to whom she had seen him go yesterday again with the wine-jar?

Sirona's husband, Phœbicius, as Miriam well knew, was upon the mountain, and offering sacrifice by moonlight to Mithras with his fellow-heathen in a cave which she had long known. She had seen the Gaul quit the court during the time of evening prayer with a few soldiers, two of whom carried after him a huge coffer, out of which rose the handle of a mighty caldron, and a skin full of water and various vessels. She knew that these men would pass the whole night in the grotto of Mithras, and there greet "the young god"—the rising sun—with strange ceremonies; for the inquisitive shepherdess had more than once listened, when she had led her goats up the mountain before the break of day, and her ear had detected that the worshipers of Mithras were performing their nocturnal solemnities. Now it flashed across her mind that Sirona was alone, and that the late visit of Hermas probably concerned her and not the senator.

She started; there was quite a pain in her heart, and, as usual, when any violent emotion agitated her mind, she involuntarily sprung to her feet, prompted by the force of her passion, and had almost reached the door when the senator's voice brought her to a pause, and recalled her to the consciousness of the impropriety of her behavior.

The sick man still lay with his inflamed wound and fever down in the court, and she knew that she should escape blame if in answer to her master's stern questioning she said that the patient needed her, but she had never told a lie, and her pride forbade her even now to speak an untruth. The other slaves stared with astonishment, as she replied,/"I wanted to get out; the supper is so long."

Petrus glanced at the window, and perceiving how high the moon stood, he shook his head as if in wonder at his own conduct, then without blaming her he offered a thanksgiving, gave the slaves the signal to leave the room, and after receiv-

ing a kiss of "good-night" from each of his children—from
among whom Polykarp the sculptor alone was missing—he
withdrew to his own room. But he did not remain alone there
for long. So soon as Dorothea had discussed the requirements
of the house for the next day with Marthana and the steward,
and had been through the sleeping-room of her younger children, casting a loving glance on the peaceful sleepers, arranging here a coverlet and there a pillow, she entered her husband's room and called his name.

Petrus stood still and looked round, and his grave eyes were
full of grateful tenderness as they met those of his wife.
Dorothea knew the soft and loving heart within the stern ex-
terior, and nodded to him with sympathetic understanding;
but before she could speak he said, "Come in, come nearer to
me; there is a heavy matter in hand, and you can not escape
your share of the burden."

"Give me my share!" cried she, eagerly. "The slim girl
of former years has grown a broad-shouldered old woman, so
that it may be easier to her to help her lord to bear the many
burdens of life. But I am seriously anxious—even before we
went to chuch something unsatisfactory had happened to you,
and not merely in the council-meeting. There must be something not right with one of the children."

"What eyes you have!" exclaimed Petrus.

"Dim gray eyes," said Dorothea, "and not even particularly keen. But when anything concerns you and the children
I could see it in the dark. You are dissatisfied with Polykarp;
yesterday, before he set out for Raithu, you looked at him
so—so—what shall I say? I can quite imagine what it is all
about, but I believe you are giving yourself groundless anxiety.
He is young, and so lovely a woman as Sirona—"

Up to this point Petrus had listened to his wife in silence.
Now he clasped his hands and interrupted her: "Things certainly are not going on quite right—but I ought to be used to
it. What I meant to have confided to you in a quiet hour you
tell me as if you knew all about it."

"And why not?" asked Dorothea. "When you graft a
scion on to a tree, and they have grown well together, the
grafted branch feels the bite of the saw that divides the stock,
or the blessing of the spring that feeds the roots, just as if the
pain or the boon were its own. And you are the tree and I
am the graft, and the magic power of marriage has made us
one. Your pulses are my pulses, your thoughts have become
mine, and so I always know before you tell me what it is that
stirs your soul."

Dorothea's kind eyes moistened as she spoke, and Petrus warmly clasped her hands in his as he said, "And if the gnarled old trunk bears from time to time some sweet fruit, he may thank the graft for it. I can not believe that the anchorites up yonder are peculiarly pleasing to the Lord because they live in solitude. Man comes to his perfect humanity only through his wife and child, and he who has them not can never learn the most glorious heights and the darkest depths of life and feeling. If a man may stake his whole existence and powers for anything, surely it is for his own house."

"And you have honestly done so for ours!" cried Dorothea.

"For ours," repeated Petrus, giving the words the strongest accent of his deep voice. "Two are stronger than one, and it is long since we ceased to say 'I' in discussing any question concerning the house or the children; and both have been touched by to-day's events."

"The senate will not support you in constructing the road?"

"No; the bishop gave the casting vote. I need not tell you how we stand toward each other, and I will not blame him, for he is a just man; but in many things we can never meet half way. You know that he was in his youth a soldier, and - his very piety is rough—I might almost say warlike. If we had yielded to his views, and if our head man, Obedianus, had not supported me, we should not have had a single picture in the church, and it would have looked like a barn rather than a house of prayer. We never have understood each other, and since I opposed his wish of making Polykarp a priest, and sent the boy to learn of the sculptor Thalassius—for even as a child he drew better than many masters in these wretched days that produce no great artists—since then, I say, he speaks of me as if I were a heathen—"

"And yet he esteems you highly; that I know," interrupted Dame Dorothea.

"I fully return his good opinion," replied Petrus, "and it is no ordinary matter that estranges us. He thinks that he only holds the true faith, and ought to fight for it; he calls all artistic work a heathen abomination; he never felt the purifying influence of the beautiful, and regards all pictures and statues as tending to idolatry. Still he allows himself to admire Polykarp's figures of angels and the Good Shepherd, but the lions put the old warrior in a rage. 'Accursed idols and works of the devil,' are what he calls them."

"But there were lions even in the temple of Solomon," cried Dorothea.

"I urged that, and also that in the schools of the catechists, and in the educational history of animals which we possess and teach from, the Saviour himself is compared to a lion, and that Mark, the evangelist, who brought the doctrine of the gospel to Alexandria, is represented with a lion. But he withstood me more and more violently, saying that Polykarp's works were to adorn no sacred place but the Cæsareum, and that to him is nothing but a heathen edifice, and the noble works of the Greeks that are preserved there he calls revolting images by which Satan insnares the souls of Christian men. The other senators can understand his hard words, but they can not follow mine; and so they vote with him, and my motion to construct the roadway was thrown over, because it did not become a Christian assembly to promote idolatry and to smooth a way for the devil.''

"I can see that you must have answered them sharply."

"Indeed I believe so," answered Petrus, looking down. "Many painful things were no doubt said, and it was I that suffered for them. Agapitus, who was looking at the deacon's reports, was especially dissatisfied with the account that I laid before them; they blamed us severely because you gave away as much bread to heathen households as to Christians. It is no doubt true, but—"

"But," cried Dorothea, eagerly, "hunger is just as painful to the unbaptized, and their Christian neighbors do not help them, and yet they, too, are our flesh and blood. I should ill fulfill my office if I were to let them starve, because the highest comfort is lacking to them."

"And yet," said Petrus, "the council decided that, for the future, you must apply at the most a fourth part of the grain allotted to their use. You need not fear for them; for the future some of our own produce may go to them out of what we have hitherto sold. You need not withdraw even a loaf from any one of your protégés, but certainly may now be laid by the plans for the road. Indeed there is no hurry for its completion, for Polykarp will now hardly be able to go on with his lions here among us. Poor fellow! with what delight he formed the clay models, and how wonderfully he succeeded in reproducing the air and aspect of the majestic beasts. It is as if he were inspired by the spirit of the old Athenian masters. We must now consider whether in Alexandria—"

"Rather let us endeavor," interrupted Dorothea, "to induce him at once to put aside his models, and to execute other more pious works. Agapitus has keen eyes, and the heathen work is only too dear to the lad's heart."

The senator's brow grew dark at the last words, and he said, not without some excitement, "Everything that the heathen do is not to be condemned. Polykarp must be kept busy, constantly and earnestly occupied, for he has set his eyes where they should not be set. Sirona is the wife of another, and even in sport no man should try to win his neighbor's wife. Do you think the Gaulish woman is capable of forgetting her duty?"

Dorothea hesitated, and after some reflection answered: "She is a beautiful and vain child—a perfect child; I mean in nature, and not in years, although she certainly might be the grandchild of her strange husband, for whom she feels neither love nor respect, nor, indeed, anything but utter aversion. I know not what, but something frightful must have come between them even in Rome, and I have given up all attempts to guide her heart back to him. In everything else she is soft and yielding, and often, when she is playing with the children, I can not imagine where she finds her reckless gayety. I wish she were a Christian, for she is very dear to me—why should I deny it? It is impossible to be sad when she is by, and she is devoted to me, and dreads my blame, and is always striving to win my approbation. Certainly she tries to please every one, even the children; but, so far as I can see, not Polykarp more than any one else, although he is such a fine young man. No, certainly not."

"And yet the boy gazes at her," said Petrus, "and Phœbicius has noticed it; he met me yesterday when I came home, and, in his sour, polite manner, requested me to advise my son, when he wished to offer a rose, not to throw it into his window, as he was not fond of flowers, and preferred to gather them himself for his wife."

The senator's wife turned pale, and then exclaimed, shortly and positively, "We do not need a lodger, and much as I should miss his wife, the best plan will be for you to request him to find another dwelling."

"Say no more, wife," Petrus said, sternly, and interrupting her with a wave of his hand. "Shall we make Sirona pay for it because our son has committed a folly for her sake? You yourself said that her intercourse with the children, and her respect for you, preserve her from evil; and now shall we show her the door? By no means. The Gauls may remain in my house so long as nothing occurs that compels me to send them out of it. My father was a Greek, but through my mother I have Amalekite blood in my veins, and I should dishonor myself if I drove from my threshold any with whom I had once broken bread under my roof. Polykarp shall be warned, and ✿

shall learn what he owes to us, to himself, and to the laws of
God. I know how to value his noble gifts, and I am his
friend, but I am also his master, and I will find means of pre-
venting my son from introducing the light conduct of the
capital beneath his father's roof."

The last words were spoken with weight and decision, like
the blows of a hammer, and stern resolve sparkled in the
senator's eyes. Nevertheless, his wife went fearlessly up to
him, and said, laying her hand on his arm, " It is indeed well
that a man can keep his eyes set on what is just, when we
women should follow the hasty impulse of our heart. Even in
wrestling, men only fight with lawful and recognized means,
while fighting women use their teeth and nails. You men
understand better how to prevent injustice than we do, and
that you have once more proved to me, but, in carrying justice
out, you are not our superiors. The Gauls may remain in our
house, and do you take Polykarp severely to task, but in the
first instance as his friend. Or would it not be better if you
left it to me? He was so happy in thinking of the completion
of his lions, and in having to work for the great building in
the capital, and now it is all over. I wish you had already
broken that to him; but love stories are women's affairs, and
you know how good the boy is to me. A mother's word sometimes has more effect than a father's blow, and it is in life as
it is in war—the light forces of archers go first into the field,
and the heavily armed division stays in the background to support them; then, if the enemy will not yield, it comes forward
and decides the battle. First let me speak to the lad. It may
be that he threw the rose into Sirona's window only in sport,
for she plays with his brothers and sisters as if she herself were
one of them. I will question him; for if it is so, it would be
neither just nor prudent to blame him. Some caution is
needed even in giving a warning; for many a one who would
never have thought of stealing has become a thief through
false suspicion. A young heart that is beginning to love is
like a wild boy who always would rather take the road he is
warned to avoid; and when I was a girl, I myself first discovered how much I liked you when the senator Aman's wife
—who wanted you for her own daughter—advised me to be on
my guard with you. A man who has made such good use of
his time among all the temptations of the Greek Sodom as
Polykarp, and who has won such high praise from all his
teachers and masters, can not have been much injured by the
light manners of the Alexandrians. It is in a man's early years
that he takes the bent which he follows throughout his later

life, and that he had done before he left our house. Nay—
even if I did not know what a good fellow Polykarp is—I need
only look at you to say, ' A child that was brought up by this
father could never turn out a bad man.'"

Petrus sadly shrugged his shoulders, as though he regarded
his wife's flattering words as mere idle folly, and yet he smiled
as he asked:

" Whose school of rhetoric did you go to? So be it, then;
speak to the lad when he returns from Raithu. How high the
moon is already; come to rest—Antonius is to place the altar
in the early dawn, and I wish to be present."

CHAPTER IX.

MIRIAM'S ears had not betrayed her. While she was detained at supper, Hermas had opened the court-yard gate; he
came to bring the senator a noble young buck that he had
killed a few hours before, as a thank-offering for the medicine
to which his father owed his recovery. It would no doubt
have been soon enough the next morning, but he could find
no rest up on the mountain, and did not—and indeed did not
care to—conceal from himself the fact that the wish to give
expression to his gratitude attracted him down into the oasis
far less than the hope of seeing Sirona and of hearing a word
from her lips.

Since their first meeting he had seen her several times, and
had even been into her house, when she had given him the
wine for his father, and when he had taken back the empty
flask. Once, as she was filling the bottle which he held out
of the large jar, her white fingers had touched his, and her inquiry whether he were afraid of her, or if not, why his hands
which looked so strong should tremble so violently, dwelt still
in his mind. The nearer he approached Petrus's house the
more vehemently his heart beat; he stood still in front of the
gate-way to take breath and to collect himself a little, for he
felt that, agitated as he was, he would find it difficult to utter
any coherent words.

At last he laid his hand on the latch and entered the yard.
The watch-dogs already knew him, and only barked once as
he stepped over the threshold.

He brought a gift in his hand, and he wanted to take nothing away, and yet he appeared to himself just like a thief as
he looked round, first at the main building lighted up by the
moon, and then at the Gaul's dwelling-house, which, veiled in
darkness, stood up as a vague silhouette, and threw a broad-

dark shadow on the granite flags of the pavement, which was
trodden to shining smoothness. There was not a soul to be
seen, and the reek of the roast sheep told him that Petrus and
his household were assembled at supper.

"I might come inopportunely on the feasters," said he to
himself, as he threw the buck over from his left to his right
shoulder, and looked up at Sirona's window, which he knew
only too well.

It was not lighted up, but a whiter and paler something appeared within its dark stone frame, and this something attracted his gaze with an irresistible spell; it moved, and
Sirona's greyhound set up a sharp barking.

It was she—it must be she! Her form rose before his fancy
in all its brilliant beauty, and the idea flashed through his
mind that she must be alone, for he had met her husband
and the old slave woman among the worshipers of Mithras on
their way to the mountain. The pious youth, who so lately
had punished his flesh with the scourge to banish seductive
dream-figures, had in these few days become quite another
man. He would not leave the mountain for his father's sake,
but he was quite determined no longer to avoid the way of the
world; nay, rather to seek it. He had abandoned the care of
his father to the kindly Paulus, and had wandered about
among the rocks; there he had practiced throwing the discus,
he had hunted the wild goats and beasts of prey, and from
time to time—but always with some timidity—he had gone
down into the oasis to wander round the senator's house and
catch a glimpse of Sirona.

Now that he knew that she was alone he was irresistibly
drawn to her. What he desired of her he himself could not
have said, and nothing was clear 'to his mind beyond the wish
to touch her fingers once more.

Whether this were a sin or not was all the same to him: the
most harmless play was called a sin, and every thought of the
world for which he longed; and he was fully resolved to take
the sin upon himself, if only he might attain his end. Sin
after all was nothing but a phantom terror with which they
frighten children, and the worthy Petrus had assured him that
he might be a man capable of great deeds. With a feeling
that he was venturing on an unheard-of act, he went toward
Sirona's window, and she at once recognized him as he stood
in the moonlight.

"Hermas!" he heard her say softly. He was seized with
such violent terror that he stood as if spell-bound, the goat
slipped from his shoulders, and he felt as if his heart had

ceased to beat. And again the sweet woman's voice called
"Hermas, is it you? What brings you to us at such a late
hour?"

He stammered an incoherent answer, and she said, "I do
not understand; come a little nearer."

Involuntarily he stepped forward into the shadow of the
house and close up to her window. She wore a white robe
with wide, open sleeves, and her arms shone in the dim light
as white as her garment. The greyhound barked again; she
quieted it, and then asked Hermas how his father was, and
whether he needed some more wine. He replied that she was
very kind, angelically kind, but that the sick man was recovering fast, and that she had already given him far too much.
Neither of them said anything that might not have been heard
by everybody, and yet they whispered as if they were speaking
of some forbidden thing.

"Wait a moment," said Sirona, and she disappeared within
the room; she soon reappeared, and said, softly and sadly, "I
would ask you to come into the house, but Phœbicius has
locked the door. I am quite alone; hold the flask, so that I
may fill it through the open window."

With these words she leaned over with the large jar; she
was strong, but the wine-jar seemed to her heavier than on
other occasions, and she said, with a sigh, "The amphora is
too heavy for me."

He reached up to help her; again his fingers met hers, and
again he felt the ecstatic thrill which had haunted his memory
day and night ever since he first had felt it. At this instant
there was a sudden noise in the house opposite; the slaves were
coming out from supper. Sirona knew what was happening;
she started and cried out, pointing to the senator's door, "For
all the gods' sake! they are coming out, and if they see you
here I am lost!"

Hermas looked hastily round the court, and listened to the
increasing noise in the other house, then, perceiving that there
was no possible escape from the senator's people, who were
close upon him, he cried out to Sirona, in a commanding tone,
"Stand back!" and flung himself up through the window into
the Gaul's apartment. At the same moment the door opposite
opened, and the slaves streamed out into the yard.

In front of them all was Miriam, who looked expectantly
all round the wide space seeking something, and disappointed.
He was not there, and yet she had heard him come in; and
the gate had not opened and closed a second time, of that she
was perfectly certain. Some of the slaves went to the stables,

others went outside the gate into the street to enjoy the coolness of the evening; they sat in groups on the ground, looking
up at the stars, chattering or singing. Only the shepherdess
remained in the court-yard seeking him on all sides, as if she
were hunting for some lost trinket. She searched even behind
the mill-stones, and in the dark sheds in which the stone-
workers' tools were kept. Then she stood still a moment and
clinched her hands; with a few light bounds she sprung into
the shadow of the Gaul's house. Just in front of Sirona's
window lay the steinbock; she hastily touched it with her
slender naked toes, but quickly withdrew her foot with a
shudder, for it had touched the beast's fresh wound, wet with
its blood. She rapidly drew the conclusion that he had killed
it, and had thrown it down here, and that he could not be far
off. Now she knew where he was in hiding—and she tried to
laugh, for the pain she felt seemed too acute and burning for
tears to allay or cool it. But she did not wholly lose her
power of reflection. "They are in the dark," thought she,
"and they would see me if I crept under the window to
listen; and yet I must know what they are doing there together."   .

She hastily turned her back on Sirona's house, slipped into
the clear moonlight, and after standing there for a few minutes, went into the slaves' quarters. An instant after she
slipped out behind the mill-stones, and crept as cleverly and
as silently as a snake along the ground under the darkened
base of the centurion's house, and lay close under Sirona's
window.

Her loudly beating heart made it difficult for even her sharp
ears to hear, but though she could not gather all that he said,
she distinguished the sound of his voice; he was no longer in
Sirona's room, but in the room that looked out on the street.

Now she could venture to raise herself and to look in at the
open window. The door of communication between the two
rooms was closed, but a streak of light showed her that in the
further room, which was the sitting-room, a lamp was burning.   .

She had already put up her hand in order to hoist herself
up into the dark room, when a gay laugh from Sirona fell
upon her ear. The image of her enemy rose up before her
mind, brilliant and flooded with light as on that morning
when Hermas had stood just opposite, bewildered by her fascination. And now—now—he was actually lying at her feet,
and saying sweet flattering words to her, and he would speak

to her of love, and stretch out his arm to clasp her—but she had laughed.

Now she laughed again. Why was all so still again? Had she offered her rosy lips for a kiss? No doubt—no doubt. And Hermas did not wrench himself from her white arms, as he had torn himself from hers that noon by the spring—torn himself away never to return.

Cold drops stood on her brow, she buried her hands in her thick, black hair, and a loud cry escaped her—a cry like that of a tortured animal. A few minutes more and she had slipped through the stable and the gate by which they drove the cattle in; and no longer mistress of herself, was flying up the mountain to the grotto of Mithras to warn Phœbicius.

The anchorite Gelasius saw from afar the figure of the girl flying up the mountain in the moonlight, and her shadow flitting from stone to stone, and he threw himself on the ground, and signed a cross on his brow, for he thought he saw a goblin form, one of the myriad gods of the heathen—an Oread pursued by a Satyr.

Sirona had heard the girl's shriek.

· "What was that?" she asked the youth, who stood before her in the full-dress uniform of a Roman officer, as handsome as the young god of war, though awkward and unsoldierly in his movements.

"An owl screamed—" replied Hermas. "My father must at last tell me from what house·we are descended, and I will go to Byzantium, the new Rome, and say to the emperor, 'Here am I, and I will fight for you among your warriors.'"

"I like you so!" exclaimed Sirona.

"If that is the truth," cried Hermas, "prove it to me! Let me once press my lips to your shining gold hair. You are beautiful: as sweet as a flower, as gay and bright as a bird, and yet as hard as our mountain rock. If you do not grant me one kiss I shall long till I am sick and weak before I can get away from here, and prove my strength in battle."

"And if I yield," laughed Sirona, "you will be wanting another and another kiss, and at last not get away at all. No, no, my friend—I am the wiser of us two. Now go into the dark room; I will look out and see whether the people are gone in again, and whether you can get off unseen from the street window, for you have been here much too long already. Do you hear?—I command you."

Hermas obeyed with a sigh; Sirona opened the shutter and looked out. The slaves were coming back into the court, and she called out a friendly word or two, which were answered

with equal friendliness, for the Gaulish lady, who never overlooked even the humblest, was dear to them all. She took in
the night air with deep-drawn breaths, and looked up con-
tentedly at the moon, for she was well content with herself.

When Hermas had swung himself up into her room she had
started back in alarm; he had seized her hand, and pressed his
burning lips to her arm, and she let him do it, for she was
overcome with strange bewilderment. Then she heard Dame
Dorothea calling out, "Directly—directly; I will only say good-
night first to the children."

These simple words, uttered in Dorothea's voice, had a
magical effect on the warm-hearted woman—badly used and
suspected as she was, and yet so well formed for happiness,
love, and peace. When her husband had locked her in, taking
even her slave with him, at first she had raved, wept, meditated
revenge and flight, and at last, quite broken down, had seated
herself by the window in silent thought of her beautiful home,
her brothers and sisters, and the dark olive groves of Arelas.

Then Hermas appeared. It had not escaped her that the
young anchorite passionately admired her; and she was not
displeased, for she liked him, and the confusion with which
he had been overcome at the sight of her flattered her and
seemed to her doubly precious, because she knew that the
hermit in his sheep-skin, on whom she had bestowed a gift of
wine, was in fact a young man of distinguished rank. And
how truly to be pitied was the poor boy, who had had his
youth spoiled by a stern father. A woman easily bestows
some tender feeling on the man that she pities; perhaps because she is grateful to him for the pleasure of feeling herself
the stronger, and because through him and his suffering she
finds gratification for the noblest happiness of a woman's
heart—that of giving tender and helpful care; women's hearts
are softer than ours. In men's hearts love is commonly extinguished when pity begins, while admiration acts like sun-
shine on the budding plant of a woman's inclination, and pity
is the glory which radiates from her heart.

Neither admiration nor pity, however, would have been
needed to induce Sirona to call Hermas to her window; she
felt so unhappy and lonely that any one must have seemed
welcome from whom she might look for a friendly and encouraging word to revive her deeply wounded self-respect. And
there came the young anchorite, who forgot himself and everything else in her presence, whose looks, whose movement,
whose very silence seemed to do homage to her. And then his
bold spring into her room, and his eager wooing—"This is

love," said she to herself. Her cheeks glowed, and when Hermas clasped her hand, and pressed her arm to his lips, she could not repulse him, till Dorothea's voice reminded her of the worthy lady and of the children, and through them of her own far-off sisters.

The thought of these pure beings flowed over her troubled spirit like a purifying stream, and the question passed through her mind, "What should I be without those good folks over there? and is this great love-sick boy, who stood before Polykarp just lately looking like a school-boy—is he so worthy that I should for his sake give up the right of looking them boldly in the face?" And she pushed Hermas roughly away, just as he was venturing for the first time to apply his lips to her perfumed gold hair, and desired him to be less forward, and to release her hand.

She spoke in a low voice, but with such decision that the lad, who was accustomed to the habit of obedience, unresistingly allowed her to push him into the sitting-room. There was a lamp burning on the table, and on a bench by the wall of the room, which was lined with colored stucco, lay the helmet, the centurion's staff, and the other portions of the armor which Phœbicius had taken off before setting out for the feast of Mithras, in order to assume the vestments of one of the initiated of the grade of "Lion."

The lamp-light revealed Sirona's figure, and as she stood before him in all her beauty, with glowing cheeks, the lad's heart began to beat high, and with increased boldness he opened his arms and endeavored to draw her to him; but Sirona avoided him and went behind the table, and, leaning her hands on its polished surface while it protected her like a shield, she lectured him in wise and almost motherly words against his rash, intemperate, and unbecoming behavior.

Any one who was learned in the heart of woman might have smiled at such words from such lips and in such an hour; but Hermas blushed and cast down his eyes, and knew not what to answer. A great change had come over the Gaulish lady. She felt a great pride in her virtue, and in the victory she had won over herself; and while she sunned herself in the splendor of her own merits, she wished that Hermas, too, should feel and recognize them. She began to expatiate on all that she had to forego and to endure in the oasis, and she discoursed of virtue and the duties of a wife, and of the wickedness and audacity of men.

Hermas, she said, was no better than the rest, and because she had shown herself somewhat kind to him, he fancied already

that he had a claim on her liking; but he was greatly mistaken, and if only the court-yard had been empty, she would
long ago have shown him the door.

The young hermit was soon only half listening to all she
said, for his attention had been riveted by the armor which
lay before him, and which gave a new direction to his excited
feelings. He involuntarily put out his hand toward the gleaming helmet, and interrupted the pretty preacher with the question, " May I try it on?"

Sirona laughed out loud and exclaimed, much amused and
altogether diverted from her train of thought, " To be sure.
You ought to be a soldier. How well it suits you! Take off
your nasty sheep-skin, and let us see how the anchorite looks
as a centurion."

Hermas needed no second telling: he decked himself in the
Gaul's armor with Sirona's help. We human beings must indeed be in a deplorable plight; otherwise how is it that from our
earliest years we find such delight in disguising ourselves; that
is to say, in sacrificing our own identity to the tastes of another,
whose aspect we borrow? The child shares this inexplicable
pleasure with the sage, and the stern man who should condemn it would not therefore be the wiser, for he who wholly
abjures folly is a fool all the more certainly the less he fancies
himself one. Even dressing others has a peculiar charm, especially for women; it is often a question which has the greatest
pleasure, the maid who dresses her mistress or the lady who
wears the costly garment.

Sirona was devoted to every sort of masquerading. If it had
been needful to seek a reason why the senator's children and
grandchildren were so fond of her, by no means last or least
would have been the fact that she would willingly and cheerfully allow herself to be tricked out in colored kerchiefs, rib-
bons, and flowers, and on her part could contrive the most fan-
tastic costumes for them. So soon as she saw Hermas with
the helmet on, the fancy seized her to carry through the trav-
esty he had begun. She eagerly and in perfect innocence
pulled the coat of armor straight, helped him to buckle the
breast-plate and to fasten on the sword, and as she performed
the task, at which Hermas proved himself unskillful enough,
her gay and pleasant laugh rang out again and again. When
he sought to seize her hand, as he not seldom did, she hit him
sharply on the fingers, and scolded him.

Hermas's embarrassment thawed before this pleasant sport,
and soon he began to tell her how hateful the lonely life on the
mountain was to him. He told her that Petrus himself had

advised him to try his strength out in the world, and he confided to her that if his father got well, he meant to be a soldier, and do great deeds. She quite agreed with him, praised
and encouraged him, then she criticized his slovenly deport-
ment, showed him with comical gravity how a warrior ought
to stand and walk, called herself his drill-master, and was de-
lighted at the zeal with which he strove to imitate her.

In such play the hours passed quickly. Hermas was proud
of himself in his soldierly garb, and was happy in her presence
and in the hope of future triumphs; and Sirona was gay, as
she had usually been only when playing with the children, so
that even Miriam's wild cry, which the youth explained to be
the scream of an owl, only for a moment reminded her of the
danger in which she was placing herself. Petrus's slaves had
long gone to rest before she began to weary of amusing herself
with Hermas, and desired him to lay aside her husband's equip-
ment, and to leave her. Hermas obeyed while she warily
opened the shutters, and turning to him, said, "You can not
venture through the court-yard; you must go through this window into the open street. But there is some one coming down
the road; let him pass first, it will not be long to wait, for he
is walking quickly."

She carefully drew the shutters to, and laughed to see how
clumsily Hermas set to work to unbuckle the greaves; but the
gay laugh died upon her lips when the gate flew open, the
greyhound and the senator's watch-dogs barked loudly, and
she recognized her husband's voice as he ordered the dogs to
be quiet.

"Fly—fly—for the gods' sake!" she cried in a trembling
voice. With that ready presence of mind with which destiny
arms the weakest woman in great and sudden danger, she extinguished the lamp, flung open the shutter, and pushed Hermas to the window. The boy did not stay to bid her farewell,
but swung himself with a strong leap down into the road, and,
followed by the barking of the dogs, which roused all the
neighboring households, he flew up the street to the little
church.

He had not got more than half way when he saw a man
coming toward him; he sprung into the shadow of a house,
but the belated walker accelerated his steps, and came straight
up to him. He set off running again, but the other pursued
him, and kept close at his heels till he had passed all the houses
and began to go up the mountain path. Hermas felt that he
was outstripping his pursuer, and was making ready for a
spring over a block of stone that encumbered the path, when

he heard his name called behind him, and he stood still, for he recognized the voice of the man from whom he was flying as that of his good friend Paulus.

" You, indeed!" said the Alexandrian, panting for breath. " Yes, you are swifter than I. Years hang lead on our heels, but do you know what it is that lends them the swiftest wings? You have just learned it! It is a bad conscience; and pretty things will be told about you; the dogs have barked it all out loud enough to the night."

" And so they may!" replied Hermas, defiantly, and trying in vain to free himself from the strong grasp of the anchorite, who held him firmly. " I have done nothing wrong."

" Thou shalt not covet thy neighbor's wife!" interrupted Paulus, in a tone of stern severity. " You have been with the centurion's pretty wife, and were taken by surprise. Where is your sheep-skin?"

Hermas started, felt on his shoulder, and exclaimed, striking his fist against his forehead: ". Merciful Heaven! I have left it there! The raging Gaul will find it."

" He did not actually see you there?" asked Paulus, eagerly.

" No, certainly not," groaned Hermas; " but the skin—"

" Well, well," muttered Paulus. " Your sin is none the less, but something may be done in that case. Only think if it came to your father's ears; it might cost him his life."

" And that poor Sirona!" sighed Hermas.

" Leave me to settle that," exclaimed Paulus. " I will make everything straight with her. There, take my sheep-skin. You will not? Well, to be sure, the man who does not fear to commit adultery would make nothing of becoming his father's murderer. There, that is the way! fasten it together over your shoulders; you will need it, for you must quit this spot, and not for to-day and to-morrow only. You wanted to go out into the world, and now you will have the opportunity of showing whether you really are capable of walking on your own feet. First go to Raithu and greet the pious Nikon in my name, and tell him that I remain here on the mountain, for after long praying in the Church I have found myself unworthy of the office of elder which they offered me. Then get yourself carried by some ship's captain across the Red Sea, and wander up and down the Egyptian coast. The hordes of the Blemmyes have lately shown themselves there; keep your eye on them, and when the wild bands are plotting some fresh outbreak you can warn the watch on the mountain peaks; how to cross the sea and so outstrip them, it will be your business to find out. Do you feel bold enough and capable of accomplishing this task? Yes? So I expected! Now may the Lord guide you. I will take care of your father, and his blessing and your mother's will rest upon you if you sincerely repent, and if you now do your duty."

"You shall learn that I am a man," cried Hermas, with sparkling eyes. "My bow and arrows are lying in your cave; I will fetch them and then—ay! you shall see whether you sent the right man on the errand. Greet my father, and once more give me your hand."

Paulus grasped the boy's right hand, drew him to him and kissed his forehead with fatherly tenderness. Then he said: "In my cave, under the green stone, you will find six gold pieces; take three of them with you on your journey. You will probably need them—at any rate to pay your passage. Now be off, and get to Raithu in good time."

Hermas hurried up the mountain, his head full of the important task that had been laid upon him; dazzling visions of the great deeds he was to accomplish eclipsed the image of the fair Sirona, and he was so accustomed to believe in the superior insight and kindness of Paulus that he feared no longer for Sirona now that his friend had made her affair his own.

The Alexandrian looked after him, and breathed a short prayer for him; then he went down again into the valley.

It was long past midnight, and the moon was sinking; it grew cooler and cooler, and since he had given his sheep-skin to Hermas he had nothing on but his threadbare coat. Nevertheless he went slowly onward, stopping every now and then, moving his arms and speaking incoherent words in a low tone to himself.

He thought of Hermas and Sirona, of his own youth, and of how in Alexandria he himself had tapped at the shutters of the dark-haired Aso and the fair Simaitha.

"A child—a mere boy," he murmured. "Who would have thought it? The Gaulish woman no doubt may be handsome, and as for him, it is a fact that as he threw the discus I was myself surprised at his noble figure. And his eyes—ay, he has Magdalen's eyes! If the Gaul had found him with his wife, and had run his sword through his heart, he would have gone unpunished by the earthly judge—however, his father is spared this sorrow. In this desert the old man thought that his darling could not be touched by the world and its pleasures. And now? These brambles I once thought lay dried up on the earth, and could never get up to the top of the palm-tree where the dates ripen; but a bird flew by, and picked up the berries, and carried them into its nest at the highest point of the tree.

Who can point out the road that another will take, and say to-
day, ' To-morrow I shall find him thus and not otherwise?'
We fools flee into the desert in order to forget the world, and
the world pursues us and clings to our skirts. Where are the
shears that are keen enough to cut the shadow from beneath
our feet? What is the prayer that can effectually release us—
born of the flesh—from the burden of the flesh? My Redeemer, Thou Only One, who knowest it, teach it to me, the
basest of the base.''

CHAPTER X.

WITHIN a few minutes after Hermas had flung himself out
of the window into the roadway, Phœbicius walked into his
sleeping-room. Sirona had had time to throw herself on to
her couch; she was terribly frightened, and had turned her
face to the wall. Did he actually know that some one had
been with her? And who could have betrayed her and have
called him home? Or could he have come home by accident
sooner than usual?

It was dark in the room, and he could not see her face, and
yet she kept her eyes shut as if asleep, for every fraction of a
minute in which she could still escape seeing him in his fury
seemed a reprieve; and yet her heart beat so violently that it
seemed to her that he must hear it, when he approached the
bed with a soft step that was peculiar to him. She heard him
walk up and down, and at last go into the kitchen that adjoined
the sleeping-room. In a few moments she perceived, through
her half-closed eyes, that he had brought in a light; he had
lighted a lamp at the hearth, and now searched both the rooms.

As yet he had not spoken to her nor opened his lips to utter
a word.

Now he was in the sitting-room, and now—involuntarily she
drew herself into a heap and pulled the coverlet over her head
—now he laughed aloud, so loud and scornfully that she felt
her hands and feet turn cold, and a rushing crimson mist floated before her eyes. Then the light came back into the bedroom, and came nearer and nearer. She felt her head pushed
by his hard hand, and with a feeble scream she flung off the
coverlet and sat up.

Still he did not speak a word, but what she saw was quite
enough to smother the last spark of her courage and hope, for
her husband's eyes showed only the whites, his sallow features
were ashy pale, and on his brow the branded mark of Mithras

stood out more clearly than ever. In his right hand he held
the lamp, in his left Hermas's sheep-skin.

As his haggard eye met hers he held the anchorite's matted
garments so closely to her face that it touched her. Then he
threw it violently on the floor, and asked, in a low, husky
voice: "What is that?"

She was silent. He went up to the little table near her bed;
on it stood her night-draught in a pretty colored glass, that
Polykarp had brought her from Alexandria as a token, and with
the back of his hand swept it from the table, so that it fell on
the dais, and flew with a crash into a thousand fragments. She
screamed, the greyhound sprung up and barked at the Gaul.
He seized the little ·beast's collar and flung it so violently
across the room that it uttered a pitiful cry of pain. The dog
had belonged to Sirona since she was quite a girl, it had come
with her to Rome, and from thence to the oasis; it clung to
her with affection, and she to it, for Iambe liked no one to
caress and stroke her so much as her mistress. She was so
much alone, and the greyhound was always with her, and not
only entertained her by such tricks as any other dog might
have learned, but was to her a beloved, dumb, but by no means
deaf, companion from her early home, who would prick its ears
when she spoke the name of her dear little sister in distant
Arelas, from whom she had not heard for years; or it would
look sadly in her face, and kiss her white hands when longing
forced tears into her eyes.

In her solitary, idle, childless existence, Iambe was much,
very much, to her, and now, as she saw her faithful companion
and friend creep, ill-treated and whining, up to her bed—as the
supple animal tried in vain to spring up and take refuge in
her lap, and held out to his mistress his trembling, perhaps
broken, little paw, fear vanished from the miserable young
woman's heart—she sprung from her couch, took the little dog
in her arms, and exclaimed, with a glance which flashed with
anything rather than fear or repentance:

"You do not touch the poor little beast again, if you take
my advice."

"I will drown it to-morrow morning," replied Phœbicius
with perfect indifference, but with an evil smile on his flaccid
lips. "So many two-legged lovers make themselves free to
my house that I do not see why I should share your affections
with a quadruped into the bargain. How came this sheep-
skin here?"

Sirona vouchsafed no answer to this last question, but she
exclaimed, in great excitement: "By God—by your god—by

the mighty Rock, and by all the gods! if you do the little
beast a harm, it will be the last day I stop in your house!"

"Hear her!" said the centurion; "and where do you propose to travel to? The desert is wide, and there is room and
to spare to starve in it, and for your bones to bleach there.
How grieved your lovers would be—for their sakes I will take
care before drowning the dog to lock in its mistress."

"Only try to touch me!" screamed Sirona, beside herself,
and springing to the window. "If you lay a finger on me I
will call for help, and Dorothea and her husband will protect
me against you."

"Hardly," answered Phœbicius, dryly. "It would suit you
no doubt to find yourself under the same roof as that great boy
who brings you colored glass, and throws roses into your window, and perhaps has strewed the road with them by which he
found his way to you to-day. But there are nevertheless laws
which protect the Roman citizen from criminals and impudent
seducers. You were always a great deal too much in the house
over there, and you have exchanged your games with the little
screaming beggars for one with the grown-up child, the rose-
thrower—the fop, who, for your sake, and not to be recognized,
covers up his purple coat with a sheep-skin! Do you think
you can teach me anything about love-sick night-wanderers and
women? I see through it all! Not one step do you set hence-
forth across Petrus's threshold. There is the open window—
scream—scream as loud as you will, and let all the people know
of your disgrace. I have the greatest mind to carry this sheep-
skin to the judge the first thing in the morning. I shall go
now, and set the room behind the kitchen in order for you;
there is no window there through which men in sheep-skin can
get into my house. You shall live there till you are tamed,
and kiss my feet, and confess what has been going on here to-
night. I shall learn nothing from the senator's slaves, that I
very well know; for you have turned all their heads too—they
grin with delight when they see you. All friends are made
welcome by you, even when they wear nothing but sheep-skin.
But they may do what they please—I have the right keeper for
you in my own hand. I am going at once—you may scream if
you like, but I should myself prefer that you should keep quiet.
As to the dog, we have not yet heard the last of the matter;
for the present I will keep him here. If you are quiet and
come to your senses, he may live for aught I care; but if you
are refractory, a rope and a stone can soon be found, and the
stream runs close below. You know I never jest—least of all
just now."

Sirona's whole frame was in the most violent agitation. Her breath came quickly, her limbs trembled, but she could not find words to answer him.

Phœbicius saw what was passing in her mind, and he went on: "You may snort proudly now; but an hour will come when you will crawl up to me like your lame dog and pray for mercy. I have another idea—you will want a couch in the dark room, and it must be soft, or I shall be blamed. I will spread out the sheep-skin for you. You see I know how to value your adorer's offerings."

The Gaul laughed loud, seized the hermit's garments, and went with the lamp into the dark room behind the kitchen, in which vessels and utensils of various sorts were kept. These he set on one side to turn it into a sleeping-room for his wife, of whose guilt he was fully convinced.

Who the man was for whose sake she had dishonored him, he knew not, for Miriam had said nothing more than, "Go home, your wife is laughing with her lover."

While her husband was still threatening and storming, Sirona had said to herself that she would rather die than live any longer with this man. That she herself was not free from fault never occurred to her mind. He who is punished more severely than he deserves, easily overlooks his own fault in his feeling for the judge's injustice.

Phœbicius was right; neither Petrus nor Dorothea had it in their power to protect her against him, a Roman citizen. If she could not contrive to help herself she was a prisoner, and without air, light, and freedom she could not live. During his last speech her resolution had been quickly matured, and hardly had he turned his back and crossed the threshold than she hurried up to her bed, wrapped the trembling greyhound in the coverlet, took it in her arms like a child, and ran into the sitting-room with her light burden. The shutters of the window were still open through which Hermas had fled into the open. With the help of a stool she took the same way, let herself slip down from the sill into the street, and hastened on without aim or goal—inspired only by the wish to escape durance in the dark room, and to burst every bond that tied her to her hated mate—up the church hill and along the road which leads over the mountain to the sea.

Phœbicius gave her a long start, for after having arranged her prison he remained some time in the little room behind the kitchen, not in order to give her time, to collect his thoughts or to reflect on his future action, but simply because he felt utterly exhausted.

The centurion was nearly sixty years of age, and his frame, originally a powerful one, was now broken by every sort of dissipation, and could no longer resist the effects of the strain and excitement of this night.

The lean, wiry, and very active man did not usually fall into these fits of total enervation excepting in the day-time, for after sundown a wonderful change would come over the gray-headed veteran, who nevertheless displayed much youthful energy in the exercise of his official duties. At night his drooping eyelids, that almost veiled his eyes, opened more widely, his flaccid hanging under lip closed firmly, his long neck and narrow elongated head were held erect, and when, at a later hour, he went out to drinking-bouts or to the service in honor of Mithras, he might often still be taken for a fine, indomitable young man.

But when he was drunk he was no longer gay, but wild, braggart, and noisy. It frequently happened that before he left the carouse, while he was still in the midst of his boon companions, the syncope would come upon him which had so often alarmed Sirona, and from which he could never feel perfectly safe even when he was on duty at the head of his soldiers.

The vehement big man in such moments offered a terrible image of helpless impotence; the paleness of death would over-spread his features, his back was as if it was broken, and he lost his control over every limb. His eyes only continued to move, and now and then a shudder shook his frame. His people said that when he was in this condition the centurion's ghastly demon had entered into him, and he himself believed in this evil spirit, and dreaded it; nay, he had attempted to be released through heathen spells, and even through Christian exorcisms. Now he sat in the dark room on the sheep-fell, which in scorn of his wife he had spread on a hard wooden bench. His hands and feet turned cold, his eye glowed, and the power to move even a finger had wholly deserted him; only his lips twitched, and his inward eye, looking back on the past with preternaturally sharpened vision, saw far away and beyond the last frightful hour.

"If," thought he, "after my mad run down the oasis, which few younger men could have vied with, I had given the reins to my fury instead of restraining it, the demon would not have mastered me so easily. How that devil Miriam's eyes flashed as she told me that a man was betraying me. She certainly must have seen the wearer of the sheep-skin, but I lost sight of her before I reached the oasis; I fancy she turned and went up the mountain. What indeed might not Sirona have done to her? That woman snares all hearts with her eyes as a bird-catcher snares birds with his flute. How the fine gentlemen ran after her in Rome! Did she dishonor me there, I wonder? She dismissed the legate Quintillus, who was so anxious to please me—I may thank that fool of a woman that he became my enemy—but he was older even than I, and she likes young men best. She is like all the rest of them, and I of all men might have known it. It is the way of the world; to-day one gives a blow and to-morrow takes one."

A sad smile passed over his lips, then his features settled into a stern gravity, for various unwelcome images rose clearly before his mind, and would not be got rid of.

His conscience stood in inverse relation to the vigor of his body. When he was well, his too darkly stained past life troubled him little; but when he was unmanned by weakness, he was incapable of fighting the ghastly demon that forced upon his memory in painful vividness those very deeds which he would most willingly have forgotten. In such hours he must need remember his friend, his benefactor, and superior officer, the tribune Servianus, whose fair young wife he had tempted with a thousand arts to forsake her husband and child and fly with him into the wide world; and at this moment a bewildering illusion made him fancy that he was the tribune Servianus and yet at the same time himself. Every hour of pain, and the whole bitter anguish that his betrayed benefactor had suffered through his act when he had seduced Glycera, he himself now seemed to realize, and at the same time the enemy that had betrayed him, Servianus, was none other than himself, Phœbicius, the Gaul. He tried to protect himself, and meditated revenge against the seducer, and still he could not altogether lose the sense of his own identity.

This whirl of mad imagining, which he vainly endeavored to make clear to himself, threatened to distract his reason, and he groaned aloud; the sound of his own voice brought him back to actuality.

He was Phœbicius again and not another, that he knew now, and yet he could not completely bring himself to comprehend the situation. The image of the lovely Glycera, who had followed him to Alexandria, and whom he had there abandoned when he had squandered his last piece of money and her last costly jewels in the Greek city, no longer appeared to him alone, but always side by side with his wife Sirona.

Glycera had been a melancholy sweetheart, who had wept much and laughed little after running away from her husband; he fancied he could hear her speaking soft words of re-

4

proach, while Sirona defied him with loud threats, and dared
to nod and signal to the senator's son Polykarp.

The weary dreamer angrily shook himself, collected his
thoughts, doubled his fist and lifted it angrily; this movement
was the first sign of returning physical energy; he stretched
his limbs like a man awaking from sleep, rubbed his eyes,
pressed his hands to his temples; by degrees full consciousness
returned to him, and with it the recollection of all that had occurred in the last hour or two.

He hastily left the dark room, refreshed himself in the
kitchen with a gulp of wine, and went up to the open window
to gaze at the stars.

It was long past midnight; he was reminded of his companions now sacrificing on the mountains, and addressed a long
prayer " to the crown," " the invincible sun-god," " the great
light," " the god begotten of the rock," and to many other
names of Mithras; for since he had belonged to the mystics of
this divinity, he had become a zealous devotee, and could fast,
too, with extraordinary constancy. He had already passed
through several of the eighty trials, to which a man had to subject himself before he could attain to the highest grades of the
initiated, and the weakness which had just now overpowered
him, had attacked him for the first time after he had for a
whole week lain for hours in the snow, besides fasting severely
in order to attain the grade of " Lion."

Sirona's rigorous mind was revolted by all these practices,
and the decision with which she had always refused to take
any part in them had widened the breach which, without that,
parted her from her husband. Phoebicius was, in his fashion,
very much in earnest with all these things; for they alone
saved him in some measure from himself, from dark memories,
and from the fear of meeting the reward of his evil deeds in a
future life, while Sirona found her best comfort in the remem-
brance of her early life, and so gathered courage to endure the
miserable present cheerfully, and to hold fast to hope for better times.

Phoebicius ended his prayer to-day—a prayer for strength to
break his wife's strong spirit, for a successful issue to his revenge on her seducer—ended it without haste, and with careful observance of all the prescribed forms. Then he took two
strong ropes from the wall, pulled himself up, straight and
proud, as if he were about to exhort his soldiers to courage before a battle, cleared his throat like an orator in the Forum
before he begins his discourse, and entered the bedroom with a
dignified demeanor. Not the smallest suspicion of the possi-

bility of her escape troubled his sense of security when, not finding Sirona in the sleeping-room, he went into the sitting-room to carry out the meditated punishment. Here again—no one.

He paused in astonishment; but the thought that she could have fled appeared to him so insane that he immediately and decisively dismissed it. No doubt she feared his wrath, and was hidden under her bed or behind the curtain which covered his clothes. "The dog," thought he, "is still cowering by her—" and he began to make a noise, half whistling, and half hissing, which Iambe could not bear, and which always provoked her to bark angrily—but in vain. All was still in the vacant room, still as death. He was now seriously anxious; at first deliberately, and then with rapid haste, he threw the light under every vessel, into every corner, behind every cloth, and rummaged in places that not even a child—nay, hardly a frightened bird—could have availed itself of for concealment. At last his right hand fairly dropped the ropes, and his left, in which he held the lamp, began to tremble. He found the shutters of the sleeping-room open, where Sirona had been sitting on the seat looking at the moon, before Hermas had come upon the scene. "Then she is not here!" he muttered, and setting the lamp on the little table, from which he had just now flung Polykarp's glass, he tore open the door, and hurried into the court-yard. That she could have swung herself into the road, and have set out in the night for the open desert, had not yet entered into his mind. He shook the door that closed in the homestead, and found it locked; the watch-dogs roused themselves, and gave tongue, when Phœbicius turned to Petrus's house, and began to knock at the door with the brazen knocker, at first softly and then with growing anger; he considered it as certain that his wife had sought and found protection under the senator's roof. He could have shouted with rage and anguish, and yet he hardly thought of his wife and danger of losing her, but only of Polykarp and the disgrace he had wrought him and the reparation he would exact from him and his parents, who had dared to tamper with his household rights—his, the imperial centurion's.

What was Sirona to him? In the flush of an hour of excitement he had linked her destiny to his.

At Arelas, about two years since, one of his comrades had joined their circle of boon companions, and had related that he had been the witness of a remarkable scene. A number of young fellows had surrounded a boy and had unmercifully beaten him—he himself knew not wherefore. The little one had defended himself bravely, but was at last overcome by numbers. "Then suddenly," continued the soldier, "the door of a house near the circus opened, and a young girl with long golden hair flew out, and drove the boys to flight, and released the victim, her brother, from his tormentors. She looked like a lioness," cried the narrator; "Sirona she is called, and of all the pretty girls of Arelas, she is beyond a doubt the prettiest." This opinion was confirmed on all sides, and Phœbicius, who at that time had just been admitted to the grade of "Lion" among the worshipers of Mithras, and liked very well to hear himself called "the Lion," exclaimed, "I have long been seeking a Lioness, and here it seems to me that I have found one. Phœbicius and Sirona—the two names sound very finely together."

On the following day he asked Sirona of her father for his wife, and as he had to set out for Rome in a few days the wedding was promptly celebrated. She had never before quitted Arelas, and knew not what she was giving up when she took leave of her father's house perhaps forever. In Rome Phœbicius and his young wife met again; there many admired the beautiful woman, and made every effort to obtain her favor, but to him she was only a lightly won, and therefore lightly valued, possession; nay, ere long no more than a burden, ornamental no doubt, but troublesome to guard. When presently his handsome wife attracted the notice of the legate, he endeavored to gain profit and advancement through her, but Sirona had rebuffed Quintillus with such insulting disrespect, that his superior officer became the centurion's enemy, and contrived to procure his removal to the oasis, which was tantamount to banishment.

From that time he had regarded her, too, as his enemy, and firmly believed that she designedly showed herself most friendly to those who seemed most obnoxious to him, and among these he reckoned Polykarp.

Once more the knocker sounded on the senator's door; it opened, and Petrus himself stood before the raging Gaul, a lamp in his hand.

————

CHAPTER XI.

THE unfortunate Paulus sat on a stone bench in front of the senator's door, and shivered; for, as dawn approached, the night-air grew cooler, and he was accustomed to the warmth of the sheep-skin, which he had now given to Hermas. In his hand he held the key of the church, which he had promised the door-keeper to deliver to Petrus; but all was so still in the senator's house that he shrunk from rousing the sleepers.

"What a strange night this has been!" he muttered to himself, as he drew his short and tattered tunic closer together. "Even if it were warmer, and if, instead of this threadbare rag, I had a sack of feathers to wrap myself in, still I should feel a cold shiver if the spirits of hell that wander about here were to meet me again. Now I have actually seen one with my own eyes. Demons in women's form rush up the mountain out of the oasis to tempt and torture us in our sleep. What could it have been that the goblin in a white robe and with flowing hair held in its arms? Very likely the stone with which the incubus loads our breast when he torments us. The other one seemed to fly, but I did not see its wings. That side building must be where the Gaul lives with his ungodly wife, who has ensnared my poor Hermas. I wonder whether she is really so beautiful! But what can a youth who has grown up among rocks and caves know of the charms of women? He would, of course, think the first who looked kindly at him the most enchanting of her sex. Besides, she is fair, and therefore a rare bird among the sun-burned bipeds of the desert. The centurion surely can not have found the sheep-skin, or all would not be so still here; once since I have been here an ass has brayed, once a camel has groaned, and now already the first cock is crowing; but not a sound have I heard from human lips, not even a snore from the stout senator or his buxom wife Dorothea, and it would be strange indeed if they did not both snore."

He rose, went up to the window of Phœbicius's dwelling, and listened at the half-open shutters, but all was still.

An hour ago Miriam had been listening under Sirona's room; after betraying her to Phœbicius she had followed him at a distance, and had slipped back into the court-yard through the stables. She felt that she must learn what was happening within, and what fate had befallen Hermas and Sirona at the hands of the infuriated Gaul. She was prepared for anything, and the thought that the centurion might have killed them both with the sword filled her with bitter-sweet satisfaction. Then, seeing the light through the crack between the partly open wooden shutters, she softly pushed them further apart, and, resting her bare feet against the wall, she raised herself to look in.

She saw Sirona sitting up upon her couch, and opposite to her the Gaul with pale distorted features; at his feet lay the sheep-skin; in his right hand he held the lamp, and its light

fell on the paved floor in front of the bed, and was reflected in
a large dark-red pool.

"That is blood," thought she, and she shuddered and closed
her eyes.

When she reopened them she saw Sirona's face, with crimson
cheeks, turned toward her husband; she was unhurt—but
Hermas?

"That is his blood!" she thought, with anguish, and a voice
seemed to scream in her very heart, "I, his murderess, have
shed it."

Her hands lost their hold of the shutters, her feet touched
the pavement of the yard, and, driven by her bitter anguish of
soul, she fled out by the way she had come—out into the open
and up to the mountain. She felt that rather would she defy
the prowling panthers, the night-chill, hunger and thirst, than
appear again before Dame Dorothea, the senator, and Marthana with this guilt on her soul; and the flying Miriam was
one of the goblin forms that had terrified Paulus.

The patient anchorite sat down again on the stone seat.
"The frost is really cruel," thought he, "and a very good
thing is such a woolly sheep-skin; but the Saviour endured far
other sufferings than these, and for what did I quit the world
but to imitate Him, and to endure to the end here that I may
win the joys of the other world. There, where angels soar,
man will need no wretched ram's-fell, and this time certainly
selfishness has been far from me, for I really and truly suffer
for another—I am freezing for Hermas, and to spare the old
man pain. I would it were even colder! Nay, I will never,
absolutely never again, lay a sheep-skin over my shoulders."

Paulus nodded his head as if to signify assent to his own resolve; but presently he looked graver, for again it seemed to
him that he was walking in a wrong path.

"Ay! Man achieves a handful of good, and forthwith his
heart swells with a camel-load of pride. What though my
teeth are chattering, I am none the less a most miserable creature. How it tickled my vanity, in spite of all my meditations
and scruples, when they came from Raithu and offered me the
office of elder; I felt more triumphant the first time I won with
the quadriga, but I was scarcely more puffed up with pride
then than I was yesterday. How many who think to follow
the Lord strive only to be exalted as He is; they keep well out
of the way of His abasement. Thou, oh, Thou Most High,
art my witness that I earnestly seek it, but so soon as the
thorns tear my flesh the drops of blood turn to roses, and if I
put them aside, others come and still fling garlands in my

way. I verily believe that it is as hard here on earth to find pain without pleasure as pleasure without pain."

While thus he meditated his teeth chattered with cold, but suddenly his reflections were interrupted, for the dogs set up a loud barking. Phœbicius was knocking at the senator's door.

Paulus rose at once and approached the gate-way. He could hear every word that was spoken in the court-yard: the deep voice was the senator's, the high sharp tones must be the centurion's.

Phœbicius was demanding his wife back from Petrus, as she had hidden in his house, while Petrus positively declared that Sirona had not crossed his threshold since the morning of the previous day.

In spite of the vehement and indignant tones in which his lodger spoke, the senator remained perfectly calm, and presently went away to ask his wife whether she by chance, while he was asleep, had opened the house to the missing woman. Paulus heard the soldier's steps as he paced up and down the court-yard, but they soon ceased, for Dame Dorothea appeared at the door with her husband, and on her part emphatically declared that she knew nothing of Sirona.

"Your son Polykarp, then," interrupted Phœbicius, "will be better informed of her whereabouts."

"My son has been since yesterday at Raithu on business," said Petrus, resolutely but evasively; "we expect him home to-day only."

"It would seem that he has been quick, and has returned much sooner," retorted Phœbicius. "Our preparations for sacrificing on the mountain were no secret, and the absence of the master of the house is the opportunity for thieves to break in—above all, for lovers who throw roses into their ladies' windows. You Christians boast that you regard the marriage tie as sacred, but it seems to me that you apply the rule only to your fellow-believers. Your sons may make free to take their pleasure among the wives of the heathen; it only remains to be proved whether the heathen husbands will be trifled with or not. So far as I am concerned, I am inclined for anything rather than jesting. I would have you to understand that I will never let Cæsar's uniform, which I wear, be stained by disgrace, and that I am minded to search your house, and if I find my undutiful wife and your son within its walls, I will carry them and you before the judge, and sue for my rights."

"You will seek in vain," replied Petrus, commanding himself with difficulty. "My word is yea or nay, and I repeat once more no, we harbor neither her nor him. As for Dorothea and myself, neither of us is inclined to interfere in your concerns, but neither will we permit another—be he whom he may—to interfere in ours. This threshold shall never be crossed by any but those to whom I grant permission, or by the emperor's judge, to whom I must yield. You I forbid to enter. Sirona is not here, and you would do better to seek her elsewhere than to fritter away your time here."

" I do not require your advice!" cried the centurion, wrathfully.

"And I," retorted Petrus, " do not feel myself called upon to arrange your matrimonial difficulties. Besides you can get back Sirona without our help, for it is always more difficult to keep a wife safe in the house than to fetch her back when she has run away."

" You shall learn whom you have to deal with!" threatened the centurion, and he threw a glance round at the slaves, who had collected in the court, and who had been joined by the senator's eldest son. " I shall call my people together at once, and if you have the seducer among you we will intercept his escape."

" Only wait an hour," said Dorothea, now taking up the word, while she gently touched her husband's hand, for his self-control was almost exhausted, " and you will see Polykarp ride home on his father's horse. Is it only from the roses that my son threw into your wife's window that you suppose him to be her seducer—she plays so kindly with all his brothers and sisters—or are there other reasons which move you to insult and hurt us with so heavy an accusation?"

Often when wrathful men threaten to meet with an explosion, like black thunder-clouds, a word from the mouth of a sensible woman gives them pause, and restrains them like a breath of soft wind.

Phœbicius had no mind to listen to any speech from Polykarp's mother, but her question suggested to him for the first time a rapid retrospect of all that had occurred, and he could not conceal from himself that his suspicions rested on weak grounds. And at the same time he now said to himself that if indeed Sirona had fled into the desert instead of to the senator's house he was wasting time, and letting the start, which she had already gained, increase in a fatal degree.

But few seconds were needed for these reflections, and as he was accustomed, when need arose, to control himself, he said:

" We must see—some means must be found—" and then without any greeting to his host, he slowly returned to his own house. But he had not reached the door, when he heard hoofs on the road, and Petrus called after him, "Grant us a few minutes longer, for here comes Polykarp, and he can justify himself to you in his own person."

The centurion paused, the senator signed to old Jethro to open the gate; a man was heard to spring from his saddle, but it was an Amalekite—and not Polykarp—who came into the court.

"What news do you bring?" asked the senator, turning half to the messenger and half to the centurion.

"My lord Polykarp, your son," replied the Amalekite—a dark brown man of ripe years with supple limbs, and a sharp tongue—"sends his greetings to you and to the mistress, and would have you to know that before midday he will arrive at home with eight workmen, whom he has engaged in Raithu. Dame Dorothea must be good enough to make ready for them all and to prepare a meal."

"When did you part from my son?" inquired Petrus.

"Two hours before sundown."

Petrus heaved a sigh of relief, for he had not till now been perfectly convinced of his son's innocence; but, far from triumphing or making Phœbicius feel the injustice he had done him, he said kindly—for he felt some sympathy with the Gaul in his misfortune:

"I wish the messenger could also give some news of your wife's retreat; she found it hard to accommodate herself to the dull life here in the oasis, perhaps she has only disappeared in order to seek a town which may offer more variety to such a beautiful young creature than this quiet spot in the desert."

Phœbicius waved his hand with a negative movement, implying that he knew better, and said:

"I will show you what your nice night-bird left in my nest. It may be that you can tell me to whom it belongs."

Just as he hastily stepped across the court-yard to his own dwelling Paulus entered by the now open gate; he greeted the senator and his family, and offered Petrus the key of the church.

The sun meanwhile had risen, and the Alexandrian blushed to show himself in Dame Dorothea's presence in his short and ragged undergarment, which was quite inefficient to cover the still athletic mold of his limbs. Petrus had heard nothing but good of Paulus, and yet he measured him now with no friendly eye, for all that wore the aspect of extravagance repelled his temperate and methodical nature. Paulus was made conscious of what was passing in the senator's mind when, without vouchsafing a single word, he took the key from his hand. It was not a matter of indifference to him that this man should think ill of him, and he said, with some embarrassment:

"We do not usually go among people without a sheep-skin, but I have lost mine."

Hardly had he uttered the words, when Phœbicius came back with Hermas's sheep-skin in his hand, and cried out to Petrus:

"This I found on my return home, in our sleeping-room."

"And when have you ever seen Polykarp in such a mantle?" asked Dorothea.

"When the gods visit the daughters of men," replied the centurion, "they have always made choice of strange disguises. Why should not a perfumed Alexandrian gentleman transform himself for once into one of those rough fools on the mountain? However, even old Homer sometimes nodded—and I confess that I was in error with regard to your son. I meant no offense, senator! You have lived here longer than I; who can have made me a present of this skin, which still seems to be pretty new—horns and all?"

Petrus examined and felt the skin. "This is an anchorite's garment," he said; "the penitents on the mountain are all accustomed to wear such."

"It is one of those rascals then that has found his way into my house!" exclaimed the centurion. "I bear Cæsar's commission, and I am to exterminate all vagabonds that trouble the dwellers in the oasis, or travelers in the desert. Thus run the orders which I brought with me from Rome. I will drive the low fellows together like deer for hunting, for they are all rogues and villains, and I shall know how to torture them until I find the right one."

"The emperor will ill-requite you for that," replied Petrus. "They are pious Christians, and you know that Constantine himself—"

"Constantine!" exclaimed the centurion, scornfully. "Perhaps he will let himself be baptized, for water can hurt no one, and he can not, like the great Diocletian, exterminate the masses who run after the crucified miracle-monger, without depopulating the country. Look at these coins; here is the image of Cæsar, and what is this on the other side? Is this your Nazarene, or is it the old god, the immortal and invincible sun? And is that man one of your creed, who in Constantinople adores Tyche and the Dioscuri Castor and Pollux? The water he is baptized with to-day he will wipe away to-morrow, and the old gods will be his defenders, if in more peaceful times he maintains them against your superstitions."

"But it will be a good while till then," said Petrus coolly.

"For the present, at least, Constantine is the protector of the Christians. I advise you to put your affair into the hands of Bishop Agapitus."

"That he may serve me up a dish of your doctrine, which is bad even for women," said the centurion, laughing; "and that I may kiss my enemies' feet? They are a vile rabble up there, I repeat, and they shall be treated as such till I have found my man. I shall begin the hunt this very day."

"And this very day you may end it, for the sheep-skin is mine."

It was Paulus who spoke these words in a loud and decided tone; all eyes were at once turned on him and on the centurion.

Petrus and the slaves had frequently seen the anchorite, but never without a sheep-skin similar to that which Phœbicius held in his hand. The anchorite's self-accusation must have appeared incredible, and indeed scarcely possible, to all who knew Paulus and Sirona; and nevertheless no one, not even the senator, doubted it for an instant. Dame Dorothea only shook her head incredulously, and though she could find no explanation for the occurrence, she still could not but say to herself that this man did not look like a lover, and that Sirona would hardly have forgotten her duty for his sake. She could not indeed bring herself to believe in Sirona's guilt at all, for she was heartily well-disposed toward her; besides—though it, no doubt, was not right—her motherly vanity inclined her to believe that if the handsome young woman had indeed sinned, she would have preferred her fine tall Polykarp—whose roses and flaming glances she blamed in all sincerity—to this shaggy, wild-looking gray beard.

Quite otherwise thought the centurion. - He was quite ready to believe in the anchorite's confession, for the more unworthy the man for whom Sirona had broken faith, the greater seemed her guilt, and the more unpardonable her levity; and to his man's vanity it seemed to him easier—particularly in the presence of such witnesses as Petrus and Dorothea—to bear the fact that his wife should have sought variety and pleasure at any cost, even at that of devoting herself to a ragged beggar, than that she should have given her affections to a younger, handsomer, and worthier man than himself. He had sinned much against her, but all that lay like feathers on his side of the scales, while that which she had done weighed down hers like a load of lead. He began to feel like a man who, in wading through a bog, has gained firm ground with one foot, and all these feelings gave him energy to walk up to the anchorite

with a self-control of which he was not generally master, excepting when on duty at the head of his soldiers.

He approached the Alexandrian with an assumption of dignity and a demeanor which testified to his formerly having
taken part in the representations of tragedies in the theaters
of great cities. Paulus, on his part, did not retreat by a single
step, but looked at him with a smile that alarmed Petrus and
the rest of the by-standers. The law put the anchorite absolutely into the power of the outraged husband, but Phœbicius
did not seem disposed to avail himself of his rights, and nothing but contempt and loathing were perceptible in his tone, as
he said:

. . " A man who takes hold of a mangy dog in order to punish
him only dirties his hand. The woman who betrayed me for
your sake, and you—you dirty beggar—are worthy of each
other. I could crush you like a fly that can be destroyed
by a blow of my hand if I chose, but my sword is Cæsar's, and
shall never be soiled by such foul blood as yours; however, the
beast shall not have cast off his skin for nothing; it is thick,
and so you have only spared me the trouble of tearing it off before giving you your due. You shall find no lack of blows.
Confess where your sweetheart has fled to and they shall be
few, but if you are slow to answer they will be many. Lend
me that thing there, fellow!"

With these words he took a whip of hippopotamus hide out
of a camel-driver's hand, went close up to the Alexandrian,
and asked: " Where is Sirona?"

" Nay, you may beat me," said Paulus. " However hard
your whip may fall on me, it can not be heavy enough for my
sins; but as to where your wife is hiding, that I really can not
tell you—not even if you were to tear my limbs with pincers
instead of stroking me with that wretched thing."

There was something so genuinely honest in Paulus's voice
and tone, that the centurion was inclined to believe him; but
it was not his way to let a threatened punishment fail of execution, and this strange beggar should learn by experience that
when his hand intended to hit hard, it was far from " stroking." And Paulus did experience it, without uttering a cry,
and without stirring from the spot where he stood.

When at last Phœbicius dropped his weary arm and breathlessly repeated his question, the ill-used man replied:

" I told you before I do not know, and therefore I can not
reveal it."

Up to this moment Petrus, though he had felt strongly impelled to rush to the rescue of his severely handled fellow-be-

liever, had nevertheless allowed the injured husband to have his way, for he seemed disposed to act with unusual mildness, and the Alexandrian to be worthy of all punishment; but at this point Dorothea's request would not have been needed to prompt him to interfere.

He went up to the centurion, and said to him in an undertone:

"You have given the evil-doer his due, and if you desire that he should undergo a severer punishment than you can inflict, carry the matter—I say once more—before the bishop. You will gain nothing more here. Take my word for it. I know the man and his fellow-men; he actually knows nothing of where your wife is hiding, and you are only wasting the time and strength which you would do better to save in order to search for Sirona. I fancy she will have tried to reach the sea, and to get to Egypt or possibly to Alexandria; and there—you know what the Greek city is—she will fall into utter ruin."

"And so," laughed the Gaul, "find what she seeks—variety and every kind of pleasure. For a young thing like that, who loves amusement, there is no pleasant occupation but vice. But I will spoil her game; you are right, it is not well to give her too long a start. If she has found the road to the sea, she may already— Hey, here Talib!" He beckoned to Polykarp's Amalekite messenger. "You have just come from Raithu; did you meet a flying woman on the way, with yellow hair and a white face?"

The Amalekite, a free man with sharp eyes, who was highly esteemed in the senator's house, and even by Phœbicius himself, as a trustworthy and steady man, had expected this question, and eagerly replied: ·

"At two stadia beyond El Heswe I met a large caravan from Petria, which rested yesterday in the oasis here; a woman, such as you describe, was running with it. When I heard what had happened here I wanted to speak, but who listens to a cricket while it thunders?"

"Had she a lame greyhound with her?" asked Phœbicius, full of expectation.

"She carried something in her arms," answered the Amalekite. "In the moonlight I took it for a baby. My brother, who was escorting the caravan, told me the lady was no doubt running away, for she had paid the charge for the escort not in ready money, but with a gold signet-ring."

The Gaul remembered a certain gold ring with a finely carved onyx, which long years ago he had taken from Glycera's finger,

for she had another one like it, and which he had given to
Sirona on the day of their marriage.

"It is strange!" thought he; "what we give to women to
bind them to us they use as weapons to turn against us, be it
to please some other man, or to smooth the path by which they
escape from us. It was with a bracelet of Glycera's that I paid
the captain of the ship that brought us to Alexandria; but the
soft-hearted fool, whose dove flew after me, and I are men of a
different stamp; I will follow my flown bird, and catch it
again."

He spoke the last words aloud, and then desired one of the
senator's slaves to give his mule a good feed and drink, for his
own groom and the superior decurion who during his absence
must take his place, were also worshipers of Mithras, and had
not yet returned from the mountain.

Phœbicius did not doubt that the woman who had joined the
caravan—which he himself had seen yesterday—was his fugitive
wife, and he knew that his delay might have reduced his earnest
wish to overtake her and punish her to the remotest proba-
bility; but he was a Roman soldier, and would rather have laid
violent hands on himself than have left his post without a
deputy. When at last his fellow-worshipers came from their
sacrifice and worship of the rising sun, his preparations for his
long journey were completed.

Phœbicius carefully impressed on the decurion all he had to
do during his absence, and how he was to conduct himself;
then he delivered the key of his house into Petrus's keeping as
well as the black slave-woman, who wept loudly and passionately over the flight of her mistress; he requested the senator
to bring the anchorite's misdeed to the knowledge of the
bishop, and then, guided by the Amalekite Talib, who rode
before him on his dromedary, he trotted hastily away in pursuit of the caravan, so as to reach the sea, if possible, before
its embarkation.

As the hoofs of the mule sounded fainter and fainter in the
distance, Paulus also quitted the senator's court-yard; Dorothea
pointed after him as he walked toward the mountain. "In
truth, husband," said she, "this has been a strange morning;
everything that has occurred looks as clear as day, and yet I
can not understand it all. My heart aches when I think what
may happen to the wretched Sirona if her enraged husband
overtakes her. It seems to me that there are two sorts of marriage; one was instituted by the most loving of the angels, nay,
by the All-Merciful himself, but the other—it is not to be
thought of! How can those two live together for the future?

And that under our roof! Their closed house looks to me as though ruined and burned out, and we have already seen the nettles spring up which grow everywhere among the ruins of human dwellings.''

————o————

PART II.

CHAPTER I.

THE path of every star is fixed and limited, every plant bears flowers and fruit which in form and color exactly resemble their kind, and in all the fundamental characteristics of their qualities and dispositions, of their instinctive bent and external impulse, all animals of the same species resemble each other; thus, the hunter who knows the red deer in his fathers' forest, may know in every forest on earth how the stag will behave in any given case. The better a genus is fitted for variability in the comformation of its individuals, the higher is the rank it is entitled to hold in the graduated series of creatures capable of development; and it is precisely that wonderful many-sidedness of his inner life, and of its outward manifestation, which assigns to man his superiority over all other animated beings.

Some few of our qualities and activities can be fitly symbolized in allegorical fashion by animals; thus, courage finds an emblem in the lion, gentleness in the dove, but the perfect human form has satisfied a thousand generations, and will satisfy a thousand more, when we desire to reduce the divinity to a sensible image, for, in truth, our heart is as surely capable of comprehending " God in us "—that is in our feelings— as our intellect is capable of comprehending His outward manifestation in the universe.

Every characteristic of every finite being is to be found again in man, and no characteristic that we can attribute to the Most High is foreign to our own soul, which, in like manner, is infinite and immeasurable, for it can extend its investigating feelers to the very utmost boundary of space and time. Hence, the roads which are open to the soul are numberless as those of the divinity. Often they seem strange, but the initiated very well know that these roads are in accordance to fixed laws, and that even the most exceptional emotions of the soul may be traced back to causes which were capable of giving rise to them and to no others.

Blows hurt, disgrace is a burden, and unjust punishment embitters the heart; but Paulus's soul had sought and found a way to which these simple propositions did not apply.

He had been ill-used and contemned, and, though perfectly innocent, ere he left the oasis he was condemned to the severest penance. As soon as the bishop had heard from Petrus of all that had happened in his house, he had sent for Paulus, and as he could answer nothing to the accusation, he had expelled him from his flock—to which the anchorites belonged—forbidden him to visit the church on week days, and declared that this his sentence should be publicly proclaimed before the assembled congregation of the believers.

And how did this affect Paulus as he climbed the mountain, lonely and proscribed?

A fisherman from the little sea-port of Pharan, who met him half way and exchanged a greeting with him, thought to himself as he looked after him, "The great gray-beard looks as happy as if he had found a treasure." Then he walked on into the valley with his scaly wares, reminded, as he went, of his son's expression of face when his wife bore him his first little one.

Near the watch-tower at the edge of the defile, a party of anchorites were piling some stones together. They had already heard of the bishop's sentence on Paulus, the sinner, and they gave him no greeting. He observed it and was silent, but when they could no longer see him he laughed to himself and muttered, while he rubbed a weal that the centurion's whip had left upon his back, "If they think that a Gaul's cudgel has a pleasant flavor they are mistaken; however I would not exchange it for a skin of Anthyllan wine; and if they could only know that at least one of the stripes which torments me is due to each one of themselves, they would be surprised! But away with pride! How they spat on Thee, Jesus my Lord, and who am I, and how mildly have they dealt with me, when I for once have taken on my back another's stripes. Not a drop of blood was drawn! I wish the old man had hit harder!"

He walked cheerfully forward, and his mind recurred to the centurion's speech that "he could, if he list, tread him down like a worm," and he laughed again softly, for he was quite aware that he was ten times as strong as Phœbicius, and formerly he had overthrown the braggart Arkesilaos of Kyrene and his cousin, the tall Xenophanes, both at once in the sand of the Palæstra. Then he thought of Hermas, of his sweet dead mother, and of his father, and—which was the most comforting thought of all—of how he had spared the old man this bitter sorrow.

On his path there grew a little plant with a reddish blossom. In years he had never looked at a flower, or, at any rate, had never wished to possess one; to-day he stooped down over the blossom that graced the rock, meaning to pluck it. But he did not carry out his intention, for before he had laid his hand upon it he reflected:

"To whom could I offer it? And perhaps the flowers themselves rejoice in the light, and in the silent life that is in their roots. How tightly it clings to the rock. Further away from the road flowers of even greater beauty blow, seen by no mortal eye; they deck themselves in beauty for no one but for their Creator, and because they rejoice in themselves. I, too, will withdraw from the highways of mankind; let them accuse me! so long as I live at peace with myself and my God I ask nothing of any one. He that abases himself—ay, he that abases himself! My hour, too, shall come, and above and beyond this life I shall see them all once more: Petrus and Dorothea, Agapitus and the brethren who now refuse to receive me, and then, when my Saviour himself beckons me to Him, they will see me as I am, and hasten to me and greet me with double kindness."

He looked up, proud and rejoicing as he thought thus, and painted to himself the joys of Paradise, to which this day he had earned an assured claim. He never took longer and swifter steps than when his mind was occupied with such meditations, and when he reached Stephanus's cave he thought the way from the oasis to the heights had been shorter than usual.

He found the sick man in great anxiety, for he had waited until now for his son in vain, and feared that Hermas had met with some accident—or had abandoned him, and fled out into the world. Paulus soothed him with gentle words, and told him of the errand on which he had sent the lad to the further coast of the sea.

We are never better disposed to be satisfied with even bad news than when we have expected it to be much worse; so Stephanus listened to his friend's explanation quite calmly, and with signs of approval. He could no longer conceal from himself that Hermas was not ripe for the life of an anchorite, and since he had learned that his unhappy wife—whom he had so long given up for lost—had died a Christian, he found that he could reconcile his thoughts to relinquishing the boy to the

world. He had devoted himself and his son to a life of penance, hoping and striving that so Glycera's soul might be
snatched from damnation, and now he knew that she herself
had earned her title to heaven.

"When will he come home again?" he asked Paulus.

"In five or six days," was the answer. "Ali, the fisherman—out of whose foot I took a thorn some time since—informed me secretly, as I was going to church yesterday, that
the Blemmyes are gathering behind the sulphur mountains;
when they have withdrawn it will be high time to send Hermas
to Alexandria. My brother is still alive, and for my sake he
will receive him as a blood relation, for he, too, has been baptized.

"He may attend the school of catechumens in the metropolis, and if he—if he—"

"That we shall see," interrupted Paulus. "For the present it comes to this, we must let him go from hence, and leave
him to seek out his own way. You fancy that there may be
in heaven a place of glory for such as have never been overcome, and you would fain have seen Hermas among them. It
reminds me of the physician of Corinth, who boasted that he
was cleverer than any of his colleagues, for that not one of his
patients had ever died. And the man was right, for neither
man nor beast had ever trusted to his healing arts. Let
Hermas try his young strength, and even if he be no priest,
but a valiant warrior like his forefathers, even so he may
honestly serve God. But it will be a long time before all this
comes to pass. So long as he is away I will attend on you—
you still have some water in your jar?"

"It has twice been filled for me," said the old man. "The
brown shepherdess, who so often waters her goats at our
spring, came to me the first thing in the morning and again
about two hours ago; she asked after Hermas, and then offered
of her own accord to fetch water for me so long as he was
away. She is as timid as a bird, and flew off as soon as she
had set down the jug."

"She belongs to Petrus, and can not leave her goats for
long," said Paulus. "Now, I will go and find you some herbs
for a relish; there will be no more wine in the first place.
Look me in the face—for how great a sinner now do you take
me? Think the very worst of me, and yet perhaps you will
hear worse said of me. But here come two men. Stay! one
is Hilarion, one of the bishop's acolytes, and the other is
Pachomius the Memphite, who lately came to the mountain.
They are coming up here, and the Egyptian is carrying a

small jar. I would it might hold some more wine to keep up your strength.''

The two friends had not long to remain in ignorance of their visitors' purpose. So soon as they reached Stephanus's cave both turned their backs on Paulus with conspicuously marked intention; nay, the acolyte signed his brow with the cross, as if he thought it necessary to protect himself against evil influences.

The Alexandrian understood; he drew back and was silent, while Hilarion explained to he sick man that Paulus was guilty of grave sins, and that, until he had done full penance, he must remain excluded as a rotten sheep from the bishop's flock, as well as interdicted from waiting on a pious Christian.

"We know from Petrus," the speaker went on, "that your son, father, has been sent across the sea, and as you still need waiting on, Agapitus sends you by me his blessing and this strengthening wine; this youth, too, will stay by you, and provide you with all necessaries until Hermas comes home.''

With these words he gave the wine-jar to the old man, who looked in astonishment from him to Paulus, who felt indeed cut to the heart when the bishop's messenger turned to him for an instant, and with the cry, "Get thee out from among us!'' disappeared.

How many kindly ties, how many services willingly rendered and affectionately accepted were swept away by these words— but Paulus obeyed at once. He went up to his sick friend, their eyes met and each could see that the eyes of the other were dimmed with tears.

"Paulus," cried the old man, stretching out both his hands to his departing friend, whom he felt he could forgive whatever his guilt; but the Alexandrian did not take them, but turned away, and, without looking back, hastily went up the mountain to a pathless spot, and then on toward the valley— onward and still onward, till he was brought to a pause by the steep declivity of the hollow way which led southward from the mountains into the oasis.

The sun stood high, and it was burning hot. Streaming with sweat and panting for breath he leaned against the glowing porphyry wall behind him, hid his face in his hands and strove to collect himself, to think, to pray—for a long time in vain; for instead of joy in the suffering which he had taken upon himself, the grief of isolation weighed upon his heart, and the lamentable cry of the old man had left a warning echo in his soul, and roused doubts of the rightcousness of a deed, by which even the best and purest had been deceived, and led into injustice toward him. His heart was breaking with anguish and grief, but when at last he returned to the consciousness of his sufferings, physical and mental, he began to recover his courage, and even smiled as he murmured to himself:

"It is well, it is well—the more I suffer the more surely shall I find grace. And besides, if the old man had seen Hermas go through what I have experienced it would undoubtedly have killed him. Certainly I wish it could have been done without—without—ay, it is even so—without deceit; even when I was a heathen I was truthful and held a lie, whether in myself or in another, in as deep horror as Father Abraham held murder, and yet when the Lord required him, he led his son Isaac to the slaughter. And Moses, when he beat the overseer—and Elias, and Deborah, and Judith—I have taken upon myself no less than they, but my lie will surely be forgiven me, if it is not reckoned against them that they shed blood."

These and such reflections restored Paulus to equanimity and to satisfaction with his conduct, and he began to consider, whether he should return to his old cave and the neighborhood of Stephanus, or seek for a new abode. He decided on the latter course; but first he must find fresh water and some sort of nourishment, for his mouth and tongue were quite parched.

Lower down in the valley sprung a brooklet of which he knew, and hard by it grew various herbs and roots, with which he had often allayed his hunger. He followed the declivity to its base, then turning to the left, he crossed a small table-land, which was easily accessible from the gorge, but which on the side of the oasis formed a perpendicular cliff many fathoms deep. Between it and the main mass of the mountain rose numerous single peaks, like a camp of granite tents, or a wildly tossing sea suddenly turned to stone; behind these blocks ran the streamlet, which he found after a short search.

Perfectly refreshed, and with renewed resolve to bear the worst with patience, he returned to the plateau, and from the edge of the precipice he gazed down into the desert gorge that stretched away far below his feet, and in whose deepest and remotest hollow the palm groves and tamarisk thickets of the oasis showed as a sharply defined mass of green, like a luxuriant wreath flung upon a bier. The whitewashed roofs of the little town of Pharan shone brightly among the branches and clumps of verdure, and above them all rose the new church, which he was now forbidden to enter. For a moment the thought was keenly painful that he was excluded from the

devotions of the community, from the Lord's supper, and
from congregational prayer, but then he asked, was not every
block of stone on the mountain an altar?—was not the blue
sky above a thousand times wider and more splendid than the
mightiest dome raised by the hand of man, not even excepting
the vaulted roof of the Serapeum at Alexandria? and he remembered the "Amen" of the stones that had rung out
after the preaching of the blind man. By this time he had
quite recovered himself, and he went toward the cliff in order
to find a cavern that he knew of, and that was empty—for its
gray-headed inhabitant had died some weeks since. "Verily,"
thought he, "it seems to me that I am by no means weighed
down by the burden of my disgrace, but, on the contrary,
lifted up. Here at least I need not cast down my eyes, for I
am alone with my God, and in His presence I feel I need not
be ashamed."

Thus meditating, he pressed on through a narrow space,
which divided two huge masses of porphyry, but suddenly he
stood still, for he heard the barking of a dog in his immediate
neighborhood, and a few minutes after a greyhound rushed
toward him—now indignantly flying at him, and now timidly
retreating—while it carefully held up one leg, which was
wrapped in a many-colored bandage.

Paulus recollected the inquiry which Phœbicius had addressed to the Amalekite as to a greyhound, and he immediately guessed that the Gaul's runaway wife must be not far off.
His heart beat more quickly, and although he did not immediately know how he should meet the disloyal wife, he felt
himself impelled to go and seek her. Without delay he followed the way by which the dog had come, and soon caught
sight of a light garment, which vanished behind the nearest
rock, and then behind a further, and yet a further one.

At last he came up with the fleeing woman. She was standing at the very edge of a precipice, that rose high and sheer
above the abyss—a strange and fearful sight; her long golden
hair had got tangled, and waved over her bosom and shoulders,
half plaited, half undone. Only one foot was firm on the
ground; the other—with its thin sandal all torn by the sharp
stones—was stretched out over the abyss, ready for the next
fatal step. At the next instant she might disappear over the
cliff, for though with her right hand she held on to a point of
rock, Paulus could see that the bowlder had no connection
with the rock on which she stood, and rocked to and fro.

She hung over the edge of the chasm like a sleep-walker, or
a possessed creature pursued by demons, and at the same time

her eyes glistened with such wild madness, and she drew her breath with such feverish rapidity that Paulus, who had come close up to her, involuntarily drew back. He saw that her lips moved, and though he could not understand what she said, he felt that her voiceless utterance was to warn him back.

What should he do? If he hurried forward to save her by a hasty grip, and if this maneuver failed, she would fling herself irredeemably into the abyss; if he left her to herself the stone to which she clung would get looser and looser, and as soon as it fell she would certainly fall too. He had once heard it said that sleep-walkers always threw themselves down when they heard their names spoken; this statement now recurred to his mind, and he forbore from calling out to her.

Once more the unhappy woman waved him off; his very heart stopped beating, for her movements were wild and vehement, and he could see that the stone which she was holding on by shifted its place. He understood nothing of all the words which she tried to say—for her voice, which only yesterday had been so sweet, to-day was inaudibly hoarse—except the one name "Phœbicius," and he felt no doubt that she clung to the stone over the abyss, so that, like the mountain-goat when it sees itself surprised by the hunter, she might fling herself into the depths below rather than be taken by her pursuer. Paulus saw in her neither her guilt nor her beauty, but only a child of man trembling on the brink of a fearful danger whom he must save from death at any cost; and the thought that he was at any rate not a spy sent in pursuit of her by her husband, suggested to him the first words which he found courage to address to the desperate woman. They were simple words enough, but they were spoken in a tone which fully expressed the child-like amiability of his warm heart, and the Alexandrian, who had been brought up in the most approved school of the city of orators, involuntarily uttered his words in the admirably rich and soft-chest voice which he so well knew how to use.

"Be thankful," said he, "poor dear woman—I have found you in a fortunate hour. I am Paulus, Hermas's best friend, and I would willingly serve you in your sore need. No danger is now threatening you, for Phœbicius is seeking you on a wrong road; you may trust me. Look at me! I do not look as if I could betray a poor erring woman. But you are standing on a spot where I would rather see my enemy than you; lay your hand confidingly in mine—it is no longer white and slender, but it is strong and honest—grant me this request and you will never rue it! See, place your foot here, and take care how you leave go of the rock there. You know not how suspiciously it shook its head over your strange confidence in it. Take care! there—your support has rolled it over into the abyss; how it crashes and splits. It has reached the bottom, smashed into a thousand pieces, and I am thankful that you preferred to follow me rather than that false support." While Paulus was speaking he had gone up to Sirona, as a girl whose bird has escaped from its cage, and who creeps up to it with timid care in the hope of recapturing it, he offered her his hand, and as soon as he felt hers in his grasp; he had carefully rescued her from her fearful position, and had led her down to a secure footing on the plateau. So long as she followed him unresistingly he led her on toward the mountain—without aim or fixed destination—but away, away from the abyss.

She paused by a square block of diorite, and Paulus, who had not failed to observe how heavy her steps were, desired her to sit down; he pushed up a flag of stone, which he propped with smaller ones, so that Sirona might not lack a support for her weary back. When he had accomplished this Sirona leaned back against the stone, and something of dawning satisfaction was audible in the soft sigh, which was the first sound that had escaped her tightly closed lips since her rescue. Paulus smiled at her encouragingly, and said, "Now rest a little, I see what you want; one can not defy the heat of the sun for a whole day with impunity."

Sirona nodded, pointed to her mouth, and implored wearily and very softly for "Water, a little water."

Paulus struck his hand against his forehead, and cried eagerly, "Directly—I will bring you a fresh draught. In a few minutes I will be back again."

Sirona looked after him as he hastened away. Her gaze became more and more staring and glazed, and she felt as if the rock on which she was sitting were changing into the ship which had brought her from Massilia to Ostia. Every heaving motion of the vessel, which had made her so giddy as it danced over the shifting waves, she now distinctly felt again, and at last it seemed as if a whirlpool had seized the ship, and was whirling it round faster and faster in a circle. She closed her eyes, felt vaguely and in vain in the air for some hold-fast, her head fell powerless on one side, and before her cheek sunk upon her shoulder she uttered one feeble cry of distress, for she felt as if all her limbs were dropping from her body, as leaves in autumn fall from the boughs, and she fell back unconscious on the stony couch which Paulus had constructed for her.

It was the first swoon that Sirona, with her sound physical and mental powers, had ever experienced; but the strongest of her sex would have been overcome by the excitement, the efforts, the privations, and the sufferings which had that day befallen the unfortunate fair one.

At first she had fled without any plan out into the night and up the mountain; the moon lighted her on her way, and for fully an hour she continued her upward road without any rest. Then she heard the voices of travelers who were coming toward her, and she left the beaten road and tried to get away from them, for she feared that her greyhound, which she still carried on her arm, would betray her by barking, or if they heard it whining, and saw it limp. At last she had sunk down on a stone, and had reflected on all the events of the last few hours, and on what she had to do next. She could look back dreamily on the past, and build castles in the air in a blue-skied future —this was easy enough; but she did not find it easy to reflect with due deliberation, and to think in earnest. Only one thing was perfectly clear to her; she would rather starve and die of thirst, and shame, and misery—nay, she would rather be the instrument of her own death, than return to her husband. She knew that she must in the first instance expect ill-usage, scorn, and imprisonment in a dark room at the Gaul's hands; but all that seemed to her far more endurable than the tenderness with which he from time to time approached her. When she thought of that she shuddered and clinched her white teeth, and doubled her fists so tightly that her nails cut the flesh.

·But what was she to do? If Hermas were to meet her? And yet what help could she look for from him, for what was he but a mere lad? and the thought of linking her life to his, if only for a day, appeared to her foolish and ridiculous.

Certainly she felt no inclination to repent or to blame herself; still it had been a great folly on her part to call him into the house for the sake of amusing herself with him.

Then she recollected the severe punishment she had once suffered, because, when she was still quite little, and without meaning any harm, she had taken her father's water clock to pieces, and had spoiled it.

She felt that she was very superior to Hermas, and her position was now too grave a one for her to feel inclined to play any more. She thought indeed of Petrus and Dorothea, but she could only reach them by going back to the oasis, and then she feared to be discovered by Phœbicius.

If Polykarp now could only meet her on his way back from

Raithu; but the road she had just quitted did not lead from thence, but to the gate-way that lay more to the southward.

The senator's son loved her—of that she was sure, for no one else had ever looked into her eyes with such deep delight or such tender affection; and he was no inexperienced boy, but a right earnest man, whose busy and useful life now appeared to her in a quite different light to that in which she had seen it formerly. How willingly now would she have allowed herself to be supported and guided by Polykarp! But how could she reach him? No—even from him there was nothing to be expected; she must rely upon her own strength, and she decided that so soon as the morning should blush, and the sun begin to mount in the cloudless sky, she would keep herself concealed during the day among the mountains, and then as evening came on, she would go down to the sea, and endeavor to get on board a vessel to Klysma and thence reach Alexandria. She wore a ring with a finely cut onyx on her finger, elegant ear-rings in her ears, and on her left arm a bracelet. These jewels were of virgin gold, and besides these she had with her a few silver coins and one large gold piece, that her father had given her as token out of his small store, when she had quitted him for Rome, and that she had hitherto preserved as carefully as if it were a talisman.

She pressed the token, which was sewed into a little bag, to her lips, and thought of her paternal home, and her brothers and sisters.

Meanwhile the sun mounted higher and higher; she wandered from rock to rock in search of a shady spot and a spring of water, but none was to be found, and she was tormented with violent thirst and aching hunger. By midday the strips of shade, too, had vanished, where she had found shelter from the rays of the sun, which now beat down unmercifully on her unprotected head. Her forehead and neck began to tingle violently, and she fled before the burning beams like a soldier before the shafts of his pursuer. Behind the rocks which hemmed in the plateau on which Paulus met her, at last, when she was quite exhausted, she found a shady resting-place. The greyhound lay panting in her lap, and held up its broken paw, which she had carefully bound up in the morning when she had first sat down to rest, with a strip of stuff that she had torn with the help of her teeth from her undergarment. She now bound it up afresh, and nursed the little creature, caressing it like an infant. The dog was wretched and suffering like herself, and besides it was the only being that, in spite of her helplessness, she could cherish and

be dear to.   But ere long she lost the power even to speak
caressing words or to stir a hand to stroke the dog.   It slipped
off her lap and limped away, while she sat staring blankly before her, and at last forgot her sufferings in an uneasy slumber,
till she was roused by Iambe's barking and the Alexandrian's
footstep.   Almost half dead, her mouth parched and her brain
on fire, while her thoughts whirled in confusion, she believed
that Phœbicius had found her track, and was come to seize
her.   She had already noted the deep precipice, to the edge of
which she now fled, fully resolved to fling herself over into the
depths below rather than to surrender herself prisoner.

Paulus had rescued her from the fall, but now—as he came
up to her with two pieces of stone which were slightly hollowed,
so that he had been able to bring some fresh water in them,
and which he held level with great difficulty, walking with
the greatest care—he thought that inexorable death had only
too soon returned to claim the victim he had snatched from
him, for Sirona's head hung down upon her breast, her face
was sunk toward her lap, and at the back of her head, where
her abundant hair parted into two flowing tresses, Paulus observed on the snowy neck of the insensible woman a red spot
which the sun must have burned there.

His whole soul was full of compassion for the young, fair,
and unhappy creature, and, while he took hold of her chin,
which had sunk on her bosom, lifted her white face and moistened her forehead and lips with water, he softly prayed for her
salvation.

The shallow cavity of the stones only offered room for a
very small quantity of the refreshing moisture, and so he was
obliged to return several times to the spring.   While he was
away the dog remained by his mistress, and would now lick
her hand, now put his sharp little nose close up to her mouth,
and examine her with an anxious expression, as if to ascertain
her state of health.

When Paulus had gone the first time to fetch some water
for Sirona he had found the dog by the side of the spring; and
he could not help thinking, "The unreasoning brute has
found the water without a guide, while his mistress is dying
of thirst.   Which is the wiser—the man or the brute?"   The
little dog on his part strove to merit the anchorite's good feelings toward him, for, though at first he had barked at him, he
now was very friendly to him, and looked him in the face from
time to time, as though to ask, "Do you think she will recover?"

Paulus was fond of animals, and understood the little dog's

language. When Sirona's lips began to move and to recover their rosy color, he stroked Iambe's smooth sharp head, and said, as he held a leaf that he had curled up to hold some water to Sirona's lips, "Look, little fellow, how she begins to enjoy it! A little more of this, and again a little more. She smacks her lips as if I were giving her sweet Falernian. I will go and fill the stone again; you stop here with her, I shall be back again directly, but before I return she will have opened her eyes; you are pleasanter to look upon than a shaggy old gray-beard, and she will be better pleased to see you than me when she awakes." Paulus's prognosis was justified, for when he returned to Sirona with a fresh supply of water she was sitting upright, rubbed her open eyes, stretched her limbs, clasped the greyhound in both arms, and burst into a violent flood of tears.

The Alexandrian stood aside motionless, so as not to disturb her, thinking to himself: .

"These tears will wash away a large part of her suffering from her soul."

When at last she was calmer, and began to dry her eyes, he went up to her, offered her the stone cup of water, and spoke to her kindly. She drank with eager satisfaction, and eat the last bit of bread that he could find in the pocket of his garment, soaking it in the water. She thanked him with the child-like sweetness that was peculiar to her, and then tried to rise, and willingly allowed him to support her. She was still very weary, and her head ached, but she could stand and walk.

As soon as Paulus had satisfied himself that she had no symptoms of fever he said, "Now, for to-day, you want nothing more but a warm mess of food, and a bed sheltered from the night chill; I will provide both. You sit down here; the rocks are already throwing long shadows, and before the sun disappears behind the mountain I will return. While I am away your four-footed companion here will while away the time."

He hastened down to the spring with quick steps; close to it was the abandoned cave which he had counted on inhabiting instead of his former dwelling. He found it after a short search, and in it, to his great joy, a well-preserved bed of dried plants, which he soon shook up and relaid, a hearth, and wood proper for producing fire by friction, a water-jar, and in a cellar-like hole, whose opening was covered with stones and so concealed from any but a practiced eye, there were several cakes of hard bread, and one or two pots. In one of these

were some good dates, in another gleamed some white meal, a
third was half full of sesame oil, and a fourth held some salt.

"How lucky it is," muttered the anchorite, as he quitted
the cave, "that the old anchorite was such a glutton."

By the time he returned to Sirona the sun was going down.

There was something in the nature and demeanor of Paulus
which made all distrust of him impossible, and Sirona was
ready to follow him, but she felt so weak that she could scarcely support herself on her feet.

"I feel," she said, "as if I were a little child, and must
begin again to learn to walk."

"Then let me be your nurse. I knew a Spartan dame once
who had a beard almost as rough as mine. Lean confidently
on me, and before we go down the slope we will go up and
down the level here two or three times." She took his arm,
and he led her slowly up and down.

It vividly recalled a picture of the days of his youth, and he
remembered a day when his sister, who was recovering from a
severe attack of fever, was first allowed to go out into the open
air. She had gone out, clinging to his arm into the peristyle
of his father's house; as he walked backward and forward with
poor, weary, abandoned Sirona, his neglected figure seemed by
degrees to assume the noble aspect of a high-born Greek, and
instead of the rough, rocky soil, he felt as if he were treading
the beautiful mosaic pavement of his father's court. Paulus
was Menander again, and if there was little in the presence of
the recluse which could recall his identity with the old man he
had trodden down, the despised anchorite felt, while the expelled and sinful woman leaned on his arm, the same proud
sense of succoring a woman as when he was the most distinguished youth of a metropolis, and when he had led forward
the master's much courted daughter in the midst of a shouting
troop of slaves.

Sirona had to remind Paulas that night was coming on, and
was startled, when the hermit removed her hand from his arm
with ungentle haste, and called to her to follow him with a
roughness that was quite new to him. She obeyed, and where-
over it was necessary to climb over the rocks, he supported
and lifted her, but he only spoke when she addressed him.

When they had reached their destination he showed her the
bed, and begged her to keep awake till he should have prepared a dish of warm food for her, and he shortly brought her
a simple supper, and wished her a good night's rest, after she
had taken it.

Sirona shared the bread and the salted meal-porridge with her

dog, and then lay down on the couch, where she sunk at once
into a deep, dreamless sleep, while Paulus passed the night
sitting by the hearth.

He strove to banish sleep by constant prayer, but fatigue
frequently overcame him, and he could not help thinking of
the Gaulish lady, and of the many things which, if only he
were still the rich Menander, he would procure in Alexandria
for her and for her comfort. Not one prayer could he bring
to its due conclusion, for either his eyes closed before he came
to the "Amen," or else worldly images crowded round him,
and forced him to begin his devotions again from the beginning, when he had succeeded in recollecting himself. In this
half-somnolent state he obtained not one moment of inward
collectedness, of quiet reflection; not even when he gazed up
at the starry heavens, or looked down on the oasis, veiled in
night, where many others like himself were deserted by sleep.
Which of the citizens could it be that was watching by that
light which he saw glimmering down there in unwonted brightness till he himself, overpowered by fatigue, fell asleep?

CHAPTER II.

THE light in the town which had attracted Paulus was in
Petrus's house, and burned in Polykarp's room, which formed
the whole of a small upper story, which the senator had constructed for his son over the northern portion of the spacious
flat roof of the main building.

The young man had arrived about noon with the slaves he
had just procured, had learned all that had happened in his
absence, and had silently withdrawn into his own room after
supper was ended. Here he still lingered over his work.

A bed, a table, on and under which lay a multitude of wax-
tablets, papyrus-rolls, metal-points, and writing-reeds, with a
small bench, on which stood a water-jar and basin, composed
the furniture of this room; on its white-washed walls hung
several admirable carvings in relief, and figures of men and
animals stood near them in long rows. In one corner, near a
stone water-jar, lay a large, damp-shining mass of clay.

Three lamps fastened to stands abundantly lighted this
work-room, but chiefly a figure standing on a high trestle,
which Polykarp's fingers were industriously molding.

Phœbicius had called the young sculptor a fop, and not altogether unjustly, for he loved to be well dressed, and was choice
as to the cut and color of his simple garments, and he rarely
neglected to arrange his abundant hair with care, and to

anoint it well; and yet he was almost indifferent as to whether his appearance pleased other people or not, but he knew nothing nobler than the human form, and an instinct, which he did not attempt to check, impelled him to keep his own person as nice as he liked to see that of his neighbor.

Now, at this hour of the night, he wore only a shirt of white woolen stuff, with a deep red border. His locks, usually so well-kept, seemed to stand out from his head separately, and instead of smoothing and confining them, he added to their wild disorder, for, as he worked, he frequently passed his hand through them with a hasty movement. A bat, attracted by the bright light, flew in at the open window—which was screened only at the bottom by a dark curtain—and fluttered round the ceiling; but he did not observe it, for his work absorbed his whole soul and mind. In this eager and passionate occupation, in which every nerve and vein in his being seemed to bear a part, no cry for help would have struck his ear—even a flame breaking out close to him would not have caught his eye. His cheeks glowed, a fine dew of glistening sweat covered his brow, and his very gaze seemed to become more and more firmly riveted to the sculpture as it took form under his hand. Now and again he stepped back from it, and leaned backward from his hips, raising his hands to the level of his temples, as if to narrow the field of vision; then he went up to the model, and clutched the plastic mass of clay, as though it were the flesh of his enemy.

He was now at work on the flowing hair of the figure before him, which had already taken the outline of a female head, and he flung the bits of clay, which he removed from the back of it on to the ground, as violently as though he were casting them at an antagonist at his feet. Again his finger-tips and modeling tool were busy with the mouth, nose, cheeks, and eyes, and his own eyes took a softer expression, which gradually grew to be a gaze of ecstatic delight, as the features he was molding began to agree more and more with the image, which at this time excluded every other from his imagination.

At last, with glowing cheeks, he had finished rounding the soft form of the shoulders, and drew back once more to contemplate the effect of the completed work; a cold shiver seized him, and he felt himself impelled to lift it up, and dash it to the ground with all his force. But he soon had mastered this stormy excitement, he pushed his hand through his hair again and again, and posted himself, with a melancholy smile and with folded hands, in front of his creation; sunk deeper and deeper in his contemplation of it, he did not observe that the door behind him was opened, although the flame of his lamps flickered in the draught, and that his mother had entered the work-room, and by no means endeavored to approach him un-heard, or to surprise him. In her anxiety for her darling, who had gone through so many bitter experiences during the past day, she had not been able to sleep. Polykarp's room lay above her bedroom, and when his steps overhead betrayed that, though it was now near morning, he had not yet gone to rest, she had risen from her bed without waking Petrus, who seemed to be sleeping. She obeyed her motherly impulse to encourage Polykarp with some loving words, and climbing up the narrow stair that led to the roof, she went into his room. Surprised, irresolute and speechless, she stood for some time behind the young man, and looked at the strongly illuminated and beautiful features of the newly formed bust, which was only too like its well-known prototype. At last she laid her hand on her son's shoulder and spoke his name.

Polykarp stepped back, and looked at his mother in be-wilderment, like a man roused from sleep; but she interrupted the stammering speech with which he tried to greet her, by saying, gravely and not without severity, as she pointed to the statue:

"What does this mean?"

"What should it mean, mother?" answered Polykarp, in a low tone, and shading his head sadly. "Ask me no more at present, for if you gave me no rest, and even if I tried to ex-plain to you how to-day—this very day—I have felt impelled and driven to make this woman's image, still you could not understand me—no, nor any one else."

"God forbid that I should ever understand it!" cried Dorothea. "'Thou shalt not covet thy neighbor's wife,' was the commandment of the Lord on the mountain. And you? You think I could not understand you? Who should under-stand you, then, if not your mother? This I certainly do not comprehend, that a son of Petrus and of mine should have thrown all the teaching and the example of his parents so utterly to the wind. But what you are aiming at with this statue it seems to me is not hard to guess. As the forbidden fruit hangs too high for you, you degrade your art, and make to yourself an image that resembles her according to your taste. Simply and plainly it comes to this: as you can no longer see the Gaul's wife in her own person, and yet can not exist without the sweet presence of the fair one, you make a portrait of clay to make love to, and you will carry on idolatry before it, as once the Jews did before the golden calf and the brazen serpent."

Polykarp submitted to his mother's angry blame in silence, but in painful emotion. Dorothea had never before spoken to him thus, and to hear such words from the very lips which were used to address him with such heartfelt tenderness gave him unspeakable pain. Hitherto she had always been inclined to make excuses for his weaknesses and little faults; nay, the zeal with which she had observed and pointed out his merits and performances before strangers as well as before their own family, had often seemed to him embarrassing. And now? She had indeed reason to blame him, for Sirona was the wife of another; she had never even noticed his admiration, and now, they all said, had committed a crime for the sake of a stranger. It must seem both a mad and a sinful thing in the eyes of men that he of all others should sacrifice the best he had—his art—and how little could Dorothea, who usually endeavored to understand him, comprehend the overpowering impulse which had driven him to this task.

He loved and honored his mother with his whole heart, and feeling that she was doing herself an injustice by her false and low estimate of his proceedings, he interrupted her eager discourse, raising his hands imploringly to her.

" No, mother, no!" he exclaimed. " As truly as God is my helper, it is not so. It is true that I have molded this head, but not to keep it and to commit the sin of worshiping it, but rather to free myself from the image that stands before my mind's eye by day and by night, in the city and in the desert, whose beauty distracts my mind when I think, and my devotions when I try to pray. To whom is it given to read the soul of man? And is not Sirona's form and face the loveliest image of the Most High? So to represent it, that the whole charm that her presence exercises over me might also be felt by every beholder is a task that I have set myself ever since her arrival in our house. I had to go back to the capital, and the work I longed to achieve took a clearer form; at every hour I discovered something to change and to improve in the pose of the head, the glance of the eye or the expression of the mouth. But still I lacked courage to put the work in hand, for it seemed too audacious to attempt to give reality to the glorious image in my soul, by the aid of gray clay and pale cold marble; to reproduce it so that the perfect work should delight the eye of sense, no less than the image enshrined in my breast delights my inward eye. At the same time I was not idle, I gained the prize for the model of the lions, and if

I have succeeded with the Good Shepherd blessing the flock, which is for the sarcophagus of Comes, and if the master could praise the expression of devoted tenderness in the look of the Redeemer, I know—nay, do not interrupt me, mother, for what I felt was a pure emotion and no sin—I know that it was because I was myself so full of love that I was enabled to inspire the very stone with love. At last I had no peace, and even without my father's orders I must have returned home; then I saw her again, and found her even more lovely than the image which reigned in her soul. I heard her voice, and her silvery bell-like laughter—and then—and then— You know very well what I learned yesterday. The unworthy wife of an unworthy husband, the woman Sirona is gone from me forever, and I was striving to drive her image from my soul, to annihilate it and dissipate it—but in vain! and by degrees a wonderful stress of creative power came upon me. I hastily placed the lamps, took the clay in my hand, and feature by feature I brought forth with bitter joy the image that is deeply graven in my heart, believing that thus I might be released from the spell. There is the fruit which was ripened in my heart, but there, where it so long has dwelt, I feel a dismal void, and if the husk which so long tenderly infolded this image were to wither and fall asunder, I should not wonder at it. To that thing there clings the best part of my life."

"Enough!" exclaimed Dorothea, interrupting her son, who stood before her in great agitation and with trembling lips. "God forbid that that mask there should destroy your life and soul. I suffer nothing impure within my house, and you should not in your heart. That which is evil can never more be fair, and however lovely the face there may look to you, it looks quite as repulsive to me when I reflect that it probably smiled still more fascinatingly on some strolling beggar. If the Gaul brings her back I will turn her out of my house, and I will destroy her image with my own hands if you do not break it in pieces on the spot."

Dorothea's eyes were swimming in tears as she spoke these words. She had felt with pride and emotion during her son's speech how noble and high-minded he was, and the idea that this rare and precious treasure should be spoiled or perhaps altogether ruined for the sake of a lost woman, drove her to desperation, and filled her motherly heart with indignation.

Firmly resolved to carry out her threat, she stepped toward the figure, but Polykarp placed himself in her way, raising his arm imploringly to defend it, and saying, "Not to-day—not yet, mother! I will cover it up, and will not look at it again

5

till to-morrow, but once—only once—I must see it again by sunlight."

"So that to-morrow the old madness may revive you!" cried Dorothea. "Move out of my way or take the hammer yourself."

"You order it, and you are my mother," said Polykarp.

He slowly went up to the chest in which his tools and instruments lay, and bitter tears ran down his cheeks as he took his heaviest hammer in his hand.

When the sky has shone for many days in summer-blue, and then suddenly the clouds gather for a storm, when the first silent but fearful flash, with its noisy but harmless associate, the thunder-clap, has terrified the world, a second and third thunder-bolt immediately follow. Since the stormy night of yesterday had broken in on the peaceful, industrious and monotonous life by the senator's hearth, many things had happened that had filled him and his wife with fresh anxiety.

In other houses it was nothing remarkable that a slave should run away, but in the senator's it was more than twenty years since such a thing had occurred, and yesterday the goatherd Miriam had disappeared. This was vexatious, but the silent sorrow of his son Polykarp was a greater anxiety to Petrus. It did not please him that the youth, who was usually so vehement, should submit unresistingly and almost indifferently to the Bishop Agapitus, who prohibited his completing his lions. His son's sad gaze, his crushed and broken aspect were still in his mind when at last he went to rest for the night; it was already late, but sleep avoided him even as it had avoided Dorothea. While the mother was thinking of her son's sinful love and the bleeding wound in his young and betrayed heart, the father grieved for Polykarp's baffled hopes of exercising his heart on a great work, and recalled the saddest, bitterest day of his own youth; for he, too, had served his apprenticeship under a sculptor in Alexandria, had looked up to the works of the heathen as noble models, and striven to form himself upon them. He had already been permitted by his master to execute designs of his own, and out of the abundance of subjects which offered themselves he had chosen to model an Ariadne, waiting and longing for the return of Theseus, as a symbolic image of his own soul awaiting its salvation. How this work had filled his mind! how delightful had the hours of labor seemed to him!—when, suddenly, his stern father had come to the city, had seen his work before it was quite finished, and instead of praising it had scorned it;

had abused it as a heathen idol, and had commanded Petrus to return home with him immediately and to remain there, for that his son should be a pious Christian, and a good stone-mason withal—not half a heathen, and a maker of false gods.

Petrus had much loved his art, but he offered no resistance to his father's orders; he followed him back to the oasis, there to superintend the work of the slaves who hewed the stone, to measure the granite blocks for sarcophagi and pillars, and to direct the cutting of them.

His father was a man of steel, and he himself a lad of iron, and when he saw himself compelled to yield to his father and to leave his master's workshop, to abandon his cherished and unfinished work and to become an artisan and a man of busi-ness, he swore never again to take a piece of clay in his hand, or to wield a chisel. And he kept his word even after his father's death; but his creative instincts and love of art con-tinued to live and work in him, and were transmitted to his two sons.

Antonius was a highly gifted artist, and if Polykarp's master was not mistaken, and if he himself were not misled by father-ly affection, his second son was on the high-road to the very first rank in art—to a position reached only by elect spirits.

Petrus knew the models for the Good Shepherd and for the lions, and declared to himself that these last were unsurpassa-ble in truth, power, and majesty. How eagerly must the young artist long to execute them in hard stone, and to see them placed in the honored though indeed pagan spot which was intended for them. And now the bishop forbade him to work, and the poor fellow might well be feeling just as he himself had felt thirty years ago, when he had been com-manded to abandon the immature first-fruits of his labor.

Was the bishop indeed right? This and many other ques-tions agitated the sleepless father, and as soon as he heard that his wife had risen from her bed to go to her son, whose foot-steps he, too, could hear overhead, he got up and followed her. He found the door of the work-room open, and, himself un-seen and unheard, he was witness to his wife's vehement speech, and to the lad's justification, while Polykarp's work stood in the full light of the lamps, exactly in front of him.

His gaze was spell-bound to the mass of clay; he looked and looked, and was not weary of looking, and his soul swelled with the same awe-struck sense of devout admiration that it had experienced when, for the first time in his early youth, he saw with his own eyes the works of the great old Athenian masters in Cæsareum.

And this head was his son's work!

He stood there greatly overcome, his hands clasped together, holding his breath till his mouth was dry, and swallowing his tears to keep them from falling. At the same time he listened with anxious attention, so as not to lose one word of Poly-karp's.

"Ay, thus and thus only are great works of art begotten," said he to himself, "and if the Lord had bestowed on me such gifts as on this lad, no father, nay, no god, should have compelled me to leave my Ariadne unfinished. The attitude of the body is not bad, I should say—but the head, the face—ay, the man who can mold such a likeness as that has his hand and eye guided by the holy spirits of art. He who has done that head will be praised in the latter days together with the great Athenian masters—and he, yes, he, merciful Heaven! he is my own beloved son!"

A blessed sense of rejoicing, such as he had not felt since his early youth, filled his heart, and Dorothea's ardor seemed to him half pitiful and half amusing.

It was not till his duteous son took the hammer in his hand that he stepped between his wife and the bust, saying, kindly:

"There will be time enough to-morrow to destroy the work. Forget the model, my son, now that you have taken advantage of it so successfully. I know of a better mistress for you—Art—to whom belongs everything of beauty that the Most High has created—Art in all its breadth and fullness, not fettered and narrowed by any Agapitus."

Polykarp flung himself into his father's arms, and the stern man, hardly master of his emotions, kissed the boy's forehead, his eyes, and his cheeks.

CHAPTER III.

AT noon of the following day the senator went to the women's room, and while he was still on the threshold he asked his wife—who was busy at the loom—

"Where is Polykarp? I did not find him with Antonius, who is working at the placing of the altar, and I thought I might find him here."

"After going to the church," said Dorothea, "he went up the mountain. Go down to the workshops, Marthana, and see if your brother is come back."

Her daughter obeyed quickly and gladly, for her brother was to her the dearest, and seemed to her to be the best of men. As soon as the pair were alone together Petrus said, while he held out his hand to his wife with genial affection, "Well, mother—shake hands." Dorothea paused for an instant, looking him in the face, as if to ask him, "Does your pride at last allow you to cease doing me an injustice?" It was a reproach, but in truth not a severe one, or her lips would hardly have trembled so tenderly, as she said: "You can not be angry with me any longer, and it is well that all should once more be as it ought."

All certainly had not been "as it ought," for since the husband and wife had met in Polykarp's work-room they had behaved to each other as if they were strangers. In their bedroom, on the way to church, and at breakfast, they had spoken to each no more than was absolutely necessary, or than was requisite in order to conceal their difference from the servants and children. Up to this time an understanding had always subsisted between them that had never taken form in words, and yet that had scarcely in a single case been infringed, that neither should ever praise one of their children for anything that the other thought blameworthy, and *vice versâ*.

But on this night her husband had followed up her severest condemnation by passionately embracing the wrong-doer. Never had she been so stern in any circumstances, while on the other hand her husband, so long as she could remember, had never been so soft-hearted and tender to his son, and yet she had controlled herself so far as not to contradict Petrus in Polykarp's presence, and to leave the work-room in silence with her husband.

"When we are once alone together in the bedroom," thought she, "I will represent to him his error as I ought, and he will have to answer for himself."

But she did not carry out this purpose, for she felt that something must be passing in her husband's mind that she did not understand; otherwise how could his grave eyes shine so mildly and kindly, and his stern lips smile so affectionately after all that had occurred when he, lamp in hand, had mounted the narrow stair. He had often told her that she could read his soul like an open book, but she did not conceal from herself that there were certain sides of that complex structure whose meaning she was incapable of comprehending. And, strange to say, she ever and again came upon these incomprehensible phases of his soul, when the images of the gods, and the idolatrous temples of the heathen, or when their sons' enterprises and work were the matters in hand. And yet Petrus was the son of a pious Christian; but his grandfather had been a Greek heathen, and hence perhaps a certain

something wrought in his blood which tormented her, because
she could not reconcile it with Agapitus's doctrine, but which
she nevertheless dared not attempt to oppose because her taci-
turn husband never spoke out with so much cheerfulness and
frankness as when he might talk of these things with his sons
and their friends, who often accompanied them to the oasis.
Certainly it could be nothing sinful that at this particular
moment seemed to light up her husband's face and restore his
youth.

"They just are men," said she to herself, "and in many
things they have the advantage of us women. The old man
looks as he did on his wedding-day! Polykarp is the very
image of him, as every one says, and now, looking at the
father, and recalling to my mind how the boy looked when he
told me how he could not refrain from making Sirona's portrait, I must say that I never saw such a likeness in the whole
course of my life."

He bid her a friendly good-night and extinguished the lamp.
She would willingly have said a loving word to him, for his
contented expression touched and comforted her, but that
would just then have been too much after what she had gone
through in her son's work-room. In former years it had happened pretty often that, when one of them had caused dis-
satisfaction to the other, and there had been some quarrel
between them, they had gone to rest unreconciled, but the
older they grew the more rarely did this occur, and it was now
a long time since any shadow had fallen on the perfect serenity
of their married life.

Three years ago, on the occasion of the marriage of their
eldest son, they had been standing together, looking up at the
starry sky, when Petrus had come close up to her, and had
said: .

"How calmly and peacefully the wanderers up there follow
their roads without jostling or touching one another! As I
walked home alone from the quarries by their friendly light, I
thought of many things. Perhaps there was once a time when
the stars rushed wildly about in confusion, crossing each
other's path, while many a star flew in pieces at the impact.
Then the Lord created man, and love came into the world,
and filled the heavens and the earth, and He commanded the
stars to be our light by night; then each began to respect the
path of the other, and the stars more rarely came into collision
till even the smallest and swiftest kept to its own path and its
own period, and the shining host above grew to be as harmoni-
ous as it is numberless. Love and a common purpose worked

this marvel, for he who loves another will do him no injury, and he who is bound to perfect a work with the help of another will not hinder nor delay him. We two have long since found the right road, and if at any time one of us is inclined to cross the path of the other we are held back by love and by our common duty, namely, to shed a pure light on the path of our children.''

Dorothea had never forgotten these words, and they came into her mind now again when Petrus held out his hand to her so warmly; as she laid hers in it she said:

"For the sake of dear peace, well and good—but one thing I can not leave unsaid. Soft-hearted weakness is not usually your defect, but you will utterly spoil Polykarp."

"Leave him, let us leave him as he is," cried Petrus, kissing his wife's brow. "It is strange how we have exchanged parts! Yesterday you were exhorting me to mildness toward the lad, and to-day—"

"To-day I am severer than you," interrupted Dorothea. "Who, indeed, could guess that an old gray-beard would derogate from the duties of his office as father and as judge for the sake of a woman's smiling face in clay—as Esau sold his birth-right for a mess of pottage?"

"And to whom would it occur," asked Petrus, taking up his wife's tone, "that so tender a mother as you would condemn her favorite son, because he labored to earn peace for his soul by a deed—by a work for which his master might envy him?"

"I have indeed observed,"· interrupted Dorothea, "that Sirona's image has bewitched you, and you speak as if the boy had achieved some great miracle. I do not know much about modeling and sculpture, and I will not contradict you, but if the fair-haired creature's face were less pretty, and if Polykarp had not executed anything remarkable, would it have made the smallest difference in what he has done and felt wrong? Certainly not. But that is just like men; they only care for success."

"And with perfect justice," answered Petrus, "if the success is attained, not in mere child's play, but by a severe struggle. 'To him that hath shall more be given,' says the scripture, and he who has a soul more richly graced than others have—he who is helped by good spirits—he shall be forgiven many things that even a mild judge would be unwilling to pardon in a man of poor gifts, who torments and exerts himself and yet brings nothing to perfection. Be kind to the boy again. Do you know what prospect lies before you through him? You yourself in your life have done much good and spoken much wisdom, and I, and the children, and the people in this place, will never forget it all. But I can promise you the gratitude of the best and noblest who now live or who will live in centuries to come—for that you are the mother of Polykarp!"

"And people say," cried Dorothea, "that every mother has four eyes for her children's merits. If that is true, then fathers no doubt have ten, and you as many as Argus, of whom the heathen legends speaks— But here comes Polykarp."

Petrus went forward to meet his son, and gave him his hand, but in quite a different manner to what he had formerly shown; at least it seemed to Dorothea that her husband received the youth, no longer as his father and master, but as a friend greets a friend who is his equal in privileges and judgment. When Ploykarp turned to greet her also she colored all over, for the thought flashed through her mind that her son, when he thought of the past night, must regard her as unjust or foolish; but she soon recovered her own calm equanimity, for Polykarp was the same as ever, and she read in his eyes that he felt toward her the same as yesterday and as ever.

"Love," thought she, "is not extinguished by injustice, as fire is by water. It blazes up brighter or less bright, no doubt, according to the way the wind blows, but it can not be wholly smothered—least of all by death."

Polykarp had been up the mountain, and Dorothea was quite satisfied when he related what had led him thither. He had long since planned the execution of a statue of Moses, and when his father had left him he could not get the tall and dignified figure of the old man out of his mind. He felt that he had found the right model for his work. He must, he would forget—and he knew that he could only succeed if he found a task which might promise to give some new occupation to his bereaved soul. Still, he had seen the form of the mighty man of God which he proposed to model only in vague outline before his mind's eye, and he had been prompted to go to a spot whither many pilgrims resorted, and which was known as the Place of Communion, because it was there that the Lord had spoken to Moses. There Polykarp had spent some time, for there, if anywhere—there, where the Law-giver himself had stood, must he find right inspiration.

"And you have accomplished your end?" asked his father.

Polykarp shook his head.

"If you go often enough to the sacred spot it will come to

you," said Dorothea. "The beginning is always the chief difficulty; only begin at once to model your father's head."

"I have already begun it," replied Polykarp, "but I am still tired from last night."

"You look pale and have dark lines under your eyes," said Dorothea, anxiously. "Go upstairs and lie down to rest. I will follow you and bring you a beaker of old wine."

"That will not hurt him," said Petrus, thinking as he spoke—"A draught of Lethe would serve him even better."

When, an hour later, the senator sought his son in his work-room, he found him sleeping, and the wine stood untouched on the table, Petrus softly laid his hand on his son's forehead and found it cool and free from fever. Then he went quietly up to the portrait of Sirona, raised the cloth with which it was covered, and stood before it a long time sunk in thought. At last he drew back, covered it up again, and examined the models which stood on a shelf fastened to the wall.

A small female figure particularly fixed his attention, and he was taking it admiringly in his hand when Polykarp awoke.

"That is the image of the Goddess of Fate—that is a Tyche," said Petrus.

"Do not be angry with me, father," entreated Polykarp. "You know, the figure of a Tyche is to stand in the hand of the statue of the Cæsar that is intended for the new city of Constántine, and so I have tried to represent the goddess. The drapery and pose of the arms, I think, are a success, but I failed in the head."

Petrus, who had listened to him with attention, glanced involuntarily at the head of Sirona, and Polykarp followed his eyes, surprised and almost startled.

The father and son had understood each other, and Polykarp said:

"I had already thought of that."

Then he sighed bitterly, and said to himself:

"Yes and verily, she is the goddess of my fate." But he dared not utter this aloud.

But Petrus had heard him sigh, and said, "Let that pass. This head smiles with sweet fascination, and the countenance of the goddess that rules the actions of the immortals should be stern and grave."

Polykarp could contain himself no longer.

"Yes, father," he exclaimed; "Fate is terrible—and yet I will represent the goddess with a smiling mouth, for that which is most terrible in her is, that she rules not by stern laws, but smiles while she makes us her sport."

CHAPTER IV.

It was a splendid morning; not a cloud dimmed the sky which spread high above the desert, mountain, and oasis, like an arched tent of uniform deep-blue silk. How delicious it is to breathe the pure, light, aromatic air on the heights before the rays of the sun acquire their midday power, and the shadows of the heated porphyry cliffs, growing shorter and shorter, at last wholly disappear.

With what delight did Sirona inhale this pure atmosphere, when after a long night—the fourth that she had passed in the anchorite's dismal cave—she stepped out into the air. Paulus sat by the hearth, and was so busily engaged with some carving that he did not observe her approach.

"Kind, good man!" thought Sirona, as she perceived a steaming pot on the fire, and the palm branches which the Alexandrian had fastened up by the entrance to the cave, to screen her from the mountain sun. She knew the way without a guide to the spring from which Paulus had brought her water at their first meeting, and she now slipped away, and went down to it with a pretty little pitcher of burned clay in her hand. Paulus did indeed see her, but he pretended that he neither saw nor heard, for he knew she was going there to wash herself, and to dress and smarten herself as well as might be—for was she not a woman! When she returned she looked not less fresh and charming than on that morning when she had been seen and watched by Hermas. True, her heart was sore; true, she was perplexed and miserable, but sleep and rest had long since effaced from her healthy, youthful and elastic frame all traces left by that fearful day of flight; and fate, which often means best by us when it shows us a hostile face, had sent her a minor anxiety to divert her from her graver cares.

Her greyhound was very ill, and it seemed that in the ill-treatment it had experienced, not only its leg had been broken, but that it had suffered some internal injury. The brisk, lively little creature fell down powerless whenever it tried to stand, and when she took it up to nurse it comfortably in her lap, it whined pitifully, and looked up at her sorrowfully, and as if complaining to her. It would take neither food nor drink; its little nose was hot; and when she left the cave Iambe lay panting on the fine woolen coverlet which Paulus had spread upon the bed, unable even to look after her.

Before taking the dog the water she had fetched in the graceful jar—which was another gift from her hospitable friend—she went up to Paulus and greeted him kindly. He looked up from his work, thanked her, and a few minutes later, when she came out of the cave again, asked her, " How is the poor little creature?"

Sirona shrugged her shoulders, and said, sadly, " She has drunk nothing, and does not even know me, and pants as rapidly as last evening. If I were to lose the poor little beast—"

She could say no more for emotion, but Paulus shook his head.

" It is sinful," he said, " to grieve so for a beast devoid of reason."

" Iambe is not devoid of reason," replied Sirona. " And even if she were, what have I left if she dies? She grew up in my father's house, where all loved me; I had her first when she was only a few days old, and I brought her up on milk on a little bit of sponge. Many a time when I heard the little thing whining for food, have I got out of bed at night with bare feet; and so she came to cling to me like a child, and could not do without me. No one can know how another feels about such things. My father used to tell us of a spider that beautified the life of a prison, and what is a dirty dumb creature like that to my clever, graceful little dog! I have lost my home, and here every one believes the worst of me, although I have done no one any harm, and no one—no one loves me but Iambe."

" But I know of one who loves every one with a divine and equal love," interrupted Paulus.

" I do not care for such a one," answered Sirona. " Iambe follows no one but me; what good can a love do me that I must share with all the world! But you mean the crucified God of the Christians? He is good and pitiful, so says Dame Dorothea; but He is dead—I can not see Him, nor hear Him, and, certainly, I can not long for one who only shows me grace. I want one to whom I can count for something, and to whose life and happiness I am indispensable."

A scarcely perceptible shudder thrilled through the Alexandrian as she spoke these words, and he thought, as he glanced at her face and figure with a mingled expression of regret and admiration, " Satan, before he fell, was the fairest among the pure spirits, and he still has power over this woman. She is still far from being ripe for salvation, and yet she has a gentle heart, and even if she has erred she is not lost."

Sirona's eyes had met his, and she said with a sigh, " You

look at me so compassionately—if only Iambe were well, and
if I succeeded in reaching Alexandria, my destiny would perhaps take a turn for the better."

Paulus had risen while she spoke, and had taken the pot
from the hearth; he now offered it to his guest, saying:

"For the present we will trust to this broth to compensate
you for the delights of the capital; I am glad that you
relish it. But tell me now, have you seriously considered what
danger may threaten a beautiful, young, and unprotected
woman in the wicked city of the Greeks? Would it not be
better that you should submit to the consequences of your
guilt, and return to Phœbicius, to whom, unfortunately, you
belong?"

Sirona, at these words, had set down the vessel out of which
she was eating, and rising in passionate haste, she exclaimed:

"That shall never, never be! And when I was sitting up
there half dead, and took your step for that of Phœbicius, the
gods showed me a way to escape from him, and from you or
any one who would drag me back to him. When I fled to the
edge of the abyss I was raving and crazed, but what I then
would have done in my madness I would do now in cold blood
—as surely as I hope to see my own people in Arelas once
more! What was I once, and to what have I come through
Phœbicius! Life was to me a sunny garden with golden trel-
lises and shady trees, and waters as bright as crystal, with rosy
flowers and singing birds; and he—he has darkened its light,
and fouled its springs, and broken down its flowers. All now
seems dumb and colorless, and if the abyss is my grave, no
one will miss me nor mourn for me."

"Poor woman!" said Paulus. "Your husband then showed
you very little love."

"Love," laughed Sirona, "Phœbicius and love! Only
yesterday I told you how cruelly he used to torture me after
his feasts, when he was drunk or when he recovered from one
of his swoons. But one thing he did to me, one thing which
broke the last thread of a tie between us. No one yet has
ever heard a word of it from me; not even Dorothea, who
often blamed me when I let slip a hard word against my husband. It was well for her to talk—if I had found a husband
like Petrus I might perhaps have been like Dorothea. It is a
marvel, which I myself do not understand, that I did not grow
wicked with such a man, a man who—why should I conceal
it?—who, when we were at Rome, because he was in debt, and
because he hoped to get promotion through his legate Quintillus, sold me—me—to him. He himself brought the old man

—who had often followed me about—into his house, but our hostess, a good woman, had overheard the matter, and betrayed it all to me. It is so base, so vile—it seems to blacken my soul only to think of it! The legate got little enough in return for his sesterces, but Phœbicius did not restore his wages of sin, and his rage against me knew no bounds when he was transferred to the oasis at the instigation of his betrayed chief. Now you know all; and never advise me again to return to that man to whom my misfortune has bound me. Only listen how the poor little beast in there is whining. It wants to come to me, and has not the strength to move."

Paulus looked after her sympathetically as she disappeared under the opening in the rock, and he awaited her return with folded arms. He could not see into the cave, for the space in which the bed stood was closed at the end by the narrow passage which formed the entrance, and which joined it at an angle, as the handle of a scythe joins the blade. She remained a long time, and he could hear now and then a tender word with which she tried to comfort the suffering creature. Suddenly he was startled by a loud and bitter cry from Sirona; no doubt the poor woman's affectionate little companion was dead, and in the dim twilight of the cave she had seen its dulled eye, and felt the stiffness of death overspreading and paralyzing its slender limbs. He dared not go into the cavern, but he felt his eyes fill with tears, and he would willingly have spoken some word of consolation to her.

At last she came out, her eyes red with weeping. Paulus had guessed rightly, for she held the body of little Iambe in her arms.

" How sorry I am," said Paulus; " the poor little creature was so pretty."

Sirona nodded, sat down, and unfastened the prettily embroidered band from the dog's neck, saying, half to herself and half to Paulus:

" My little Agnes worked this collar. I myself had taught her to sew, and this was the first piece of work that was all her own." She held the collar up to the anchorite. " This clasp is of real silver," she went on, " and my father himself gave it to me. He was fond of the poor little dog, too. Now it will never leap and spring again, poor thing."

She looked sadly down at the dead dog. Then she collected herself, and said, hurriedly:

" Now I will go away from here. Nothing—nothing keeps me any longer in this wilderness, for the senator's house, where I have spent many happy hours, and where every one was fond

of me, is closed against me, and must ever be so long as he
lives there. If you have not been kind to me only to do me
harm in the end, let me go to-day, and help me to reach
Alexandria."

"Not to-day, in any case not to-day," replied Paulus.
"First I must find out when a vessel sails for Klysma or for
Berenike, and then I have many other things to see to for
you. You owe me an answer to my question as to what you
expect to do and to find in Alexandria. Poor child—the
younger and the fairer you are—"

"I know all you would say to me," interrupted Sirona.
"Wherever I have been I have attracted the eyes of men, and
when I have read in their looks that I pleased them it has
greatly pleased me—why should I deny it? Many a one has
spoken fair words to me or given me flowers, and sent old
women to my house to win me for them; but even if one has
happened to please me better than another, still I have never
found it hard to send them home again as was fitting."

"Till Hermas laid his love at your feet," said Paulus.
"He is a bold lad—"

"A pretty, inexperienced boy," said Sirona, "neither more
nor less. It was a heedless thing, no doubt, to admit him to
my rooms, but no Vestal need be ashamed to own to such
favor as I showed him. I am innocent, and I will remain so,
that I may stand in my father's presence without a blush
when I have earned money enough in the capital for the long
journey."

Paulus looked in her face astonished and almost horrified.

Then he had in fact taken on himself guilt which did not
exist, and perhaps the senator would have been slower to condemn Sirona if it had not been for his falsely acknowledging
it. He stood before her, feeling like a child that would fain
put together some object of artistic workmanship, and who
has broken it to pieces for want of skill. At the same time
he could not doubt a word that she said, for the voice within
him had long since plainly told him that this woman was no
common criminal.

For some time he was at a loss for words; at last he said,
timidly:

"What do you propose doing in Alexandria?"

"Polykarp says that all good work finds a purchaser
there," she answered. "And I can weave particularly well,
and embroider with gold thread. Perhaps I may find shelter
under some roof where there are children, and I would willingly attend to them during the day. In my free time and at

night I could work at my frame, and when I have scraped enough together I shall soon find a ship that will carry me to Gaul, to my own people. Do you not see that I can not go back to Phœbicius, and can you help me?"

"Most willingly, and better perhaps than you fancy," said Paulus. "I can not explain this to you just now; but you need not request me, but may rather feel that you have a good right to demand of me that I should rescue you."

She looked at him in surprised inquiry, and he continued:

"First let me carry away the little dog, and bury it down there. I will put a stone over the grave, that you may know where it lies. It must be so; the body can not lie here any longer. Take the thing, which lies there. I had tried before to cut it out for you, for you complained yesterday that your hair was all in a tangle because you had not a comb, so I tried to carve you one out of bone. There were none at the shop in the oasis, and I am myself only a wild creature of the wilderness, a sorry, foolish animal, and do not use one. Was that a stone that fell? Ay, certainly, I hear a man's step; go quickly into the cave and do not stir till I call you."

Sirona withdrew into her rock dwelling, and Paulus took the body of the dog in his arms to conceal it from the man who was approaching. He looked round, undecided, and seeking a hiding place for it, but two sharp eyes had already detected him and his small burden from the height above him; before he had found a suitable place stones were rolling and crashing down from the cliff to the right of the cavern, and at the same time a man came springing down with rash boldness from rock to rock, and without heeding the warning voice of the anchorite, flung himself down the slope, straight in front of him, exclaiming, while he struggled for breath and his face was hot with hatred and excitement:

"That—I know it well—that is Sirona's greyhound—where is its mistress? Tell me this instant, where is Sirona—I must and will know."

Paulus had frequently seen, from the penitent's room in the church, the senator and his family in their places near the altar, and he was much astonished to recognize in the daring leaper, who rushed upon him like a mad man with disheveled hair and fiery eyes, Polykarp, Petrus's second son.

The anchorite found it difficult to preserve his calm and composed demeanor, for since he had been aware that he had accused Sirona falsely of a heavy sin, while at the same time he had equally falsely confessed himself the partner of her misdeed, he felt an anxiety that amounted to anguish, and a

leaden oppression checked the rapidity of his thoughts. He
at first stammered out a few unintelligible words, but his opponent was in fearful earnest with his question; he seized the
collar of the anchorite's coarse garment with terrible violence,
and cried, in a husky voice: "Where did you find the dog?
Where is—"

But suddenly he let go his hold of the Alexandrian, looked
at him from head to foot, and said, softly and slowly:

"Can it be possible? Are you Paulus, the Alexandrian?"

The anchorite nodded assent. Polykarp laughed loud and
bitterly, pressed his hand to his forehead, and exclaimed, in a
tone of the deepest disgust and contempt:

"And is it so, indeed! and such a repulsive ape, too! But
I will not believe that she ever held out a hand to you, for the
mere sight of you makes me dirty."

Paulus felt his heart beating like a hammer within his
breast, and there was a singing and roaring in his ears. When
once more Polykarp threatened him with his fist he involuntarily took the posture of an athlete in a westling match, he
stretched out his arms to try to get a good hold of his adversary, and said, in a hollow, deep tone of angry warning:
"Stand back, or something will happen to you that will not
be good for your bones." The speaker was indeed Paulus,
and yet not Paulus; it was Menander, the pride of the Palæstra, who had never let pass a word of his comrades that did
not altogether please him. And yet yesterday in the oasis he
had quietly submitted to far worse insults than Polykarp had
offered him, and accepted them with contented cheerfulness.
Whence then to-day this wild sensitiveness and eager desire to
fight?.

When, two days since, he had gone to his old cave to fetch
the last of his hidden gold pieces, he had wished to greet old
Stephanus, but the Egyptian attendant had scared him off like
an evil spirit with angry curses, and had thrown stones after
him. In the oasis he had attempted to enter the church, in
spite of the bishop's prohibition, there to put up a prayer; for
he thought that the antechamber, where the spring was and
in which penitents were wont to tarry, would certainly not be
closed even to him; but the acolytes had driven him away with
abusive words, and the doorkeeper, who a short time since had
trusted him with the key, spitted in his face, and yet he had not
found it difficult to turn his back on his persecutors without
anger or complaint.

At the counter of the dealer of whom he had bought the
woolen coverlet, the little jug, and many other things for

Sirona, a priest had passed by, had pointed to his money, and had said:

"Satan takes care of his own."

Paulus had answered him nothing, had returned to his charge with an uplifted and grateful heart, and had heartily rejoiced once more in the exalted and encouraging consciousness that he was enduring disgrace and suffering for another in humble imitation of Christ. What was it, then, that made him so acutely sensitive with regard to Polykarp, and once more snapped those threads, which long years of self-denial had twined into fetters for his impatient spirit? Was it that to the man who mortified his flesh in order to free his soul from its bonds it seemed a lighter matter to be contemned as a sinner, hated of God, than to let his person and his manly dignity be treated with contempt? Was he thinking of the fair listener in the cave, who was a witness to his humiliation? Had his wrath blazed up because he saw in Polykarp, not so much an exasperated fellow-believer, as merely a man who with bold scorn had put himself in the path of another man?

The lad and the gray-bearded athlete stood face to face like mortal enemies ready for the fight, and Polykarp did not waver, although he, like most Christian youths, had been forbidden to take part in the wrestling-games in the Palæstra, and though he knew that he had to deal with a strong and practiced antagonist. He himself was indeed no weakling, and his stormy indignation added to his desire to measure himself against the hated seducer.

"Come on—come on!" he cried, his eyes flashing, and leaning forward with his neck outstretched and ready on his part for the struggle. "Grip hold! you were a gladiator, or something of that kind, before you put on that filthy dress that you might break into houses at night, and go unpunished. Make this sacred spot an arena, and if you succeed in making an end of me I will thank you, for what made life worth having to me you have already ruined, whether or no. Only come on. Or perhaps you think it easier to ruin the life of a woman than to measure your strength against her defender? Clutch hold, I say, clutch hold, or—"

"Or you will fall upon me," said Paulus, whose arms had dropped by his side during the youth's address. He spoke in a quite altered tone of indifference. "Throw yourself upon me, and do with me what you will; I will not prevent you. Here I shall stand, and I will not fight, for you have so far hit the truth—this holy place is not an arena. But the Gaulish

lady belongs neither to you nor to me, and who gives you a
claim—"

"Who gives me a right over her?" interrupted Polykarp,
stepping close up to his questioner with sparkling eyes. "He
who permits the worshiper to speak of *his* God. Sirona is
mine, as the sun, and moon, and stars are mine, because they
shed a beautiful light on my murky path. My life is mine—
and she was the life of my life, and therefore I say boldly, and
would say if there were twenty such as Phœbicius here, she
belongs to me. And because I regarded her as my own, and
so regard her still, I hate you and fling my scorn in your teeth
—you are like a hungry sheep that has got into the gardener's
flower-bed, and stolen from the stem the wonderful, lovely
flower that he has nurtured with care, and that only blooms
once in a hundred years—like a cat that has sneaked into some
marble hall, and that to satisfy its greed has strangled some
rare and splendid bird that a traveler has brought from a distant land. But you, you hypocritical robber, who disregard
your own body with beastly pride and sacrifice it to low brutal-
ity, what should you know of the magic charm of beauty—of
that daughter of heaven, that can touch even thoughtless children, and before whom the gods themselves do homage! I
have a right to Sirona; for hide her where you will—or even if
the centurion were to find her and to fetter her to himself
with chains and rivets and brass—still that which makes her
the noblest work of the Most High—the image of her beauty
—lives in no one, in no one as it lives in me. This hand has
never even touched your victim, and yet God has given Sirona
to no man as he has given her wholly to me, for to no man can
she be what she is to me, and no man can love her as I do!
She has the nature of an angel and the heart of a child; she is
without spot, and as pure as the diamond, or the swan's breast,
or the morning-dew in the bosom of a rose. And though she
has let you into her house a thousand times, and though my
father even, and my own mother, and every one—every one
pointed at her and condemned her, I would never cease to believe in her purity. It is you who have brought her to shame;
it is you—"

"I kept silence while all condemned her," said Paulus, with
warmth, "for I believed that she was guilty, just as you believe that I am, just as every one that is bound by no ties of
love is more ready to believe evil than good. Now I know, ay,
know for certain, that we did the poor woman an injustice.
If the splendor of the lovely dream that you call Sirona has
been clouded by my fault—"

"Clouded? And by you?" laughed Polykarp. "Can the toad that plunges into the sea cloud its shining blue? can the black bat that flits across the night cloud the pure light of the full moon?"

An emotion of rage again shot through the anchorite's heart, but he was by this time on his guard against himself, and he only said, bitterly, and with hardly won composure:

"And how was it, then, with the flower and with the bird that were destroyed by beasts without understanding? I fancy you meant no absent third person by that beast, and yet now you declare that it is not within my power even to throw a shadow over your day-star! You see you contradict yourself in your anger, and the son of a wise man, who himself has not long since left the school of rhetoric, should try to avoid that. You might regard me with less hostility, for I will not offend you; nay, I will repay your evil words with good—perhaps the very best indeed that you ever heard in your life. Sirona is a worthy and innocent woman, and at the time when Phœbicius came out to seek her, I had never even set eyes upon her nor had my ears ever heard a word pass her lips."

At these words Polykarp's threatening manner changed, and feeling at once incapable of understanding the matter, and anxious to believe, he eagerly exclaimed:

"But yet the sheep-skin was yours, and you let yourself be thrashed by Phœbicius without defending yourself."

"So filthy an ape," said Paulus, imitating Polykarp's voice, "needs many blows, and that day I could not venture to defend myself because—because— But that is no concern of yours. You must subdue your curiosity for a few days longer, and then it may easily happen that the man whose very aspect makes you feel dirty—the bat, the toad—"

"Let that pass now," said Polykarp. "Perhaps the excitement which the sight of you stirred up in my bruised and wounded heart led me to use unseemly language. Now, indeed, I see that your matted hair sits round a well-featured countenance. Forgive my violent and unjust attack. I was beside myself, and I opened my whole soul to.you, and now that you know how it is with me, once more I ask you, where is Sirona?"

Polykarp looked Paulus in the face with anxious and urgent entreaty, pointing to the dog, as much as to say, "You must know, for here is the evidence."

The Alexandrian hesitated to answer; he glanced by chance at the entrance of the cave, and seeing the gleam of Sirona's white robe behind the palm-branches, he said to himself that if Polykarp lingered much longer he could not fail to discover her—a consummation to be avoided.

There were many reasons which might have made him resolve to stand in the way of a meeting between the lady and the young man, but not one of them occurred to him, and though he did not even dream that a feeling akin to jealousy had begun to influence him, still he was conscious that it was his lively repugnance to seeing the two sink into each other's arms before his very eyes that prompted him to turn shortly round, to take up the body of the little dog, and to say to the inquirer:

"It is true, I do know where she is hiding, and when the time comes you shall know it too. Now I must bury the animal, and if you will you can help me."

Without waiting for any objection on Polykarp's part, he hurried from stone to stone up to the plateau on the precipitous edge of which he had first seen Sirona. The younger man followed him breathlessly, and only joined him when he had already begun to dig out the earth with his hands at the foot of a cliff. Polykarp was now standing close to the anchorite, and repeated his question with vehement eagerness, but Paulus did not look up from his work, and only said, digging faster and faster:

"Come to this place again to-morrow, and then it may perhaps be possible that I should tell you."

"You think to put me off with that," cried the lad. "Then you are mistaken in me, and if you cheat me with your honest-sounding words I will—"

But he did not end his threat, for a clear, longing cry distinctly broke the silence of the deserted mountain.

"Polykarp—Polykarp!" It sounded nearer and nearer, and the words had a magic effect on him for whose ear they were intended.

With his head erect, and trembling in every limb, the young man listened eagerly. Then he cried out, "It is her voice! I am coming, Sirona, I am coming." And without paying any heed to the anchorite, he was on the point of hurrying off to meet her. But Paulus placed himself closely in front of him, and said, sternly:

"You stay here."

"Out of my way," shouted Polykarp, beside himself. "She is calling to me out of the hole where you are keeping her—you slanderer—you cowardly liar! Out of the way I say! You will not? Then defend yourself, you hideous toad, or I will tread you down, if my foot does not fear to be soiled with your poison."

Up to this moment Paulus had stood before the young man with outspread arms, motionless, but immovable as an oak-tree; now Polykarp first hit him. This blow shattered the anchorite's patience, and, no longer master of himself, he exclaimed: "You shall answer to me for this," and before a third and fourth call had come from Sirona's lips, he had grasped the artist's slender body, and with a mighty swing he flung him backward over his own broad and powerful shoulders on to the stony ground.

After this mad act he stood over his victim with outstretched legs, folded arms, and rolling eyes, as if rooted to the earth. He waited till Polykarp had picked himself up, and, without looking round, but pressing his hands to the back of his head, had tottered away like a drunken man.

Paulus looked after him till he disappeared over the cliff at the edge of the level ground; but he did not see how Polykarp fell senseless to the ground with a stifled cry, not far from the very spring whence his enemy had fetched the water to refresh Sirona's parched lips.

CHAPTER V.

"She will attract the attention of Damianus or Salathiel or one of the others up there," thought Paulus, as he heard Sirona's call once more, and, following her voice, he went hastily and excitedly down the mountain side.

"We shall have peace for to-day at any rate from that audacious fellow," muttered he to himself, "and perhaps to-morrow too, for his blue bruises will be a greeting from me. But how difficult it is to forget what we have once known! The grip with which I flung him, I learned—how long ago?—from the chief gymnast at Delphi. My marrow is not yet quite dried up, and that I will prove to the boy with these fists, if he comes back with three or four of the same mettle."

But Paulus had not long to indulge in such wild thoughts, for on the way to the cave he met Sirona.

"Where is Polykarp?" she called out from afar.

"I have sent him home," he answered.

"And he obeyed you?" she asked again.

"I gave him striking reasons for doing so," he replied, quickly.

"But he will return?"

"He has learned enough up here for to-day. We have now to think of your journey to Alexandria."

"But it seems to me," replied Sirona, blushing, "that I am safely hidden in your cave, and just now you yourself said—" ⸴

"I warned you against the dangers of the expedition," interrupted Paulus. "But since then it has occurred to me that I know of a shelter and of a safe protector for you. There, we are at home again. Now go into the cave, for very probably some one may have heard you calling, and if other anchorites were to discover you here they would compel me to take you back to your husband."

"I will go directly," sighed Sirona, "but first explain to me—for I heard all that you said to each other "—and she colored—"how it happened that Phœbicius took Hermas's sheep-skin for yours, and why you let him beat you without giving any explanation?"

"Because my back is even broader than that great fellow's," replied the Alexandrian, quickly. "I will tell you all about it in some quiet hour, perhaps on our journey to Klysma. Now go into the cave, or you may spoil everything. I know, too, what you lack most since you heard the fair words of the senator's son."

"Well—what?" asked Sirona.

"A mirror!" laughed Paulus.

"How much you are mistaken!" said Sirona; and she thought to herself: "The woman that Polykarp looks at as he does at me does not need a mirror."

An old Jewish merchant lived in the fishing-town on the western declivity of the mountain; he shipped the charcoal for Egypt, which was made in the valleys of the peninsula by burning the sajal acacia, and he had formerly supplied fuel for the drying-room of the papyrus factory of Paulus's father. He now had a business connection with his brother, and Paulus himself had had dealings with him. He was prudent and wealthy, and whenever he met the anchorite he blamed him for his flight from the world, and implored him to put his hospitality to the test, and to command his resources and means as if they were his own.

This man was now to find a boat, and to provide the means of flight for Sirona. The longer Paulus thought it over the more indispensable it seemed to him that he should himself accompany the Gaulish lady to Alexandria, and in his own person find her a safe shelter. He knew that he was free to dis-

pose of his brother's enormous fortune—half of which in fact
was his—as though it were all his own, and he began to rejoice
in his possessions for the first time for many years.   Soon he
was occupied in thinking of the furnishing of the house which
he intended to assign to the fair Sirona.   At first he thought
of a simple citizen's dwelling, but by degrees he began to picture the house intended for her as fitted with shining gold,
white and colored marble, many-colored Syrian carpets, nay,
even with vain works of the heathen, with statues, and a lux-
urious bath.   In increasing unrest he wandered from rock to
rock, and many times as he went up and down he paused in
front of the cave where Sirona was.   Once he saw her light
robe, and its conspicuous gleam led him to the reflection that
it would be imprudent to conduct her to the humble fishing-
village in that dress.   If he meant to conceal her traces from
the search of Phœbicius and Polykarp, he must first provide
her with a simple dress, and a veil that should hide her shining
hair and fair face, which even in the capital could find no
match.

The Amalekite, from whom he had twice bought some goat's
milk for her, lived in a hut which Paulus could easily reach.
He still possessed a few drachmas, and with these, he could
purchase what he needed from the wife and daughter of the
goat-herd.   Although the sky was now covered with mist and
a hot sweltering south wind had risen, he prepared to start at
once.   The sun was no longer visible, though its scorching heat
could be felt, but Paulus paid no heed to this sign of an approaching storm.

Hastily, and with so little attention that he confused one
object with another in the little store-cellar, he laid some
bread, a knife, and some dates in front of the entrance to the
cave, called out to his guest that he should soon return, and
hurried at a rapid pace up the mountain.

Sirona answered him with a gentle word of farewell, and
did not even look round after him, for she was glad to be
alone, and so soon as the sound of his step had died away she
gave herself up once more to the overwhelming torrent of new
and deep feelings which had flooded her soul ever since she had
heard Polykarp's ardent hymn of love.

Paulus, in the last few hours, was Menander again, but the
lonely woman in the cavern—the cause of this transformation
—the wife of Phœbicius, had undergone an even greater change
than he.   She was still Sirona, and yet not Sirona.

When the anchorite had commanded her to retire into the
cave she had obeyed him willingly, nay, she would have with-

drawn even without his desire, and have sought for solitude;
for she felt that something mighty, hitherto unknown to her,
and incomprehensible even to herself, was passing in her soul,
and that a nameless but potent something had grown up in
her heart, had struggled free, and had found life and motion;
a something that was strange and yet precious to her, fright-
ening and yet sweet—a pain, and yet unspeakably delightful.
An emotion such as she had never before known had mastered
her, and she felt, since hearing Polykarp's speech, as if a new
and purer blood was flowing rapidly through her veins. Every
nerve quivered like the leaves of the poplars in her former
home when the wind blows down to meet the Rhone, and she
found it difficult to follow what Paulus said, and still more so
to find the right answer to his questions.

As soon as she was alone she sat down on her bed, rested her
elbows on her knees and her head in her hand, and the grow- ·
ing and surging flood of her passion broke out in an abundant
stream of warm tears.

She had never wept so before; no anguish, no bitterness was
infused into the sweet refreshing dew of those tears. Fair
flowers of never dreamed of splendor and beauty blossomed in
the heart of the weeping woman, and when at length her tears
ceased there was a great silence, but also a great glory within
her and around her. She was like a man who has grown up
in an under-ground room, where no light of day can ever shine,
and who at last is allowed to look at the blue heavens, at the
splendor of the sun, at the myriad flowers and leaves in the
green woods and on the meadows.

She was wretched, and yet a happy woman.

"That is love!" were the words that her heart sung in tri-
umph, and as her memory looked back on the admirers who
had approached her in Arelas when she was still little more
than a child, and afterward in Rome, with tender words and
looks, they all appeared like phantom forms carrying feeble
tapers, whose light paled pitifully, for Polykarp had now come
on the scene, bearing the very sun itself in his hands.

"They—and he," she murmured to herself, and she beheld
as it were a balance, and on one of the scales lay the homage
which in her vain fancy she had so coveted. It was of no more
weight than chaff, and its whole mass was like a heap of straw,
which flew up as soon as Polykarp laid his love—a hundred-
weight of pure gold—in the other scale.

"And if all the nations and kings of the earth brought their
treasures together," thought she, "and laid them at my feet,
they could not make me as rich as he has made me; and if all

the stars were fused into one, the vast globe of light which they would form could not shine so brightly as the joy that fills my soul. Come now what may, I will never complain after that hour of delight."

Then she thought over each of her former meetings with. Polykarp, and remembered that he had never spoken to her of love. What must it not have cost him to control himself thus; and a great triumphant joy filled her heart at the thought that she was pure, and not unworthy of him, and an unutterable sense of gratitude rose up in her soul. The love she bore this man seemed to take wings, and it spread itself over the common life and aspect of the world, and rose to a spirit of devotion. With a deep sigh she raised her eyes and hands to heaven, and in her longing to prove her love to every living being, nay, to every created thing, her spirit sought the mighty and beneficent Power to whom she owed such exalted happiness.

In her youth her father had kept her very strictly, but still he had allowed her to go through the streets of the town with her young companions, wreathed with flowers, and all dressed in their best, in the procession of maidens at the feast of Venus of Arelas, to whom all the women of her native town were wont to turn with prayers and sacrifices when their hearts were touched by love.

Now she tried to pray to Venus, but again and again the wanton jests of the men who were used to accompany the maidens came into her mind, and memories of how she herself had eagerly listened for the only too frequent cries of admiration, and had enticed the silent with a glance, or thanked the more clamorous with a smile. To-day certainly she had no. mind for such sport, and she recollected the stern words which had fallen from Dorothea's lips on the worship of Venus, when she had once told her how well the natives of Arelas knew how to keep their feasts.

And Polykarp, whose heart was nevertheless so full of love, he no doubt thought like his mother, and she pictured him as she had frequently seen him following his parents by the side of his sister Marthana—often hand in hand with her—as they went to church. The senator's son had always had a kindly glance for her, excepting when he was one of this procession to the temple of the God of whom they said that He was love itself, and whose votaries indeed were not poor in love; for in Petrus's house, if anywhere, all hearts were united by a tender affection. It then occurred to her that Paulus had just now advised her to turn to the crucified God of the Christians, who was full of an equal and divine love to all men. To him Poly-karp also prayed—was praying perhaps at this very hour; and if she now did the same her prayers would ascend together with his, and so she might be in some sort one with that beloved friend, from whom everything else conspired to part her.

She knelt down and folded her hands, as she had so often seen Christians do, and she reflected on the torments that the poor Man who hung with pierced hands on the cross had so meekly endured, though He suffered innocently; she felt the deepest pity for Him, and softly said to herself, as she raised her eyes to the low roof of her cave dwelling:

" Thou poor good Son of God, Thou knowest what it is when all men condemn us unjustly, and surely Thou canst understand when I say to Thee how sore my heart is! And they say, too, that of all hearts Thine is the most loving, and so Thou wilt know how it is that, in spite of all my misery, it still seems to me that I am a happy woman. The very breath of a God must be rapture, and that Thou must have learned when they tortured and mocked Thee, for Thou hast suffered out of love. They say that Thou wast wholly pure and per-fectly sinless. Now I—I have committed many follies, but not a sin—a real sin—no, indeed, I have not; and Thou must know it, for Thou art a God, and knowest the past, and canst read hearts. And, indeed, I also would fain remain innocent, and yet how can that be when I can not help being devoted to Polykarp,'and yet I am another man's wife. But am I indeed the true and lawful wife of that horrible wretch who sold me to another? He is as far from my heart—as far as if I had never seen him with these eyes. And yet, believe me, I wish him no ill, and I will be quite content if only I need never go back to him.

" When I was a child I was afraid of frogs; my brothers and sisters knew it, and once my brother Licinius laid a large one, that he had caught, on my bare neck. I started, and shuddered, and screamed out loud, for it was so hideously cold and damp—I can not express it. And that is exactly how I have always felt since those days in Rome whenever Phœbicius touched me, and yet I dared not scream when he did.

" But Polykarp! oh! would that he were here, and might only grasp my hand. He said I was his own, and yet I have never encouraged him. But now! if a danger threatened him or a sorrow, and if by any means I could save him from it, indeed —indeed—though I never could bear pain well, and am afraid of death, I would let them nail me to a cross for him, as Thou was crucified for us all.

" But then he must know that I had died for him, and if he looked into my dying eyes with his strange, deep gaze, I would tell him that it is to him that I owe a love so great that it is a thing altogether different and higher than any love I have ever before seen. And a feeling that is so far above all measure of what ordinary mortals experience, it seems to me, must be divine. Can such love be wrong? I know not; but Thou knowest, and Thou, whom they name the good Shepherd, lead Thou·us—each apart from the other, if it be best so for him—but yet, if it be possible, unite us once more, if it be only for one single hour. If only he could know that I am not wicked, and that poor Sirona would willingly belong to him, and to no other, then I would be ready to die. Oh, Thou good, kind Shepherd, take me into Thy flock, and guide me."

Thus prayed Sirona, and before her fancy there floated the image of a lovely and loving youthful form; she had seen the original in the model for Polykarp's noble work, and she had not forgotten the exquisite details of the face. It seemed to her as well-known and familiar as if she had known—what in fact she could not even guess—that she herself had had some share in the success of the work.

The love which unites two hearts is like the ocean of Homer, which encircles both halves of the earth. It flows and rolls on. Where shall we seek its source—here or there—who can tell?

It was Dame Dorothea who in her motherly pride had led the Gaulish lady into her son's workshop. Sirona thought of her and her husband and her house, where over the door a motto was carved in the stone which she had seen every morning from her sleeping-room. She could not read Greek, but Polykarp's sister, Marthana, had more than once told her what it meant. " Commit thy ways to the Lord, and put thy trust in Him," ran the inscription, and she repeated it to herself again and again, and then drew fancy pictures of the future in smiling day-dreams, which by degrees assumed sharper outlines and brighter colors.

She saw herself united to Polykarp, and as the daughter of Petrus and Dorothea, at home in the senator's house; she had a right now to the children who loved her, and who were so dear to her; she helped the deaconess in all her labors, and won praise and looks of approval. She had learned to use her hands in her father's house, and now she could show what she could do; Polykarp even gazed at her with surprise and admiration, and said that she was as clever as she was beautiful, and promised to become a second Dorothea. She went with him

into his workshop, and there arranged all the things that lay
about in confusion, and dusted it, while he followed her every
movement with his gaze, and at last stood before her, his arms
wide—wide open to clasp her.

She started, and pressed her hands over her eyes, and flung
herself loving and beloved on his breast, and would have
thrown her arms round his neck, while her hot tears flowed—
but the sweet vision was suddenly shattered, for a swift flash
of light pierced the gloom of the cavern, and immediately after
she heard the heavy roll of the thunder-clap, dulled by the
rocky walls of her dwelling.

Completely recalled to actuality, she listened for a moment,
and then stepped to the entrance of the cave. It was already
dusk, and heavy rain-drops were falling from the dark clouds
which seemed to shroud the mountain peaks in a vast veil
of black crape. Paulus was nowhere to be seen, but there
stood the food he had prepared for her. She had eaten nothing
since her breakfast, and she now tried to drink the milk, but
it had curdled and was not fit to use; a small bit of bread
and a few dates quite satisfied her.

As the lightning and thunder began to follow each other
more and more quickly, and the darkness fast grew deeper, a
great fear fell upon her; she pushed the food on one side, and
looked up to the mountain where the peaks were now wholly
veiled in night, now seemed afloat in a sea of flame, and more
distinctly visible than by daylight. Again and again a forked
flash like a saw-blade of fire cut through the black curtain of
cloud with terrific swiftness, again and again the thunder
sounded like a blast of trumpets through the silent wilderness,
and multiplied itself, clattering, growling, roaring, and echoing
from rock to rock. Light and sound at last seemed to be
hurled from heaven together, and the very rock in which
her cave was formed quaked.

Crushed and trembling, she drew back into the inmost depth
of her rocky chamber, starting at each flash that illumined the
darkness.

At length they occurred at longer intervals, the thunder lost
its appalling fury; and as the wind drove the storm further
and further to the southward, at last it wholly died away.

CHAPTER VI.

It was quite dark in Sirona's cavern, fearfully dark, and the
blacker grew the night which shrouded her, the more her terror increased. From time to time she shut her eyes as tightly

as she could, for she fancied she could see a crimson glare, and she longed for light in that hour as a drowning man longs for the shore. Dark forebodings of every kind oppressed her soul. What if Paulus had abandoned her, and had left her to her fate? Or if Polykarp should have been searching for her on the mountain in this storm, and in the darkness should have fallen into some abyss, or have been struck by the lightning? Supposing the mass of rock that overhung the entrance to the cave should have been loosened in the storm, and should fall and bar her exit to the open air? Then she would be buried alive, and she must perish alone, without seeing him whom she loved once more, or telling him that she had not been unworthy of his trust in her.

Cruelly tormented by such thoughts as these, she dragged herself up and felt her way out into the air and wind, for she could no longer hold out in the gloomy solitude and fearful darkness. She had hardly reached the mouth of the cave when she heard steps approaching her lurking place, and again she shrunk back. Who was it that could venture in this pitch-dark night to climb from rock to rock? Was it Paulus returning? Was it he—was it Polykarp seeking her?

She felt intoxicated; she pressed her hands to her heart and longed to cry out, but she dared not, and her tongue refused its office. She listened with the tension of terror to the sound of the steps which came straight toward her nearer and nearer, then the wanderer perceived the faint gleam of her white dress, and called out to her. It was Paulus.

She drew a deep breath of relief when she recognized his voice, and answered his call.

"In such weather as this," said the anchorite, "it is better to be within than without, it seems to me, for it is not particularly pleasant out here, so far as I have found."

"But it has been frightful here inside the cave, too," Sirona answered; "I have been so dreadfully frightened—I was so lonely in the horrible darkness. If only I had had my little dog with me, it would at least have been a living being."

"I have made haste as well as I could," interrupted Paulus. "The paths are not so smooth here as the Kanopic road in Alexandria, and as I have not three necks like Cerberus, who lies at the feet of Serapis, it would have been wiser of me to return to you a little more leisurely. The storm-bird has swallowed up all the stars as if they were flies, and the poor old mountain is so grieved at it that streams of tears are everywhere flowing over his stony cheeks. It is wet even here. Now go back into the cave, and let me lay this that I have got here for you in my arms in the dry passage. I bring you good news; to-morrow evening, when it is growing dusk, we start. I have found out a vessel which will convey us to Klysma, and from thence I myself will conduct you to Alexandria. In the sheep-skin here you will find the dress and veil of an Amalekite woman, and if your traces are to be kept hidden from Phœbicius you must accommodate yourself to this disguise; for if the people down there were to see you as I saw you to-day, they would think that Aphrodite herself had risen from the sea, and the report of the fair-haired beauty that had appeared among them would soon spread even to the oasis."

"But it seems to me that I am well hidden here," replied Sirona. "I am afraid of a sea-voyage, and even if we succeed in reaching Alexandria without impediment, still I do not know—"

"It shall be my business to provide for you there," Paulus interrupted, with a decision that was almost boastful, and that somewhat disturbed Sirona. "You know the fable of the ass in the lion's skin, but there are lions who wear the skin of an ass on their shoulders—or of a sheep; it comes to the same thing. Yesterday you were speaking of the splendid palaces of the citizens, and lauding the happiness of their owners. You shall dwell in one of those marble houses, and rule it as its mistress, and it shall be my care to procure you slaves, and litter-bearers, and a carriage with four mules. Do not doubt my word, for I am promising nothing that I can not perform. The rain is ceasing, and I will try to light a fire. You want nothing more to eat? Well, then, I will wish you good-night. The rest will all do to-morrow."

Sirona had listened in astonishment to the anchorite's promises.

How often had she envied those who possessed all that her strange protector now promised her—and now it had not the smallest charm for her; and, fully determined in any case not to follow Paulus, whom she began to distrust, she replied, as she coldly returned his greeting, "There are many hours yet before to-morrow evening in which we can discuss everything."

While Paulus was with difficulty rekindling the fire, she was once more alone, and again she began to be alarmed in the dark cavern.

She called the Alexandrian. "The darkness terrifies me so," she said. "You still had some oil in the jug this morning; perhaps you may be able to contrive a little lamp for me; it is so fearful to stay here in the dark."

Paulus at once took a shard, tore a strip from his tattered

coat, twisted it together, and laid it for a wick in the greasy fluid, lighted it at the slowly reviving fire, and putting this more than simple light in Sirona's hand, he said:

"It will serve its purpose; in Alexandria I will see that you have lamps which give more light, and which are made by a better artist."

Sirona placed the lamp in a hollow in the rocky wall at the head of her bed, and then lay down to rest.

Light scares away wild beasts and fear, too, from the resting-place of man, and it kept terrifying thoughts far away from the Gaulish woman.

She contemplated her situation clearly and calmly, and quite decided that she could neither quit the cave nor intrust her-self to the anchorite till she had once more seen and spoken to Polykarp. He no doubt knew where to seek her, and certain-ly, she thought, he would by this time have returned, if the storm and the starless night had not rendered it an impossibility to come up the mountain from the oasis.

"To-morrow I shall see him again, and then I will open my heart to him, and he shall read my soul like a book, and on every page and in every line he will find his own name. And I will tell him, too, that I have prayed to his 'Good Shepherd,' and how much good it has done me, and that I will be a Chris-tian like his sister Marthana and his mother. Dorothea will be glad indeed when she hears it, and she at any rate can not have thought that I was wicked, for she always loved me, and the children—the children—"

The bright crowd of merry faces came smiling in upon her fancy, and her thoughts passed insensibly into dreams; kindly sleep touched her heart with its gentle hand, and its breath swept every shadow of trouble from her soul. She slept, smiling and untroubled as a child whose eyes some guardian angel softly kisses, while her strange protector now turned the flickering wood on the damp hearth, and with a reddening face blew up the dying charcoal fire, and again walked restlessly up and down, and paused each time he passed the entrance to the cave to throw a longing glance at the light which shone out from Sirona's sleeping-room.

Since the moment when he had flung Polykarp to the ground, Paulus had not succeeded in recovering his self-com-mand; not for a moment had he regretted the deed, for the reflection had never occurred to him that a fall on the stony soil of the Sacred Mountain, which was as hard as iron, must hurt more than a fall on the sand of the arena.

"The impudent fellow," thought he, "richly deserved what

he got.'' Who gave him a better right over Sirona than he,
Paulus himself, had—he who had saved her life, and had taken
it upon himself to protect her?

Her great beauty had charmed him from the first moment
of their meeting, but no impure thought stirred his heart as he
gazed at her with delight, and listened with emotion to her
child-like talk. It was the hot torrent of Polykarp's words
that had first thrown the spark into his soul, which jealousy
and the dread of having to abandon Sirona to another had
soon fanned into a consuming flame. He would not give up
this woman, he would continue to care for her every need; she
should owe everything to him, and to him only. And so, without reserve, he devoted himself body and soul to the preparations for her flight. The hot breath of the storm, the thunder
and lightning, torrents of rain, and blackness of night could
not delay him, while he leaped from rock to rock, feeling his
way—soaked through, weary and in peril; he thought only of
her and of how he could most safely carry her to Alexandria,
and then surround her with all that could charm a woman's
taste. Nothing—nothing did he desire for himself, and all
that he dreamed of and planned turned only and exclusively
on the pleasure which he might afford her. When he had prepared and lighted the lamp for her he saw her again, and was
startled at the beauty of the face that the trembling flame revealed. He could observe her a few seconds only, and then
she had vanished, and he must remain alone in the darkness
and the rain. He walked restlessly up and down, and an
agonizing longing once more to see her face lighted up by the
pale flame, and the white arm that she had held out to take
the lamp, grew more and more strong in him and accelerated
the pulses of his throbbing heart. As often as he passed the
cave, and observed the glimmer of light that came from her
room, he felt prompted and urged to slip in and to gaze on
her once more. He never once thought of prayer and scourging, his old means of grace; he sought rather for a reason that
might serve him as an excuse if he went in, and it struck him
that it was cold, and that a sheep-skin was lying in the cavern.
He would fetch it, in spite of his vow never to wear a sheep-
skin again; and supposing he were thus enabled to see her,
what next?

When he had stepped across the threshold an inward voice
warned him to return, and told him that he must be treading
the path of unrighteousness, for that he was stealing in on tip-
toe like a thief; but the excuse was ready at once: '' That is
for fear of waking her, if she is asleep.''

And now all further reflection was silenced, for he had already reached the spot where, at the end of the rocky passage, the cave widened into her sleeping-room; there she lay on the hard couch, sunk in slumber and enchantingly fair.

A deep gloom reigned around, and the feeble light of the little lamp lighted up only a small portion of the dismal chamber, but the head, throat and arms that it illuminated seemed to shine with a light of their own that enhanced and consecrated the light of the feeble flame. Paulus fell breathless on his knees and fixed his eyes with growing eagerness on the graceful form of the sleeper.

Sirona was dreaming; her head, veiled in her golden hair, rested on a high pillow of herbs, and her delicately rosy face was turned up to the vault of the cave; her half-closed lips moved gently, and now she moved her bent arm and her white hand, on which the light of the lamp fell, and which rested half on her forehead and half on her shining hair.

" Is she saying anything?" asked Paulus of himself, as he pressed his brow against a projection of the rock as tightly as if he would stem the rapid rush of his blood that it might not overwhelm his bewildered brain.

Again she moved her lips. Had she indeed spoken? Had she perhaps called him?

That could not be, for she still slept; but he wished to believe it—and he would believe it, and he stole nearer to her and nearer, and bent over her, and listened—while his own strength failed him even to draw a breath—listened to the soft regular breathing that heaved her bosom. No longer master of himself, he touched her white arm with his bearded lips and she drew it back in her sleep, then his gaze fell on her parted lips and the pearly teeth that shone between them, and a mad longing to kiss them came irresistibly over him. He bent trembling over her, and was on the point of gratifying his impulse when, as if startled by a sudden apparition, he drew back and raised his eyes from the rosy lips to the hand that rested on the sleeper's brow.

The lamp-light played on a golden ring on Sirona's finger, and shone brightly on an onyx on which was engraved an image of Tyche, the tutelary goddess of Antioch, with a sphere upon her head, and bearing Amalthea's horn in her hand.

A new and strange emotion took possession of the anchorite at the sight of this stone. With trembling hands he felt in the breast of his torn garment, and presently drew forth a small iron crucifix and the ring that he had taken from the cold hand of Hermas's mother. In the golden circlet was set an onyx,

C

on which precisely the same device was visible as that on
Sirona's hand. The string with its precious jewel fell from his
grasp, he clutched his matted hair with both hands, groaned
deeply, and repeated again and again, as though to crave forgiveness, the name of "Magdalen."

Then he called Sirona in a loud voice, and as she awoke, ex-
cessively startled, he asked her, in urgent tones:

"Who gave you that ring?"

"It was a present from Phœbicius," replied she. "He said
he had had it given to him many years since in Antioch, and
that it had been engraved by a great artist. But I do not want
it any more, and if you like to have it you may."

"Throw it away!" exclaimed Paulus; "it will bring you
nothing but misfortune." Then he collected himself, went
out into the air with his head sunk on his breast, and there,
throwing himself down on the wet stones by the hearth, he
cried out: "Magdalen! dearest and purest! You, when you
ceased to be Glycera, became a saintly martyr, and found the
road to heaven; I, too, had my day of Damascus—of revelation
and conversion—and I dared to call myself by the name of
Paulus—and now—now?" Plunged in despair he beat his
forehead, groaning out, "All, all in vain!"

CHAPTER VII.

COMMON natures can only be lightly touched by the immeasurable depth of anguish that is experienced by a soul that de-
spairs of itself; but the more heavily the blow of such suffering falls, the more surely does it work with purifying power on
him who has to taste of that cup.

Paulus thought no more of the fair, sleeping woman; tortured by acute remorse, he lay on the hard stones, feeling that
he had striven in vain. When he had taken Hermas's sin and
punishment and disgrace upon himself, it had seemed to him
that he was treading in the very footsteps of the Saviour. And
now?—He felt like one who, while running for a prize, stum-
bles over a stone and grovels in the sand where he is already
close to the goal.

"God sees the will and not the deed," he muttered to himself. "What I did wrong with regard to Sirona—or what I
did not do—that matters not. When I leaned over her I had
fallen utterly and entirely into the power of the Evil One, and
was an ally of the deadliest enemy of Him to whom I had
dedicated my life and soul. Of what avail was my flight from
the world, and my useless sojourn in the desert? He who

always keeps out of the way of the battle can easily boast of being unconquered to the end—but is he therefore a hero? The palm belongs to him who in the midst of the struggles and affairs of the world clings to the heavenward road, and never lets himself be diverted from it; but as for me who walk here alone, a woman and a boy cross my path, and one threatens and the other beckons to me, and I forget my aim and stumble into the bog of iniquity. And so I can not find—no, here I can not find what I strive after. But how then—how? Enlighten me, oh, Lord, and reveal to me what I must do."

Thus thinking he rose, knelt down, and prayed fervently; when at last he came to the "Amen," his head was burning and his tongue parched.

The clouds had parted, though they still hung in black masses in the west; from time to time gleams of lightning shone luridly on the horizon and lighted up the jagged peak of mountain with a flare; the moon had risen, but its waning disk was frequently obscured by dark driving masses of cloud; blinding flashes, tender light, and utter darkness were alternating with bewildering rapidity, when Paulus at last collected himself and went down to the spring to drink and to cool his brow in the fresh water. Striding from stone to stone, he told himself that ere he could begin a new life he must do penance —some heavy penance; but what was it to be? He was standing at the very margin of the brook, hemmed in by cliffs, and was bending down to it, but before he had moistened his lips he drew back; just because he was so thirsty he resolved to deny himself drink. Hastily, almost vehemently, he turned his back on the spring, and after this little victory over himself his storm-tossed heart seemed a little calmer. Far, far from hence and from the wilderness and from the Sacred Mountain he felt impelled to fly, and he would gladly have fled then and there to a distance. Whither should he flee? It was all the same, for he was in search of suffering, and suffering, like weeds, grows on every road. And from whom? This question repeated itself again and again as if he had shouted it in the very home of echo, and the answer was not hard to find: "It is from yourself that you would flee. It is your own inmost self that is your enemy; bury yourself in what desert you will, it will pursue you, and it would be easier for you to cut off your shadow than to leave that behind."

His whole consciousness was absorbed by this sense of impotency, and now, after the stormy excitement of the last few hours, the deepest depression took possession of his mind. Exhausted, unstrung, full of loathing of himself and life, he sunk

down on a stone and thought over the occurrences of the past
few days with perfect impartiality.

"Of all the fools that I ever met," thought he, "I have
gone furthest in folly, and have thereby led things into a state
of confusion which I myself could not make straight again,
even if I were a sage—which I certainly never shall be any
more than a tortoise or a phenix. I once heard tell of a hermit who, because it is written that we ought to bury the dead,
and because he had no corpse, slew a traveler that he might
fulfill the commandment; I have acted in exactly the same
way, for, in order to spare another man suffering, and to bear
the sins of another, I have plunged an innocent woman into
misery and made myself indeed a sinner. As soon as it is
light I will go down to the oasis and confess to Petrus and
Dorothea what I have done. They will punish me, and I will
honestly help them, so that nothing of the penance that they
may lay upon me may be remitted. The less mercy I show to
myself, the more the Eternal Judge will show to me."

He rose, considered the position of the stars, and when he
perceived that morning was not far off he prepared to return
to Sirona, who was no longer any more to him than an unhappy woman to whom he owed reparation for much evil, when
a loud cry of distress in the immediate vicinity fell on his ear.

He mechanically stooped to pick up a stone for a weapon,
and listened. He knew every rock in the neighborhood of the
spring, and when the strange groan again made itself heard
he knew that it came from a spot which he knew well and
where he had often rested, because a large flat stone, supported by a stout pillar of granite, stood up far above the surrounding rocks, and afforded protection from the sun, even at noonday, when not a hand's-breadth of shade was to be found
elsewhere.

Perhaps some wounded beast had crept under the rock for
shelter from the rain. Paulus went cautiously forward. The
groaning sounded louder and more distinct than before, and
beyond a doubt it was the voice of a human being.

The anchorite hastily threw away the stone, fell upon his
knees, and soon found on the dry spot of ground under the
stone, and in the furthermost nook of the retreat, a motionless human form.

"It is most likely a herdsman that has been struck by lightning," thought he, as he felt with his hands the curly head of
the sufferer, and the strong arms that now hung down powerless. As he raised the injured man, who still uttered low
moans, and supported his head on his broad breast, the sweet

perfume of fine ointment was wafted to him from his hair, and
a fearful suspicion dawned upon his mind.

"Polykarp!" he cried, while he clasped his hands more
tightly round the body of the sufferer who, thus called upon,
moved and muttered a few intelligible words in a low tone,
but still much too clearly for Paulus, for he now knew for certain that he had guessed rightly. With a loud cry of horror he
grasped the youth's powerless form, raised him in his arms,
and carried him like a child to the margin of the spring where
he laid his noble burden down in the moist grass; Polykarp
started and opened his eyes.

Morning was already dawning, the light clouds on the eastern horizon were already edged with rosy fringes, and the coming day began to lift the dark veil from the forms and hues of
creation.

The young man recognized the anchorite, who with trembling hands was washing the wound at the back of his head,
and his eye assumed an angry glare as he called up all his remaining strength and pushed his attendant from him. Paulus
did not withdraw; he accepted the blow from his victim as a
gift or a greeting, thinking, "Ay, and I only wish you had a
dagger in your hand; I would not resist you."

The artist's wound was frightfully wide and deep, but the
blood had flowed among his thick curls and had clotted over
the lacerated veins like a thick dressing. The water with
which Paulus now washed his head reopened them and renewed the bleeding, and after the one powerful effort with
which Polykarp pushed away his enemy he fell back senseless
in his arms. The wan morning light added to the pallor of
the bloodless countenance that lay with glazed eyes in the anchorite's lap.

"He is dying!" murmured Paulus, in deadly anguish and
with choking breath, while he looked across the valley and up
to the heights, seeking help. The mountain rose in front of
him, its majestic mass glowing in the rosy dawn, while light
translucent vapor floated round the peak where the Lord had
written His laws for His chosen people, and for all peoples, on
tables of stone; it seemed to Paulus that he saw the giant form
of Moses far, far up on its sublimest height, and that from his
lips in brazen tones the strictest of all the commandments was
thundered down upon him with awful wrath, "Thou shalt not
kill!"

Paulus clasped his hands before his face in silent despair,
while his victim still lay in his lap. He had closed his eyes,
for he dared not look on the youth's pale countenance, and still

less dared he look up at the mountain; but the brazen voice
from the height did not cease, and sounded louder and louder;
half beside himself with excitement, in his inward ear he heard
it still, "Thou shalt not kill!" and then again, "Thou shalt
not covet thy neighbor's wife!" a third time, "Thou shalt
not commit adultery!" and at last a fourth, "Thou shalt
have none other gods but Me!"

He that sins against one of those laws is damned; and he—
he had broken them all, broken them while striving to tread
the thorny path to a life of blessedness.

Suddenly and wildly he threw his arms up to heaven, and
sighing deeply, gazed up at the sacred hill.

What was that? On the topmost peak of Sinai, whence the
Pharanite sentinels were accustomed to watch the distance, a
handkerchief was waving as a signal that the enemy were approaching.

He could not be mistaken, and as in the face of approaching
danger he collected himself and recovered his powers of thought
and deliberation, his ear distinctly caught the mighty floods of
stirring sound that came over the mountain from the brazen
cymbals struck by the watchmen to warn the inhabitants of
the oasis and the anchorites.

Was Hermas returned? Had the Blemmyes outstripped
him? From what quarter were the marauding hosts coming
on? Could he venture to remain here near his victim, or was
it his duty to use his powerful arms in defense of his helpless
companions? In agonized doubt he looked down at the
youth's pallid features, and deep, sorrowful compassion filled
his mind.

How promising was this young tree of humanity that his
rough fist had broken off! and these brown curls had only yesterday been stroked by a mother's hand.   His eyes filled with
tears, and he bent as tenderly as a father might over the pale
face and pressed a gentle kiss on the bloodless lips of the
senseless youth. A thrill of joy shot through him, for Polykarp's lips were indeed not cold; he moved his hand, and now
—the Lord be praised! he actually opened his eyes.

"And I am not a murderer!" A thousand voices seemed
to sing with joy in his heart, and then he thought to himself:

"First I will carry him down to his parents in the oasis, and
then go up to the brethren."

But the brazen signals rang out with renewed power, and
the stillness of the holy wilderness was broken here by the
clatter of men's voices, there by a blast of trumpets, and there
again by stifled cries. It was as if a charm had given life to

the rocks and lent them voices; as if noise and clamor were rushing like wild torrents down every gorge and cleft of the mountain-side.

"It is too late," sighed the anchorite. "If I only could—if I only knew—"

"Halloo! halloo! holy Paulus!" a shrill woman's voice, which seemed to come from high up in the air, rang out joyful and triumphant, interrupting the irresolute man's meditations. "Hermas is alive! Hermas is here again! Only look up at the heights. There flies the standard, for he has warned the sentinels. The Blemmyes are coming on, and he sent me to seek you. You must come to the strong tower on the western side of the ravine. Make haste! come at once! Do you hear? He told me to tell you. But the man in your lap—it is—yes, it is—"

"It is your master's son Polykarp," Paulus called back to her. "He is hurt unto death; hurry down to the oasis, and tell the senator; tell Dame Dorothea—"

"I have something else to do now," interrupted the shepherdess. "Hermas has sent me to warn Gelasius, Psoes, and Dulas, and if I went down into the oasis they would lock me up, and not let me come up the mountain again. What has happened to the poor fellow? But it is all the same; there is something else for you to do besides grieving over a hole in Polykarp's head. Go up to the tower, I tell you, and let him lie—or carry him up with you into your new den, and hand him over to your sweetheart to nurse."

"Demon!" exclaimed Paulus, taking up a stone.

"Let him lie!" repeated Miriam. "I will betray her hiding-place to Phœbicius if you do not do as Hermas orders you. Now I am off to call the others, and we shall meet again at the tower. And you had better not linger too long with your fair companion—pious Paulus—saintly Paulus!"

And laughing loudly, she sprung away from rock to rock as if borne up by the air.

The Alexandrian looked wrathfully after her; but her advice did not seem to be bad. He lifted the wounded man on his shoulders, and hastily carried him up toward his cave; but before he could reach it he heard steps and a loud agonized scream, and in a few seconds Sirona was by his side, crying, in passionate grief: "It is he, it is he—and oh, to see him thus! But he must live, for if he were dead your God of Love would be inexorable, pitiless, hard, cruel—it would be—"

She would say no more, for tears choked her voice, and Paulus, without listening to her lamentation, passed quickly

on in front of her, entered the cave and laid the unconscious
man down on the couch, saying gravely but kindly, as Sirona
threw herself on her knees and pressed the young man's powerless hand to her lips:

"If indeed you truly love him, cease crying and lamenting.
He yesterday got a severe wound on his head; I have washed
it; now do you bind it up with care and keep it constantly
cool with fresh water. You know your way to the spring;
when he recovers his senses rub his feet, and give him some
bread and a few drops of the wine which you will find in the
little cellar hard by; there is some oil there, too, which you will
need for a light.

"I must go up to the brethren, and if I do not return to-
morrow give the poor lad over to his mother to nurse. Only
tell her this, that I, Paulus, gave him this wound in a moment
of rage, and to forgive me if she can, she and Petrus. And
you, too, forgive me that in which I have sinned against you, and
if I should fall in the battle which awaits us, pray that the
Lord may not be too hard upon me in the day of judgment,
for my sins are great and many."

At this moment the sound of trumpets sounded even
into the deepest recess of the cave. Sirona started. "That
is the Roman tuba," she exclaimed. "I know the sound—
Phœbicius is coming this way."

"He is doing his duty," replied Paulus. "And still, one
thing more. I saw last night a ring on your hand—an onyx."

"There it lies," said Sirona; and she pointed to the furthest
corner of the cave, where it lay on the dusty soil.

"Let it remain there," Paulus begged of her; he bent over
the senseless man once more to kiss his forehead, raised his
hand toward Sirona in sign of blessing, and rushed out into
the open air.

CHAPTER VIII.

Two paths led over the mountain from the oasis to the sea;
both followed steep and stony gorges, one of which was named
the "short cut," because the traveler reached his destination
more quickly by that road than by following the better road in
the other ravine, which was practicable for beasts of burden.
Half-way up the height the "short cut" opened out on a little plateau, whose western side was shut in by a high mass of
rock with steep and precipitous flanks. At the top of this rock
stood a tower built of rough blocks, in which the anchorites

were wont to take refuge when they were threatened with a descent of their foes.

The position of this castle—as the penitents proudly styled their tower—was well chosen, for from its summit they commanded not only the "short cut" to the oasis, but also the narrow shell-strewn strip of desert which divided the western declivity of the Holy Mountain from the shore, the blue-green waters of the sea, and the distant chain of hills on the African coast.

Whatever approached the tower, whether from afar or from the neighborhood, was at once espied by them, and the side of the rock which was turned to the road-way was so precipitous and smooth that it remained inaccessible even to the natives of the desert, who, with their naked feet and sinewy arms, could climb points which even the wild goat and the jackal made a circuit to avoid. It was more accessible from the other side, and in order to secure that, a very strong wall had been built, which inclosed the level on which the castle stood in the form of a horseshoe, of which. the ends abutted on the declivity of the short road. · This structure was so roughly and inartistically heaped together that it looked as if formed by nature rather than by the hand of man. · The rough and unfinished appearance of this wall-like heap of stones was heightened by the quantity of large and small pieces of granite which were piled on the top of it, and which had been collected by the anchorites, in case of an incursion, to roll and hurl down on the invading robbers. A cistern had been dug out of the rocky soil of the plateau which the wall inclosed, and care was taken to keep it constantly filled with water.

Such precautions were absolutely necessary, for the anchorites were threatened with dangers from two sides. First from the Ishmaelite hordes of Saracens who fell upon them from the east, and secondly from the Blemmyes, the wild inhabitants of the desert country which borders the fertile lands of Egypt and Nubia, and particularly of the barren highlands that part the Red Sea from the Nile valley. They crossed the sea in light skiffs, and then poured over the mountain like a swarm of locusts.

The little stores and savings which the defenseless hermits treasured in their caves had tempted the Blemmyes again and again, in spite of the Roman garrison in Pharan, which usually made its appearance on the scene of their incursion long after they had disappeared with their scanty booty. Not many months since, the raid had been effected in which old Stephanus had been wounded by an arrow, and there was every reason to

hope that the wild marauders would not return very soon, for
Phœbicius, the commander of the Roman maniple in the oasis,
was swift and vigorous in his office, and though he had not
succeeded in protecting the anchorites from all damage, he
had followed up the Blemmyes, who fled at his approach, and
cut them off from rejoining their boats. A battle took place
between the barbarians and the Romans, not far from the
coast on the desert tract dividing the hills from the sea, which
resulted in the total annihilation of the wild tribes and gave
ground to hope that such a lesson might serve as a warning to
the sons of the desert. But if hitherto the more easily quelled
promptings of covetousness had led them to cross the sea, they
were now animated by the most sacred of all duties, by the
law which required them to avenge the blood of their fathers
and brothers, and they dared to plan a fresh incursion in
which they should put forth all their resources. They were at
the same time obliged to exercise the greatest caution, and collected their forces of young men in the valleys that lay hidden
in the long range of coast hills.

The passage of the narrow arm of the sea that parted them
from Arabia Petræa was to be effected in the first dark night;
the sun, this evening, had set behind heavy storm-clouds that
had discharged themselves in violent rain and had obscured the
light of the waning moon. So they drew their boats and rafts
down to the sea, and, unobserved by the sentinels on the
mountain who had taken shelter from the storm under their
little pent-houses, they would have reached the opposite shore,
the mountain, and perhaps even the oasis, if some one had not
warned the anchorites—and that some one was Hermas.

Obedient to the commands of Paulus, the lad had appropri-
ated three of his friend's gold pieces, had provided himself with
a bow and arrows and some bread, and then, after muttering
a farewell to his father, who was asleep in his cave, he set out
for Raithu. Happy in the sense of his strength and manhood,
proud of the task which had been set him and which he deemed
worthy of a future soldier, and cheerfully ready to fulfill it
even at the cost of his life, he hastened forward in the bright
moonlight. He quitted the path at the spot where, to render
the ascent possible, even to the vigorous desert-travelers, it
took a zigzag line, and clambered from rock to rock, up and
down, in a direct line. When he came to a level spot he flew
on as if pursuers were at his heels. After sunrise he refreshed
himself with a morsel of food, and then hurried on again, not
heeding the heat of noon, nor that of the soft sand in which his
foot sunk as he followed the line of the sea-coast.

Thus passionately hurrying onward, he thought neither of Sirona nor of his past life—only of the hills on the further shore and of the Blemmyes—how he should best surprise them, and, when he had learned their plans, how he might recross the sea and return to his own people. At last, as he got more and more weary, as the heat of the sun grew more oppressive, and as the blood rushed more painfully to his heart and began to throb more rapidly in his temples, he lost all power of thought, and that which dwelt in his mind was no more than a dumb longing to reach his destination as soon as possible.

It was the third afternoon when he saw from afar the palms of Raithu, and hurried on with revived strength. Before the sun had set he had informed the anchorite, to whom Paulus had directed him, that the Alexandrian declined their call, and was minded to remain on the Holy Mountain.

Then Hermas proceeded to the little harbor, to bargain with the fishermen of the place for the boat which he needed. While he was talking with an old Amalekite boatman, who, with his black-eyed sons, was arranging his nets, two riders came at a quick pace toward the bay in which a large merchant ship lay at anchor, surrounded by little barks. The fisherman pointed to it.

"It is waiting for the caravan from Petræa," he said. "There, on the dromedary, is the emperor's great warrior who commands the Romans in Pharan."

Hermas saw Phœbicius for the first time, and as he rode up toward him and the fisherman he started; if he had followed his first impulse, he would have turned and have taken to flight, but his clear eyes had met the dull and yet searching glance of the centurion, and, blushing at his own weakness, he stood still with his arms crossed, and proudly and defiantly awaited the Gaul, who with his companion came straight up to him.

Talib had previously seen the youth by his father's side; he recognized him and asked how long he had been there, and if he had come direct from the mountain. Hermas answered him as was becoming, and understood at once that it was not he that the centurion was seeking.

Perfectly reassured and not without curiosity he looked at the new-comer, and a smile curled his lips as he observed that the lean old man, exhausted by his long and hurried ride, could scarcely hold himself on his beast, and at the same time it struck him that this pitiable old man was the husband of the blooming and youthful Sirona. Far from feeling any remorse for his intrusion into this man's house, he yielded entirely to the audacious humor with which his aspect filled him, and when Phœbicius himself asked him as to whether he had not met on his way with a fair-haired woman and a limping greyhound, he replied, repressing his laughter with difficulty:

"Ay, indeed! I did see such a woman and her dog, but I do not think it was lame."

"Where did you see her?" asked Phœbicius, hastily.

Hermas colored, for he was obliged to tell an untruth, and it might be that he would do Sirona an injury by giving false information. He therefore ventured to give no decided answer, but inquired:

"Has the woman committed some crime, that you are pursuing her?"

"A great one!" replied Talib. "She is my lord's wife, and—"

"What she has done wrong concerns me alone," said Phœbicius, sharply interrupting his companion. "I hope this fellow saw better than you who took the crying woman with a child, from Aila, for Sirona. What is your name, boy?"

"Hermas," answered the lad. "And who are you, pray?"

The Gaul's lips were parted for an angry reply, but he suppressed it, and said:

"I am the emperor's centurion, and I ask you, what did the woman look like whom you saw, and where did you meet her?"

The soldier's fierce looks and his captain's words showed Hermas that the fugitive woman had nothing good to expect if she were caught, and as he was not in the least inclined to assist her pursuers he hastily replied, giving the reins to his audacity, "I at any rate did not meet the person whom you seek; the woman I saw is certainly not this man's wife, for she might very well be his granddaughter. She had gold hair and a rosy face, and the greyhound that followed her was called Iambe."

"Where did you meet her?" shrieked the centurion.

"In the fishing-village at the foot of the mountain," replied Hermas. "She got into a boat, and away it went!"

"Toward the north?" asked the Gaul.

"I think so," replied Hermas, "but I do not know, for I was in a hurry and could not look after her."

"Then we will try to take her in Klysma," cried Phœbicius to the Amalekite. "If only there were horses in this accursed desert!"

"It is four days' journey," said Talib, considering. "And

beyond Elim there is no water before the Wells of Moses. Certainly if we could get good dromedaries—"

"And if," interrupted Hermas, "it were not better that you, my lord centurion, should not go so far from the oasis. For over there they say that the Blemmyes are gathering, and I myself am going across as a spy so soon as it is dark."

Phœbicius looked down gloomily, considering the matter. The news had reached him, too, that the sons of the desert were preparing for a new incursion, and he cried to Talib, angrily but decidedly, as he turned his back upon Hermas, " You must ride alone to Klysma, and try to capture her. I can not and will not neglect my duty for the sake of a wretched woman."

Hermas looked after him as he went away, and laughed out loud when he saw him disappear into his inn. He hired a boat from the old man for his passage across the sea for one of the gold pieces given him by Paulus, and lying down on the nets he refreshed himself by a deep sleep of some hours' duration. When the moon rose he was roused in obedience to his orders, and helped the boy who accompanied him, and who understood the management of the sails and rudder, to push the boat, which was laid up on the sand, down into the sea. Soon he was flying over the smooth and glistening waters before a light wind, and he felt as fresh and strong in spirit as a young eagle that has just left the nest and spreads its mighty wings for the first time. He could have shouted in his new and delicious sense of freedom, and the boy at the stern shook his head in astonishment when he saw Hermas wield the oars he had intrusted to him, unskillfully it is true, but with mighty strokes.

" The wind is in our favor," he called out to the anchorite as he hauled round the sail with a rope in his hand; " we shall get on without your working so hard. You may save your strength."

" There is plenty of it, and I need not be stingy of it," answered Hermas, and he bent forward for another powerful stroke.

About half-way he took a rest, and admired the reflection of the moon in the bright mirror of the water, and he could not but think of Petrus's court-yard that had shone in the same silvery light when he had climbed up to Sirona's window. The image of the fair, white-armed woman recurred to his mind, and a melancholy longing began to creep over him.

He sighed softly again and yet again; but as his breast heaved for the third bitter sigh, he remembered the object of his journey and his broken fetters, and with eager arrogance he struck the oar flat on to the water so that it spurted high

up and sprinkled the boat and him with a shower of wet and
twinkling diamond-drops. He began to work the oars again,
reflecting as he did so that he had something better to do than
to think of a woman. Indeed, he found it easy to forget
Sirona complétely, for in the next few days he went through
every excitement in a warrior's life.

Scarcely two hours after his start from Raithu he was standing on the soil of another continent, and, after finding a hiding-place for his boat, he slipped off among the hills to watch
the movements of the Blemmyes. The very first day he went
up to the valley in which they were gathering; on the second,
after being many times seen and pursued, he succeeded in
seizing a warrior who had been sent out to reconnoiter, and in
carrying him off with him; he bound him, and by heavy
threats learned many things from him.

The number of their collected enemies was great, but Hermas had hopes of outstripping them, for his prisoner revealed
to him the spot where their boats, drawn up on shore, lay hidden under the sand and stones.

As soon as it was dusk the anchorite in his boat went toward
the place of embarkation, and when the Blemmyes, in the
darkness of midnight, drew their first bark into the water,
Hermas sailed off ahead of the enemy, landed in much danger
before the western declivity of the mountain, and hastened up
toward Sinai to warn the Pharanite watchmen on the beacon.

He gained the top of the difficult peak before sunrise, roused
the lazy sentinels who had left their post, and before they were
able to mount guard, to hoist the flags or begin to sound the
brazen cymbals, he had hurried on down the valley to his
father's cave.

Since his disappearance Miriam had incessantly hovered round
Stephanus's dwelling, and had fetched fresh water for the
old man every morning, noon and evening, even after a new
nurse, who was clumsier and more peevish, had taken Paulus's
place. She lived on roots and on the bread the sick man gave
her, and at night she lay down to sleep in a deep dry cleft of
the rock that she had long known well. She quitted her hard
bed before day-break to refill the old man's pitcher and to chat-
ter to him about Hermas.

She was a willing servant to Stephanus because, as often as
she went to him, she could hear his son's name from his lips,
and he rejoiced at her coming because she always gave him the
opportunity of talking of Hermas.

For many weeks the sick man had been so accustomed to let
himself be waited on that he accepted the shepherdess's good

offices as a matter of course, and she never attempted to account to herself for her readiness to serve him. Stephanus would have suffered in dispensing with her, and to her, her visits to the well and her conversations with the old man had become a need, nay, a necessity, for she still was ignorant whether Hermas was yet alive, or whether Phœbicius had killed him in consequence of her betrayal. Perhaps all that Stephanus told her of his son's journey of investigation was an invention of Paulus to spare the sick man, and accustom him gradually to the loss of his child; and yet she was only too willing to believe that Hermas still lived, and she quitted the neighborhood of the cave as late as possible, and filled the sick man's waterjar before the sun was up, only because she said to herself that the fugitive on his return would seek no one else so soon as his father.

She had not one really quiet moment, for if a falling stone, an approaching footstep, or the cry of a beast broke the stillness of the desert she at once hid herself, and listened with a ﹒ beating heart; much less from fear of Petrus her master, from whom she had run away, than in the expectation of hearing the step of the man whom she had betrayed into the hand of his enemy, and for whom she nevertheless painfully longed day and night.

As often as she lingered by the spring she wetted her stubborn hair to smoothe it, and washed her face with as much zeal as if she thought she should succeed in washing the dark hue out of her skin. And all this she did for him, that on his return she might charm him as much as the white woman in the oasis, whom she hated as fiercely as she loved him passionately.

During the heavy storm of last night a torrent from the mountain height had shed itself into her retreat and driven her out of it. Wet through, shelterless, tormented by remorse, fear and longing, she had clambered from stone to stone, and sought refuge and peace under first one rock, and then another; thus she had been attracted by the glimmer of light that shone out of the new dwelling of the pious Paulus; she had seen and recognized the Alexandrian, but he had not observed her as he cowered on the ground near his hearth, deeply sunk in thought.

She knew now where the excommunicated man dwelt after whom Stephanus often asked, and she had gathered from the old man's lamentations and dark hints that Paulus, too, had been insnared and brought to ruin by her enemy.

As the morning star began to pale Miriam went up to Stephanus's cave; her heart was full of tears, and yet she was unable to pour out her need and suffering in a soothing flood of weeping; she was wholly possessed with a wild desire to sink down on the earth there and die, and to be released by death from her relentless, driving torment. But it was still too early to disturb the old man—and yet she must hear a human voice, one word—even if it were a hard word—from the lips of a human being; for the bewildering feeling of distraction which confused her mind, and the misery of abandonment that crushed her heart were all too cruelly painful to be borne.

She was standing by the entrance to the cave when, high above her head, she heard the falling of stones and the cry of a human voice. She started and listened with outstretched neck and strung sinews, motionless. Then she broke suddenly into a loud and piercing shout of joy, and flinging up her arms she flew up the mountain toward a traveler who came swiftly down to meet her.

"Hermas! Hermas!" she shouted, and all the sunny delight of her heart was reflected in her cry so clearly and purely that the sympathetic chords in the young man's soul echoed the sound, and he hailed her with joyful welcome.

He had never before greeted her thus, and the tone of his voice revived her poor crushed heart like a restorative draught offered by a tender hand to the lips of the dying. Exquisite delight and a glow of gratitude such as she had never before felt flooded her soul, and as he was so good to her she longed to show him that she had something to offer in return for the gift of friendship which he offered her. So the first thing she said to him was, "I have stayed constantly near your father, and have brought him water early and late, as much as he needed."

She blushed as she thus for the first time praised herself to him, but Hermas exclaimed:

"That is a good girl! and I will not forget it. You are a wild, silly thing, but I believe that you are to be relied on by those to whom you feel kindly."

"Only try me," cried Miriam, holding out her hand to him. He took it, and as they went on together he said:

"Do you hear the brass? I have warned the watchmen up there; the Blemmyes are coming. Is Paulus with my father?"

"No, but I know where he is."

"Then you must call him," said the young man. "Him first and then Gelasius, and Psoes, and Dulas, and any more of the penitents that you can find. They must all go to the castle by the ravine. Now I will go to my father; you hurry on and show that you are to be trusted." As he spoke he put his arm round her waist, but she slipped shyly away, and, calling out: "I will take them all the message," she hurried off.

In front of the cave where she had hoped to meet with Paulus she found Sirona; she did not stop with her, but contented herself with laughing and calling, out words of abuse.

Guided by the idea that she should find the Alexandrian at the nearest well, she went on and called him, then hurrying on from cave to cave she delivered her message in Hermas's name, happy to serve him.

CHAPTER IX.

THEY were all collected behind the rough wall on the edge of the ravine—the strange men who had turned their back on life with all its joys and pains, its duties and its delights, on the community and family to which they belonged, and had fled to the desert, there to strive for a prize above and beyond this life, when they had of their own free will renounced all other effort. In the voiceless desert, far from the enticing echoes of the world, it might be easy to kill every sensual impulse, to throw off the fetters of the world, and so bring that humanity, which was bound to the dust through sin and the flesh, nearer to the pure and incorporate being of the Divinity.

All these men were Christians, and, like the Saviour, who had freely taken torments upon Himself to become the Redeemer, they, too, sought through the purifying power of suffering to free themselves from the dross of their impure human nature, and by severe penance to contribute their share of atonement for their own guilt, and for that of all their race. No fear of persecution had driven them into the desert—nothing but the hope of gaining the hardest of victories.

All the anchorites who had been summoned to the tower were Egyptians and Syrians, and among the former particularly there were many who, being already inured to abstinence and penance in the service of the old gods in their own country, now as Christians had selected as the scene of their pious exercises the very spot where the Lord must have revealed Himself to His elect.

At a later date not merely Sinai itself, but the whole tract of Arabia Petræa—through which, as it was said, the Jews at their exodus under Moses had wandered—was peopled with ascetics of like mind, who gave to their settlements the names of the resting-places of the chosen people, as mentioned in the Scriptures; but as yet there was no connection between the individual penitents, no order ruled their lives; they might still be counted by tens, though ere long they numbered hundreds and thousands.

The threat of danger had brought all these contemners of the world and of life in stormy haste to the shelter of the tower, in spite of their readiness to die. Only old Kosmas, who had withdrawn to the desert with his wife—she had found a grave there—had remained in his cave, and had declared to Gelasius, who shared his cave and who had urged him to flight, that he was content in whatever place or whatever hour the Lord should call him, and that it was in God's hands to decide whether old age or an arrow-shot should open to him the gates of heaven.

It was quite otherwise with the rest of the anchorites, who rushed through the narrow door of the watch-tower and into its inner room till it was filled to overflowing, and Paulus, who in the presence of danger had fully recovered his equanimity, was obliged to refuse admission to a new-comer in order to preserve the closely packed and trembling crowd from injury.

No murrain passes from beast to beast, no mildew from fruit with such rapidity as fear spreads from man to man. Those who had been driven by the sharpest lashings of terror had run the fastest and reached the castle first. They had received those who followed them with lamentation and outcries, and it was a pitiable sight to see how the terrified crowd, in the midst of their loud declarations of resignation to God's guidance and their pious prayers, wrung their hands, and at the same time how painfully anxious each one was to hide the little property he had saved first from the disapproval of his companions, and then from the covetousness of the approaching enemy.

With Paulus came Sergius and Jeremias, to whom, on the way, he had spoken words of encouragement. All three did their utmost to revive the confidence of the terrified men, and when the Alexandrian reminded them how zealously each of them only a few weeks since had helped to roll the blocks and stones from the wall, and down the precipice, so as to crush and slay the advancing enemy, the feeling was strong in many of them that, as he had already proved himself worthy in defense, it was due to him now to make him their leader.

The number of the men who rushed out of the tower was increasing, and when Hermas appeared with his father on his back and followed by Miriam, and when Paulus exhorted his companions to be edified by this pathetic picture of filial love, curiosity tempted even the last loiterers in the tower out into the open space.

The Alexandrian sprung over the wall, went up to Stephanus, lifted him from the shoulders of the panting youth, and, taking him on his own, carried him toward the tower; but the old warrior refused to enter the place of refuge,.and begged his friend to lay him down by the wall. Paulus obeyed his wish and then went with Hermas to the top of the tower to spy the distance from thence.

As soon as he had quitted him, Stephanus turned to the anchorites who stood near him, saying:

"These stones are loose, and though my strength is indeed small, still it is great enough to send one of them over with a push. If it comes to a battle my old soldier's eyes, dim as they are now, may with the help of yours see many things that may be useful to you, young ones. Above all things, if the game is to be a hot one for the robbers, one must command here whom the others will obey."

"It shall be you, father," interrupted Salathiel the Syrian. "You have served in Cæsar's army, and you proved your courage and knowledge of war in the last raid. You shall command us."

Stephanus sadly shook his head, and replied: "My voice is becoming too weak and low since this wound in my breast and my long illness. Not even those who stand nearest to me would understand me in the noise of battle. Let Paulus be your captain, for he is strong, cautious, and brave."

Many of the anchorites had long looked upon the Alexandrian as their best stay; for many years he had enjoyed the respect of all, and on a thousand occasions had given proof of his strength and presence of mind, but at this proposal they looked at each other in surprise, doubt and disapproval.

Stephanus saw what was passing in their minds.

"It is true he has erred gravely," he said. "And before God he is the least of the least among us; but in animal strength and indomitable courage he is superior to you all. Which of you would be willing to take his place, if you reject his guidance?"

"Orion the Saite," cried one of the anchorites, "is tall and strong. If he would—"

But Orion eagerly excused himself from assuming the dangerous office, and when Andreas and Joseph also refused with no less decision the leadership that was offered them, Stephanus said:

"You see, there is no choice left us but to beg the Alexandrian to command us here so long as the robbers threaten us, and no longer. There he comes—shall I ask him?"

A murmur of consent, though by no means of satisfaction, answered the old man, and Paulus, quite carried away by his eagerness to stake his life and blood for the protection of the weak and fevered with a soldier's ardor, accepted Stephanus's commission as a matter of course, and set to work like a general to organize the helpless wearers of sheep-skin.

Some he sent to the top of the tower to keep watch, others he charged with the transport of the stones; to a third party he intrusted the duty of hurling pieces of rock and blocks of stone down into the abyss in the moment of danger; he requested the weaker brethren to assemble themselves together, to pray for the others and to sing hymns of praise, and he concerted signs and pass-words with all; he was now here, now there, and his energy and confidence infused themselves even into the faint-hearted.

In the midst of these arrangements Hermas took leave of him and of his father, for he heard the Roman war-trumpets and the drums of the young manhood of Pharan, as they marched through the short cut to meet the enemy. He knew where the main strength of the Blemmyes lay and communicated this knowledge to the centurion Phœbicius and the captain of the Pharanites. The Gaul put a few short questions to Hermas, whom he recognized immediately, for since he had met him at the harbor of Raithu he could not forget his eyes, which reminded him of those of Glycera; and after receiving his hasty and decided answers he issued rapid and prudent orders.

A third of the Pharanites were to march forward against the enemy, drumming and trumpeting, and then retreat as far as the watch-tower as the enemy approached over the plain. If the Blemmyes allowed themselves to be tempted thither, a second third of the warriors of the oasis, that could easily lie in ambush in a cross valley, were to fall on their left flank, while Phœbicius and his maniple—hidden behind the rock on which the castle stood—would suddenly rush out and so decide the battle. The last third of the Pharanites had orders to destroy the ships of the invaders under the command of Hermas, who knew the spot where they had landed.

In the worst case the centurion and his men could retreat into the castle, and there defend themselves till the warriors of the nearest sea-ports—whither messengers were already on their way—should come to the rescue.

The Gaul's orders were immediately obeyed, and Hermas walked at the head of the division intrusted to him, as proud and as self-possessed as any of Cæsar's veterans leading his legion into the field. He carried a bow and arrows at his back, and in his hand a battle-ax that he had bought at Raithu.

Miriam attempted to follow the troops he was leading, but he observed her, and called out, "Go up to the fort, child, to my father." And the shepherdess obeyed without hesitation.

The anchorites had all crowded to the edge of the precipice; they looked at the division of the forces, and signed and shouted down. They had hoped that some part of the fighting men would be joined to them for their defense, but, as they soon learned, they had hoped in vain. Stephanus, whose feeble sight could not reach so far as the plain at the foot of the declivity, made Paulus report to him all that was going on there, and with the keen insight of a soldier he comprehended the centurion's plan. The troop led by Hermas passed by below the tower, and the youth waved and shouted a greeting up to his father. Stephanus, whose hearing remained sharper than his sight, recognized his son's voice and took leave of him with tender and loving words in as loud a voice as he could command. Paulus collected all the overflow of the old man's heart in one sentence, and called out his blessings through his two hands as a speaking-trumpet after his friend's son as he departed to battle. Hermas understood; but deeply as he was touched by this farewell he answered only by dumb signs. A father can find a hundred words of blessing sooner than a son can find one of thanks.

As the youth disappeared behind the rocks, Paulus said:

"He marches on like an experienced soldier, and the others follow him as sheep follow a ram. But hark! Certainly the foremost division of the Pharanites and the enemy have met. The outcry comes nearer and nearer."

"Then all will be well," cried Stephanus, excitedly. "If they only take the bait and let themselves be drawn on to the plateau I think they are lost. From here we can watch the whole progress of the battle, and if our side is driven back it may easily happen that they will throw themselves into the castle. Now not a pebble must be thrown in vain, for if our tower becomes the central point of the struggle, the defenders will need stones to fling.

These words were heard by several of the anchorites, and as now the war-cries and the noise of the fight came nearer and nearer, and one and another repeated to each other that their place of refuge would become the center of the combat, the frightened penitents quitted the posts assigned to them by Paulus, ran hither and thither in spite of the Alexandrian's severe prohibition, and most of them at last joined the com-

pany of the old and feeble, whose psalms grew more and more
lamentable as danger pressed closer upon them.

Loudest of all was the wailing of the Saite Orion, who cried,
with uplifted hands:

"What wilt Thou of us miserable creatures, oh, Lord?
When Moses left Thy chosen people on this very spot for only
forty days, they at once fell away from Thee; and we, we without any leader have spent all our life in Thy service, and have
given up all that can rejoice the heart, and have taken every
kind of suffering upon us to please Thee! and now these hideous heathens are surging round us again, and will kill us. Is
this the reward of victory for our striving and our long
wrestling?"

The rest joined in the lamentation of the Saite, but Paulus
stepped into their midst, blamed them for their cowardice, and
with warm and urgent speech implored them to return to their
posts, so that the wall might be guarded at least on the eastern
and more accessible side, and that the castle might not fall an
easy prey into the hands of an enemy from whom no quarter
was to be expected. Some of the anchorites were already pro-
ceeding to obey the Alexandrian's injunction, when a fearful
cry, the war-cry of the Blemmyes, who were in pursuit of the
Pharanites, rose from the foot of their rock of refuge.

They crowded together again in terror; Salathiel the Syrian
had ventured to the edge of the abyss, and had looked over old
Stephanus's shoulder down into the hollow, and when he
rushed back to his companions, crying in terror: "Our men
are flying!" Gelasius shrieked aloud, beat his breast, and tore
his rough black hair, crying out:

"Oh, Lord God, what wilt Thou of us? Is it vain then to
strike after righteousness and virtue that Thou givest us over
unto death, and does not fight for us? If we are overcome by
the heathen, ungodliness and brute force will boast themselves
as though they had won the victory over righteousness and
truth!"

Paulus had turned from the lamenting hermits, perplexed
and beside himself, and stood with Stephanus watching the
fight.

The Blemmyes had come in great numbers, and their attack,
before which the Pharanites were to have retired as a feint, fell
with such force upon the foremost division that they and their
comrades, who had rushed to their aid on the plateau, were
unable to resist it, and were driven back as far as the spot
where the ravine narrowed.

"Things are not as they should be," said Stephanus.

"And the cowardly band, like a drove of cattle," cried Paulus, in a fury, "leave the walls unprotected, and blaspheme God instead of watching or fighting."

The anchorites noticed his gestures, which were indeed those of a desperate man, and Sergius exclaimed:

"Are we then wholly abandoned? Why does not the thorn-bush light its fires and destroy the evil-doers with its flames? Why is the thunder silent, and where are the lightnings that played round the peak of Sinai? Why does not darkness fall upon us to affright the heathen? Why does not the earth open her mouth to swallow them up like the company of Korah?"

"The might of God," cried Dulas, "tarries too long. The Lord must set our piety in a doubtful light, for He treats us as though we were unworthy of all care."

"And that you are!" exclaimed Paulus, who had heard the last words, and who was dragging rather than leading the feeble Stephanus to the unguarded eastern wall. "That you are, for instead of resisting His enemies you blaspheme God, and disgrace yourselves by your miserable cowardice. Look at this sick old man who is prepared to defend you, and obey my orders without a murmur, or, by the holy martyrs, I will drag you to your posts by your hair and ears, and will—"

But he ceased speaking, for his threats were interrupted by a powerful voice which called his name from the foot of the wall.

"That is Agapitus," exclaimed Stephanus. "Lead me to the wall and set me down there."

Before Paulus could accede to his friend's wish the tall form of the bishop was standing by his side.

Agapitus the Cappadocian had in his youth been a warrior; he had hardly passed the limits of middle age, and was a vigilant captain of his congregation. When all the youth of Pharan had gone forth to meet the Blemmyes, he had no peace in the oasis, and, after enjoining on the presbyters and deacons that they should pray in the church for the fighting men with the women and the men who remained behind, he himself, accompanied by a guide and two acolytes, had gone up the mountain to witness the battle.

To the other priests and his wife, who sought to detain him, he had answered: "Where the flock is there should the shepherd be!"

Unseen and unheard he had gained the castle wall and had been a witness to Paulus's vehement speech. He now stood opposite the Alexandrian with rolling eyes, and threateningly lifted his powerful hand as he called out to him:

"And dare an outcast speak thus to his brethren? Will the champion of Satan give orders to the soldiers of the Lord? It would indeed be a joy to you if by your strong arm you could win back the good name that your soul, crippled by sin and guilt, has flung away. Come on, my friends! the Lord is with us and will help us."

Paulus had let the bishop's words pass over him in silence, and raised his hands like the other anchorites when Agapitus stepped into their midst, and uttered a short and urgent prayer.

After the "Amen" the bishop pointed out, like a general, to each man, even to the feeble and aged, his place by the wall or behind the stones for throwing, and then cried out, with a clear ringing voice that sounded above all other noise: "Show to-day that you are indeed soldiers of the Most High."

Not one rebelled, and when man by man each had placed himself at his post, he went to the precipice and looked attentively down at the fight that was raging below.

The Pharanites were now opposing the attack of the Blemmyes with success, for Phœbicius, rushing forward with his men from their ambush, had fallen upon the compact mass of the sons of the desert in flank, and, spreading death and ruin, had divided them into two bodies. The well-trained and well-armed Romans seemed to have an easy task with their naked opponents, who, in a hand to hand fight, could not avail themselves of either their arrows or their spears. But the Blemmyes had learned to use their strength in frequent battles with the imperial troops, and so soon as they perceived that they were no match for their enemies in pitched battle, their leaders set up a strange shrill cry, their ranks dissolved, and they dispersed in all directions, like a heap of feathers strewn by a gust of wind.

Agapitus took the hasty disappearance of the enemy for wild flight, he sighed deeply and thankfully and turned to go down to the field of battle, and to speak consolation to his wounded fellow-Christians.

But in the castle itself he found opportunity for exercising his pious office, for before him stood the shepherdess whom he had already observed on his arrival, and she said, with much embarrassment, but clearly and quickly: "Old Stephanus there, my lord bishop—Hermas's father for whom I carry water—bids me ask you to come to him, for his wound has reopened and he thinks his end is near." -

Agapitus immediately obeyed this call; he went with hasty steps toward the sick man, whose wound Paulus and Orion had already bound up, and greeted him with a familiarity that he was far from showing to the other penitents. He had long known the former name and the fate of Stephanus, and it was by his advice that Hermas had been obliged to join the deputation sent to Alexandria, for Agapitus was of opinion that no one ought to flee from the battle of life without having first taken some part in it.

Stephanus put out his hand to the bishop who sat down beside him, signed to the by-standers to leave them alone, and listened attentively to the feeble words of the sufferer. When he had ceased speaking, Agapitus said:

"I praise the Lord with you for having permitted your lost wife to find the ways that lead to Him, and your son will be—as you were once—a valiant man of war. Your earthly house is set in order, but are you prepared for the other, the everlasting mansion?"

"For eighteen years I have done penance, and prayed, and borne great sufferings," answered the sick man. "The world lies far behind me, and I hope I am walking in the path that leads to heaven."

"So do I hope for you and for your soul," said the bishop. "That which is hardest to endure has fallen to your lot in this world, but have you striven to forgive those who did you the bitterest wrong, and can you pray, ' Forgive us our sins as we forgive them that sin against us?' Do you remember the words, ' If ye forgive men their trespasses your heavenly Father will also forgive you?' "

"Not only have I pardoned Glycera," answered Stephanus, "but I have taken her again into my heart of hearts; but the man who basely seduced her, the wretch who, although I had done him a thousand benefits, betrayed me, robbed me and dishonored me, I wish him—,"

"Forgive him," cried Agapitus, "as you would be forgiven."

"I have striven these eighteen years to bless my enemy," replied Stephanus, "and I will still continue to strive—"

Up to this moment the bishop had devoted his whole attention to the sick anchorite, but he was now called on all sides at once, and Gelasius, who was standing by the declivity with some other anchorites, called out to him:

"Father—save us—the heathen there are climbing up the rocks."

Agapitus signed a blessing over Stephanus and then turned away from him, saying earnestly once more: "Forgive, and heaven is open to you."

Many wounded and dead lay on the plain, and the Pharanites
were retreating into the ravine, for the Blemmyes had not indeed fled, but had only dispersed themselves, and then had
climbed up the rocks which hemmed in the level ground and
shot their arrows at their enemies from thence.

"Where are the Romans?" Agapitus eagerly inquired of
Orion.

"They are withdrawing into the gorge through which the
road leads up here," answered the Saite. "But look! only
look at these heathen! The Lord be merciful to us! they are
climbing up the cliffs like wood-peckers up a tree." ·

"The stones, fly to the stones!" cried Agapitus with flashing eyes to the anchorites that stood by. "What is going on
behind the wall there? Do you hear? Yes—that is the Roman
tuba. Courage, brethren! the emperor's soldiers are guarding
the weakest side of the castle. But look here at the naked
figures in the cleft. Bring the blocks here: set your shoulders
stoutly to it, Orion! one more push, Salathiel! There it goes,
it crashes down! If only it does not stick in the rift! No!
thank God, it has bounded off—that was a leap! Well done—
there were six enemies of the Lord destroyed at once."

"I see three more yonder," cried Orion. "Come here,
Damianus, and help me."

The man he called rushed forward with several others, and
the first success raised the courage of the anchorites so rapidly
and wonderfully that the bishop soon found it difficult to re-
strain their zeal and to persuade them to be sparing with the
precious missiles.

While under the direction of Agapitus stone after stone was
hurled clattering over the steep precipice down upon the
Blemmyes, Paulus sat by the sick man, looking at the ground.

"You are not helping them?" asked Stephanus.

"Agapitus is right," replied the Alexandrian. "I have
much to expiate, and fighting brings enjoyment. How great
enjoyment I can understand by the torture it is to me to sit
still. The bishop blessed you affectionately."

"I am near the goal," sighed Stephanus, "and he promises
me the joys of Heaven if I only forgive him who stole my wife
from me. He is forgiven—yes, all is forgiven him, and may
everything that he undertakes turn to good; yea, and nothing
turn to evil—only feel how my heart throbs, it is rallying its
strength once more before it utterly ceases to beat. When it
is all over repeat to Hermas everything that I have told you,
and bless him a thousand, thousand times in my name and his
mother's; but never, never tell him that in an hour of weak-

ness she ran away with that villain—that man, that miserable man I mean—whom I forgive. Give Hermas this ring, and with it the letter that you will find under the dry herbs on the couch in my cave; they will secure him a reception from his uncle, who will also procure him a place in the army, for my brother is in high favor with Cæsar. Only listen how Agapitus urges on our men; they are fighting bravely there; that is the Roman tuba. Attend to me—the maniple will occupy the castle and shoot down on the heathen from thence; when they come carry me into the tower. I am weak and would fain collect my thoughts, and pray once more that I may find strength to forgive the man not with my lips only."

"Down there, see—there come the Romans," cried Paulus, interrupting him. "Here, up here!" he called down to the men, "the steps are more to the left."

"Here we are," answered a sharp voice. "You stay there, you people, on that projection of rock, and keep your eye on the castle. If any danger threatens call me with the trumpet. I will climb up, and from the top of the tower there I can see where the dogs come from."

During this speech Stephanus had looked down and listened; when a few minutes later the Gaul reached the wall and called out to the men inside, "Is there no one there who will give me a hand?" he turned to Paulus, saying: "Lift me up and support me—quick!"

With an agility that astonished the Alexandrian, Stephanus stood upon his feet, leaned over the wall toward the centurion —who had climbed as far as the outer foot of it—looked him in the face with eager attention, shuddered violently, and repressing his feelings with the utmost effort offered him his lean hand to help Paulus.

"Servianus!" cried the centurion, who was greatly shocked by such a meeting and in such a place, and who, struggling painfully for composure, stared first at the old man and then at him.

Not one of the three succeeded in uttering a word; but Stephanus's eyes were fixed on the Gaul's features, and the longer he looked at him the hollower grew his cheeks and the paler his lips; at the same time he still held out his hand to the other, perhaps in token of forgiveness.

So passed a long minute. Then Phœbicius recollected that he had climbed the wall in the emperor's service, and stamping with impatience at himself he took the old man's hand in a hasty grasp. But scarcely had Stephanus felt the touch of the Gaul's fingers when he started as struck by lightning, and flung himself with a hoarse cry on his enemy who was hanging on the edge of the wall.

Paulus gazed in horror at the frightful scene, and cried aloud with fervent unction: "Let him go—forgive that Heaven may forgive you."

"Heaven! what is Heaven? what is forgiveness!" screamed the old man. "He shall be damned."

Before the Alexandrian could hinder him the loose stone over which the enemies were wrestling in breathless combat gave way, and both were hurled into the abyss with the falling rock.

Paulus groaned from the lowest depth of his breast and murmured, while the tears ran down his cheeks: "He, too, has fought the fight, and he, too, has striven in vain."

CHAPTER X.

THE fight was ended; the sun as it went to its rest behind the Holy Mountain had lighted many corpses of Blemmyes, and now the stars shone down on the oasis from the clear sky.

Hymns of praise sounded out of the church, and near it, under the hill against which it was built, torches were blazing and threw their ruddy light on a row of biers, on which under green palm branches lay the heroes who had fallen in the battle against the Blemmyes.

Now the hymn ceased, the gates of the house of God opened and Agapitus led his followers toward the dead. The congregation gathered in a half circle round their peaceful brethren, and heard the blessing their pastor pronounced over the noble victims who had shed their blood in fighting the heathen. When it was ended those who in life had been their nearest and dearest went up to the dead, and many tears fell into the sand from the eyes of a mother or a wife, many a sigh went up to heaven from a father's breast. Next to the bier on which old Stephanus was resting stood another and a smaller one, and between the two Hermas knelt and wept. He raised his face, for a deep and kindly voice spoke his name.

"Petrus," said the lad, clasping the hand that the senator held out to him, "I felt forced and driven out into the world, and away from my father—and now he is gone forever, how gladly I would have been kept by him."

"He died a noble death, in battle for those he loved," said the senator, consolingly.

"Paulus was near him when he fell," replied Hermas. "My father fell from the wall while defending the tower; but look here, this girl—poor child—who used to keep your goats, died like a heroine. Poor, wild Miriam, how kind I would be to you if only you were alive now!"

Hermas as he spoke stroked the arm of the shepherdess, pressed a kiss on her small, cold hand, and softly folded it with the other across her bosom.

" How did the girl got into the battle with the men?" asked Petrus. " But you can tell me that in my own house. Come and be our guest as long as it pleases you, and until you go forth into the world; thanks are due to you from us all."

Hermas blushed and modestly declined the praises which were showered on him on all sides as the savior of the oasis. When the wailing women appeared he knelt once more at the head of his father's bier, cast a last loving look at Miriam's peaceful face, and then followed his host.

The man and boy crossed the court together. Hermas involuntarily glanced up at the window where more than once he had seen Sirona, and said, as he pointed to the centurion's house: " He, too, fell."

Petrus nodded and opened the door of his house. In the hall, which was lighted up, Dorothea came hastily to meet him, asking: " No news yet of Polykarp?"

Her husband shook his head, and she added: " How, indeed, is it possible? He will write at the soonest from Klysma or perhaps even from Alexandria. "

" That is just what I think," replied Petrus, looking down to the ground. Then he turned to Hermas and introduced him to his wife.

Dorothea received the young man with warm sympathy; she had heard that his father had fallen in the fight, and how nobly he, too, had distinguished himself. Supper was ready, and Hermas was invited to share it. The mistress gave her daughter a sign to make preparations for their guest, but Petrus detained Marthana, and said, " Hermas may fill Antonius's place; he has still something to do with some of the workmen. Where are Jethro and the house-slaves?"

" They have already eaten," said Dorothea.

The husband and wife looked at each other, and Petrus said, with a melancholy smile: " I believe they are up on the mountain. "

Dorothea wiped a tear from her eye as she replied: " They will meet Antonius there. If only they could find Polykarp! And yet I honestly say—not merely to comfort you—it is most probable that he has not met with any accident in the mountain

gorges, but has gone to Alexandria to escape the memories
that follow him here at every step. Was not that the gate?"

She rose quickly and looked into the court, while Petrus,
who had followed her, did the same, saying, with a deep sigh,
as he turned to Marthana—who, while she offered meat and
bread to Hermas was watching her parents: "It was only the
slave Anubis."

For some time a painful silence reigned round the large
table, to-day so sparsely furnished with guests.

At last Petrus turned to his guest and said: "You were to
tell me how the shepherdess Miriam lost her life in the struggle. She had run away from our house—"

"Up the mountain," added Hermas. "She supplied my
poor father with water like a daughter."

"You see, mother," interrupted Marthana, "she was not
bad-hearted; I always said so."

"This morning," continued Hermas, nodding in sad assent
to the maiden, "she followed my father to the castle, and immediately after his fall, Paulus told me, she rushed away from
it, but only to seek me, and to bring me the sad news. We
had known each other a long time; for years she had watered
her goats at our well, and while I was still quite a boy and she
a little girl, she would listen for hours when I played on my
willow-pipe the songs which Paulus had taught me. As long
as I played she was perfectly quiet, and when I ceased she
wanted to hear more and still more, until I had had too much
of it and went away. Then she would grow angry, and if I
would not do her will she would scold me with bad words.
But she always came again, and as I had no other companion
and she was the only creature who cared to listen to me, I was
very well content that she should prefer our well to all the
others. Then we grew older and I began to be afraid of her,
for she would talk in such a godless way—and she even died a
heathen. Paulus, who once overheard us, warned me against
her, and as I had long thrown away the pipe and hunted
beasts with my bow and arrow whenever my father would let
me, I was with her for shorter intervals when I went to the
well to draw water, and we became more and more strangers;
indeed, I could be quite hard to her. Only once after I came
back from the capital something happened—but that I need
not tell you. The poor child was so unhappy at being a slave,
and no doubt had first seen the light in a free house. She was
fond of me, more than a sister is of a brother—and when my
father was dead she felt that I ought not to learn the news
from any one but herself. She had seen which way I had gone

with the Pharanites and followed me up, and she soon found
me, for she had the eyes of a gazelle and the ears of a startled
bird. It was not this time difficult to find me, for when she
sought me we were fighting with the Blemmyes in the green
hollow that leads from the mountain to the sea. They roared
with fury like wild beasts, for before we could get to the sea
the fishermen in the little town below had discovered their
boats, which they had hidden under sand and stones, and had
carried them off to their harbor. The boy from Raithu who
accompanied me had by my orders kept them in sight, and
had led the fishermen to the hiding-place. The watchmen
whom they had left with the boats had fled, and had reached
their companions who were fighting round the castle, and at
least two hundred of them had been sent back to the shore to
recover possession of the boats and to punish the fishermen.
This troop met us in the green valley, and there we fell to
fighting. The Blemmyes outnumbered us; they soon surrounded us before and behind, on the right side and on the
left, for they jumped and climbed from rock to rock like
mountain-goats, and then shot down their reed-arrows from
above. Three or four touched me, and one pierced my hair
and remained hanging in it with the feather at the end of the
shaft. How the battle went elsewhere I can not tell you, for
the blood mounted to my head, and I was only conscious that
I myself snorted and shouted like a madman, and wrestled with
the heathen now here and now there, and more than once
lifted my ax to cleave a skull. At the same time I saw a part
of our men turn to fly, and I called them back with furious
words; then they turned round and followed me again. Once
in the midst of the struggle, I saw Miriam, too, clinging, pale
and trembling to a rock, and looking on at the fight. I
shouted to her to leave the spot and go back to my father,
but she stood still and shook her head with a gesture—a
gesture so full of pity and anguish—I shall never forget it.
With hands and eyes she signed to me that my father was
dead, and I understood; at least I understood that some
dreadful misfortune had happened. I had no time for reflection, for before I could gain any certain information by word of
mouth, a captain of the heathen had seized me, and we came
to a life and death struggle before Miriam's very eyes. My
opponent was strong, but I showed the girl—who had often
taunted me for being a weakling because I obeyed my father
in everything—that I need yield to no one. I could not have
borne to be vanquished before her, and I flung the heathen to
the ground and slew him with my ax. I was only vaguely

conscious of her presence, for during my severe struggle I could see nothing but my adversary. But suddenly I heard a loud scream, and Miriam sunk bleeding close before me. While I was kneeling over his comrade one of the Blemmyes had crept up to me, and had flung his lance at me from a few paces off. But Miriam—Miriam—"

"She saved you at the cost of her own life," said Petrus, completing the lad's sentence, for at the recollection of the occurrence his voice had failed and his eyes overflowed with tears.

Hermas nodded assent, and then added, softly:

"She threw up her arms and called my name as the spear struck her. The eldest son of Obedianus punished the heathen that had done it, and I supported her as she fell dying, and took her curly head on my knees and spoke her name; she opened her eyes once more, and spoke mine softly and with indescribable tenderness. I had never thought that wild Miriam could speak so sweetly; I was overcome with terrible grief, and kissed her eyes and her lips. She looked at me once more with a long, wide-open, blissful gaze, and then she was dead."

"She was a heathen," said Dorothea, drying her eyes, "but for such a death the Lord will forgive her much."

"I loved her dearly," said Marthana, "and will lay my sweetest flowers on her grave. May I cut some sprays from your blooming myrtle for a wreath?"

"To-morrow, to-morrow, my child," replied Dorothea. "Now, go to rest; it is already very late."

"Only let me stay till Antonius and Jethro come back," begged the girl.

"I would willingly help you to find your son," said Hermas, "and if you wish I will go to Raithu and Klysma, and inquire among the fishermen. Had the centurion"—and as he spoke the young soldier looked down in some embarrassment, "had the centurion found his fugitive wife of whom he was in pursuit with Talib, the Amalekite, before he died?"

"Sirona has not yet reappeared," replied Petrus, "and perhaps—but just now you mentioned the name of Paulus, who was so dear to you and your father. Do you know that it was he who so shamelessly ruined the domestic peace of the centurion?"

"Paulus!" cried Hermas. "How can you believe it?"

"Phœbicius found his sheep-skin in his wife's room," replied Petrus, gravely. "And the impudent Alexandrian recognized it as his own before us all and allowed the Gaul to punish him. He committed the disgraceful deed the very evening that you were sent off to gain intelligence."

"And Phœbicius flogged him?" cried Hermas, beside himself. "And the poor fellow bore this disgrace and your blame, and all—all for my sake. Now I understand what he meant! I met him after the battle, and he told me that my father was dead. When he parted from me he said he was of all sinners the greatest, and that I should hear it said down in the oasis. But I know better; he is great-hearted and good, and I will not bear that he should be disgraced and slandered for my sake." Hermas had sprung up with these words, and as he met the astonished gaze of his host's he tried to collect himself, and said:

"Paulus never even saw Sirona, and I repeat it, if there is a man who may boast of being good and pure and quite without sin, it is he. For me, and to save me from punishment and my father from sorrow, he owned a sin that he never committed. Such a deed is just like him—the brave, faithful friend! But such shameful suspicion and disgrace shall not weigh upon him a moment longer!"

"You are speaking to an older man," said Petrus, angrily interrupting the youth's vehement speech. "Your friend acknowledged with his own lips—"

"Then he told a lie out of pure goodness," Hermas insisted. "The sheep-skin that the Gaul found was mine. I had gone to Sirona, while her husband was sacrificing to Mithras, to fetch some wine for my father, and she allowed me to try on the centurion's armor; when he unexpectedly returned I leaped out into the street and forgot that luckless sheep-skin. Paulus met me as I fled, and said he would set it all right, and sent me away—to take my place and save my father a great trouble. Look at me as severely as you will, Dorothea, but it was only in thoughtless folly that I slipped into the Gaul's house that evening, and by the memory of my father—of whom Heaven has this day bereft me—I swear that Sirona only amused herself with me as with a boy, a child, and even refused to let me kiss her beautiful golden hair. As surely as I hope to become a warrior, and as surely as my father's spirit hears what I say, the guilt that Paulus took upon himself was never committed at all, and when you condemned Sirona you did an injustice, for she never broke her faith to her husband for me, nor still less for Paulus."

Petrus and Dorothea exchanged a meaning glance, and Dorothea said:

"Why have we to learn all this from the lips of a stranger?

It sounds very extraordinary, and yet how simple! Ay, husband, it would have become us better to guess something of this than to doubt Sirona. From the first it certainly seemed to me impossible that that handsome woman, for whom quite different people had troubled themselves, should err for this queer beggar—"

"What cruel injustice has fallen on the poor man!" cried Petrus. "If he had boasted of some noble deed we should indeed have been less ready to give him credence."

"We are suffering heavy punishment," sighed Dorothea, "and my heart is bleeding. Why did you not come to us, Hermas, if you wanted wine? How much suffering would have been spared if you had!"

The lad looked down, and was silent; but soon he recollected himself, and said, eagerly:

"Let me go and seek the hapless Paulus; I return you thanks for your kindness, but I can not bear to stay here any longer. I must go back to the mountain."

The senator and his wife did not detain him, and when the court-yard gate had closed upon him a great stillness reigned in Petrus's sitting-room. Dorothea leaned far back in her seat and sat looking in her lap while the tears rolled over her cheeks; Marthana held her hand and stroked it, and the senator stepped to the window and sighed deeply as he looked down into the dark court. Sorrow lay on all their hearts like a heavy-laden burden. All was still in the spacious room, only now and then a loud, long-drawn cry of the wailing women rang through the quiet night and reached them through the open window; it was a heavy hour, rich in vain but silent self-accusation, anxiety and short prayers; poor in hope or consolation.

Presently Petrus heaved a deep sigh, and Dorothea rose to go up to him, and to say to him some sincere word of affection; but just then the dogs in the yard barked, and the agonized father said, softly—in deep dejection, and prepared for the worst:

"Most likely it is they."

The deaconess pressed his hand in hers, but drew back when a light tap was heard at the court-yard gate.

"It is not Jethro and Antonius," said Petrus; "they have a key."

Marthana had gone up to him, and she clung to him as he leaned far out of the window and called to whoever it was that had tapped:

"Who is that knocking?"

The dogs barked so loud that neither the senator nor the women were able to hear the answer which seemed to be returned.

"Listen to Argus," said Dorothea; "he never howls like that but when you come home, or one of us, or when he is pleased."

Petrus laid his finger on his lips and sounded a clear, shrill whistle, and as the dogs, obedient to this signal, were silent, he once more called out:

"Whoever you may be, say plainly who you are, that I may open the gate."

They were kept waiting some few minutes for the answer, and the senator was on the point of repeating his inquiry, when a gentle voice timidly came from the gate to the window, saying:

"It is I, Petrus, the fugitive Sirona." Hardly had the words tremulously pierced the silence, when Marthana broke from her father, whose hand was resting on her shoulder, and flew out of the door, down the steps, and out to the gate.

"Sirona; poor, dear Sirona," cried the girl as she pushed back the bolt; as soon as she had opened the door and Sirona had entered the court, she threw herself on her neck, and kissed and stroked her as if she were her long-lost sister found again; then, without allowing her to speak, she seized her hand and drew her—in spite of the slight resistance she offered—with many affectionate exclamations up the steps and into the sitting-room. Petrus and Dorothea met her on the threshold, and the latter pressed her to her heart, kissed her forehead, and said, "Poor woman; we know now that we have done you an injustice, and will try to make it good." The senator, too, went up to her, took her hand and added his greetings to those of his wife, for he knew not whether she had as yet heard of her husband's end.

Sirona could not find a word in reply. She had expected to be expelled as a castaway when she came down the mountain, losing her way in the darkness. Her sandals were cut by the sharp rocks, and hung in strips to her bleeding feet, her beautiful hair was tumbled by the night wind, and her white robe looked like a ragged beggar's garment, for she had torn it to make bandages for Polykarp's wound.

Some hours had already passed since she had left her patient —her heart full of dread for him and of anxiety as to the hard reception she might meet with from his parents.

How her hand shook with fear of Petrus and Dorothea as she raised the brazen knocker of the senator's door, and now—

a father, a mother, a sister opened their arms to her, and an affectionate home smiled upon her. Her heart and soul overflowed with boundless emotion and unlimited thankfulness, and weeping loudly, she pressed her clasped hands to her breast.

But she spared only a few moments for the enjoyment of these feelings of delight, for there was no happiness for her without Polykarp, and it was for his sake that she had undertaken this perilous night journey. Marthana had tenderly approached her, but she gently put her aside, saying: "Not just now, dear girl. I have already wasted an hour, for I lost my way in the ravines. Get ready, Petrus, to come back to the mountain with me at once, for—but do not be startled, Dorothea; Paulus says that the worst danger is over, and if Polykarp—"

"For God's sake, do you know where he is?" cried Dorothea, and her cheeks crimsoned, while Petrus turned pale and, interrupting her, asked, in breathless anxiety:

"Where is Polykarp, and what has happened to him?"

"Prepare yourself to hear bad news," said Sirona, looking at the pair with mournful anxiety, as if to crave their pardon for the evil tidings she was obliged to bring. "Polykarp had a fall on a sharp stone, and so wounded his head. Paulus brought him to me this morning before he set out against the Blemmyes, that I might nurse him. I have incessantly cooled his wound, and toward midday he opened his eyes and knew me again, and said you would be anxious about him. After sundown he went to sleep, but he is not wholly free from fever, and as soon as Paulus came in I set out to quiet your anxiety and to entreat you to give me a cooling potion, that I may return to him with it at once." The deepest sorrow sounded in Sirona's accents as she told her story, and tears had started to her eyes as she related to the parents what had befallen their son. Petrus and Dorothea listened as to a singer, who, dressed indeed in robes of mourning, nevertheless sings a lay of return and hope to a harp wreathed with flowers.

"Quick, quick, Marthana!" cried Dorothea, eagerly, and with sparkling eyes, before Sirona had ended. "Quick! the basket with the bandages. I will mix the fever-draught myself." Petrus went up to the Gaulish woman.

"It is really no worse than you represent?" he asked, in a low voice. "He is alive? and Paulus—"

"Paulus says," interrupted Sirona, "that with good nursing the sick man will be well in a few weeks."

"And you can lead me to him?"

"I—oh, alas! alas!" Sirona cried, striking her hand against her forehead. "I shall never succeed in finding my way back, for I noticed no way-marks! But stay— Before us a penitent from Memphis, who has been dead a few weeks—"

"Old Serapion?" asked Petrus.

"That was his name," exclaimed Sirona. "Do you know his cave?"

"How should I?" replied Petrus. "But perhaps Agapitus—"

"The spring where I got the water to cool Polykarp's wound—Paulus calls it the partridge's spring."

"The partridge's spring," repeated the senator, "I know that." With a deep sigh he took his staff, and called to Dorothea:

"Do you prepare the draught, the bandages, torches, and your good litter, while I knock at our neighbor Magadon's door, and ask him to lend us slaves."

"Let me go with you," said Marthana.

"No, no; you stay here with your mother."

"And do you think that I can wait here?" asked Dorothea, "I am going with you."

"There is much here for you to do," replied Petrus, evasively, "and we must climb the hill quickly."

"I should certainly delay you," sighed the mother; "but take the girl with you; she has a light and lucky hand."

"If you think it best," said the senator, and he left the room.

While the mother and daughter prepared everything for the night expedition, and came and went, they found time to put many questions and say many affectionate words to Sirona. Marthana, even without interrupting her work, set food and drink for the weary woman on the table by which she had sunk on a seat; but she hardly moistened her lips.

When the young girl showed her the basket that she had filled with medicine and linen bandages, with wine and pure water, Sirona said: "Now lend me a pair of your strongest sandals, for mine are all torn, and I can not follow the men without shoes, for the stones are sharp and cut into the flesh."

Marthana now perceived for the first time the blood on her friend's feet; she quickly took the lamp from the table and placed it on the pavement, exclaiming, as she knelt down in front of Sirona and took her slender white feet in her hand to look at the wounds on her soles:

"Good heavens! here are three deep cuts!"

In a moment she had a basin at hand, and was carefully

bathing the wounds in Sirona's feet; while she was wrapping the injured foot in strips of linen Dorothea came up to them.

"I would," she said, "that Polykarp were only here now; this roll would suffice to bind you both." A faint flush overspread Sirona's cheeks, but Dorothea was suddenly conscious of what she had said, and Marthana gently pressed her friend's hand.

When the bandage was securely fixed Sirona attempted to walk, but she succeeded so badly that Petrus, who now came back with his friend Magadon and his sons and several slaves, found it necessary to strictly forbid her to accompany them. He felt sure of finding his son without her, for one of Magadon's people had often carried bread and oil to old Serapion, and knew his cave.

Before the senator and his daughter left the room he whispered a few words to his wife, and together they went up to Sirona.

"Do you know," he asked, "what has happened to your husband?"

Sirona nodded. "I heard it from Paulus," she answered. "Now I am quite alone in the world."

"Not so," replied Petrus. "You will find shelter and love under our roof as if it were your father's, so long as it suits you to stay with us. You need not thank us—we are deeply in your debt. Farewell till we meet again, wife. I would Polykarp were safe here, and that you had seen his wound. Come, Marthana, the minutes are precious."

When Dorothea and Sirona were alone the deaconess said: "Now I will go and make up a bed for you, for you must be very tired."

"No, no!" begged Sirona. "I will wait and watch with you, for I certainly could not sleep till I know how it is with him." She spoke so warmly and eagerly that the deaconess gratefully offered her hand to her young friend. Then she said:

"I will leave you alone for a few minutes, for my heart is so full of anxiety that I must needs go and pray for help for him, and for courage and strength for myself."

"Take me with you," entreated Sirona in a low tone. "In my need I opened my heart to your good and loving God, and I will never more pray to any other. The mere thought of Him strengthened and comforted me, and now, if ever, in this hour I need His merciful support."

"My child, my daughter!" cried the deaconess, deeply

moved. She bent over Sirona, kissed her forehead and her lips, and led her by the hand into her quiet sleeping-room. "This is the place where I most love to pray," she said, "although there is here no image and no altar. My God is everywhere present and in every place I can find Him." The two women knelt down side by side, and both besought the same God for the same mercies—not for themselves, but for another; and both in their sorrow could give thanks— Sirona, because in Dorothea she had found a. mother, and Dorothea, because in Sirona she had found a dear and loving daughter.

CHAPTER XI.

PAULUS was sitting in front of the cave that had sheltered Polykarp and Sirona, and he watched the torches whose light lessened as the bearers went further and further toward the valley. They lighted the way for the wounded sculptor, who was being borne home to the oasis, lying in his mother's easy litter, and accompanied by his father and his sister.

"Yet an hour," thought the anchorite, "and his mother will have her son again, yet a week and Polykarp will rise from his bed, yet a year and he will remember nothing of yesterday but a scar—and perhaps a kiss that he pressed on the Gaulish woman's rosy lips. I shall find it harder to forget. The ladder which for so many years I had labored to construct, on which I had thought to scale heaven, and which looked to me so lofty and so safe, there it lies broken to pieces, and the hand that struck it down was my own weakness. It would almost seem as if this weakness of mine had more power than what we call moral strength, for that which it took the one years to build up, was wrecked by the other in a moment. In weakness only am I a giant."

Paulus shivered at these words, for he was cold. Early in that morning when he had taken upon himself Hermas's guilt he had abjured wearing his sheep-skin; now his body, accustomed to the warm wrap, suffered severely, and his blood coursed with fevered haste through his veins since the efforts, night-watches, and excitement of the last few days. He drew his little coat close round him with a shiver, and muttered: "I feel like a sheep that has been shorn in midwinter, and my head burns as if I were a baker and had to draw the bread out of the oven; a child might knock me down, and my eyes are heavy. I have not even the energy to collect my thoughts for a prayer, of which I am in such sore need. My goal is undoubtedly the right one, but so soon as I seem to be nearing it, my weakness snatches it from me, as the wind swept back the fruit-laden boughs which Tantalus, parched with thirst, tried to grasp. I fled from the world to this mountain, and the world has pursued me and has flung its snares round my feet. I must seek a lonelier waste in which I may be alone—quite alone with my God and myself. There, perhaps, I may find the way I seek, if indeed the fact that the creature that I call 'I,' in which the whole world with all its agitations in little finds room—and which will accompany me even there—does not once again frustrate all my labor. He who takes his Self with him into the desert is not alone."

Paulus sighed deeply, and then pursued his reflections: "How puffed up with pride I was after I had tasted the Gaul's rods in place of Hermas, and then I was like a drunken man who falls down-stairs step by step. And poor Stephanus, too, had a fall when he was so near the goal! He failed in strength to forgive, and the senator who has just now left me, and whose innocent son I had so badly hurt, when we parted forgivingly gave me his hand. I could see that he did forgive me with all his heart, and this Petrus stands in the midst of life, and is busy early and late with mere worldly affairs."

For a time he looked thoughtfully before him, and then he went on in his soliloquy: "What was the story that old Serapion used to tell? In the Thebaid there dwelt a penitent who thought he led a perfectly saintly life and far transcended all his companions in stern virtue. Once he dreamed that there was in Alexandria a man even more perfect than himself; Phabias was his name, and he was a shoe-maker, dwelling in the White Road near the harbor of Kibotos. The anchorite at once went to the capital and found the shoe-maker, and when he asked him: 'How do you serve the Lord? How do you conduct your life?' Phabis looked at him in astonishment. 'I serve my Saviour well! I work early and late, and provide for my family, and pray morning and evening in few words for the whole city.' Petrus, it seems to me, is such a one as Phabis; but many roads lead to God, and we—and I—"

Again a cold shiver interrupted his meditation, and as morning approached the cold was so keen that he endeavored to light a fire. While he was painfully blowing the charcoal Hermas came up to him.

He had learned from Polykarp's escort where Paulus was to be found, and as he stood opposite his friend he grasped his hand, stroked his rough hair, and thanked him with deep and tender emotion for the great sacrifice he had made for him when he had taken upon himself the dishonoring punishment of his fault.

Paulus declined all pity or thanks, and spoke to Hermas of his father and of his future, until it was light, and the young man prepared to go down to the oasis to pay the last honors to the dead. To his entreaty that he would accompany him, Paulus only answered:

"No—no; not now, not now; for if I were to mix with men now I should fly asunder like a rotten wine-skin full of fermenting wine; a swarm of bees is buzzing in my head, and an ant-hill is growing in my bosom. Go now and leave me alone."

After the funeral ceremony Hermas took an affectionate leave of Agapitus, Petrus, and Dorothea, and then returned to the Alexandrian, with whom he went to the cave where he had so long lived with his dead father.

There Paulus delivered to him his father's letter to his uncle, and spoke to him more lovingly than he had ever done before. At night they both lay down on their beds, but neither of them found rest or sleep.

From time to time Paulus murmured, in a low voice, but in tones of keen anguish: "In vain—all in vain!" and again, "I seek, I seek—but who can show me the way?"

They both rose before day-break; Hermas went once more down to the well, knelt down near it, and felt as though he were bidding farewell to his father and Miriam.

Memories of every kind rose up in his soul, and so mighty is the glorifying power of love that the miserable, brown-skinned shepherdess Miriam seemed to him a thousand-fold more beautiful than that splendid woman who filled the soul of a great artist with delight.

Shortly after sunrise Paulus conducted him to the fishing-port and to the Israelite friend who managed the business of his father's house; he caused him to be bountifully supplied with gold and accompanied him to the ship laden with charcoal that was to convey him to Klysma.

The parting was very painful to him, and when Hermas saw his eyes full of tears and felt his hands tremble, he said: "Do not be troubled about me, Paulus; we shall meet again, and I will never forget you and my father."

"And your mother," added the anchorite. "I shall miss you sorely, but trouble is the very thing I look for. He who succeeds in making the sorrows of the whole world his own—he whose soul is touched by a sorrow at every breath he draws—he indeed must long for the call of the Redeemer."

Hermas fell weeping on his neck, and started to feel how burning the anchorite's lips were as he pressed them to his forehead.

At last the sailors drew in the ropes; Paulus turned once more to the youth. "You are going your own way now," he said. "Do not forget the Holy Mountain, and hear this: Of all sins three are most deadly: To serve false gods, to covet your neighbor's wife, and to raise your hands to kill; keep yourself from them. And of all virtues twó are the least conspicuous, and at the same time the greatest: Truthfulness and humility; practice these. Of all consolations these two are the best: The consciousness of wishing the right, however much we may err and stumble through human weakness, and prayer."

Once more he embraced the departing youth, then he went across the sand of the shore back to the mountain without looking round.

Hermas looked after him for a long time, greatly distressed, for his strong friend tottered like a drunken man and often pressed his hand to his head, which was no doubt as burning as his lips.

The young warrior never again saw the Holy Mountain or Paulus, but after he himself had won fame and distinction in the army he met again with Petrus's son, Polykarp, whom the emperor had sent for to Byzantium with great honor, and in whose house the Gaulish woman Sirona presided as a true and loving wife and mother.

After his parting from Hermas Paulus disappeared. The other anchorites long sought him in vain, as well as Bishop Agapitus, who had learned from Petrus that the Alexandrian had been punished and expelled in innocence, and who desired to offer him pardon and consolation in his own person. At last, ten days after, Orion the Saite found him in a remote cave. The Angel of Death had called him only a few hours before while in the act of prayer, for he was scarcely cold. He was kneeling with his forehead against the rocky wall, and his emaciated hands were closely clasped over Magdalen's ring. When his companions had laid him on his bier his noble, gentle features wore a pure and transfiguring smile.

The news of his death flew with wonderful rapidity through the oasis and the fishing town, and far and wide to the caves of the anchorites, and even to the huts of the Amalekite shepherds. The procession that followed him to his last resting-place stretched to an invisible distance; in front of all walked

Agapitus with the elders and deacons, and behind them Petrus with his wife and family, to which Sirona now belonged. Polykarp, who was now recovering, laid a palm-branch in token of reconcilement on his grave, which was visited as a sacred spot by the many whose needs he had alleviated in secret, and before long by all the penitents from far and wide.

Petrus erected a monument over his grave, on which Polykarp incised the words which Paulus's trembling fingers had traced just before his death with a piece of charcoal on the wall of his cave:

" Pray for me, a miserable man—for I was a man."

THE END.

MUNRO'S PUBLICATIONS.

The Seaside Library---Pocket Edition.

Always Unchanged and Unabridged.

WITH HANDSOME LITHOGRAPHED PAPER COVER.

Persons who wish to purchase the following works in a complete and unabridged form are cautioned to order and see that they get THE SEASIDE LIBRARY, POCKET EDITION, as works published in other libraries are frequently abridged and incomplete. Every number of THE SEASIDE LIBRARY is

ALWAYS UNCHANGED AND UNABRIDGED.

Newsdealers wishing catalogues of THE SEASIDE LIBRARY, Pocket Edition, bearing their imprint, will be supplied on sending their names addresses, and number required.

The works in THE SEASIDE LIBRARY, Pocket Edition, are printed from larger type and on better paper than any other series published.

The following works are for sale by all newsdealers, or will be sent to any address, postage free, on receipt of price, by the publisher.

GEORGE MUNRO, Munro's Publishing House,
(P. O. Box 3751.)   17 to 27 Vandewater Street, New York.

LIST OF AUTHORS.

[When ordering by mail please order by numbers.]

Robert Louis Stevenson's Works.

Julian Sturgis's Works.

Eugene Sue's Works.

George Temple's Works.

William M. Thackeray's Works.

Works by the Author of "The Two Miss Flemings."

Annie Thomas's Works.

Bertha Thomas's Works.

Count Lyof Tolstoi's Works.

Anthony Trollope's Works.

Margaret Veley's Works.

Jules Verne's Works.

L. B. Walford's Works.

F. Warden's Works.

William Ware's Works.

Persons who wish to purchase the foregoing works in a complete and unabridged form are cautioned to order and see that they get THE SEASIDE LIBRARY, Pocket Edition, as works published in other libraries are frequently abridged and incomplete. Every number of THE SEASIDE LIBRARY is

ALWAYS UNCHANGED AND UNABRIDGED.

Newsdealers wishing catalogues of THE SEASIDE LIBRARY, Pocket Edition, bearing their imprint, will be supplied on sending their names, addresses, and number required.

The works in THE SEASIDE LIBRARY, Pocket Edition, are printed from larger type and on better paper than any other series published.

The foregoing works are for sale by all newsdealers, or will be sent to any address, postage free, on receipt of price, by the publisher. Address

GEORGE MUNRO, MUNRO'S PUBLISHING HOUSE,

P. O. Box 3751.   17 to 27 Vandewater Street, N. Y.

[*When ordering by mail please order by numbers.*]

The New York Fashion Bazar Book of the Toilet.

PRICE 25 CENTS.

This is a little book which we can recommend to every lady for the Preservation and Increase of Health and Beauty. It contains full directions for all the arts and mysteries of personal decoration, and for increasing the natural graces of form and expression. All the little affections of the skin, hair, eyes and body, that detract from appearance and happiness, are made the subjects of precise and excellent recipes. Ladies are instructed how to reduce their weight without injury to health and without producing pallor and weakness. Nothing necessary to a complete toilet book of recipes and valuable advice and information has been overlooked in the compilation of this volume.

For sale by all newsdealers, or sent by mail to any address, postage prepaid, on receipt of price, 25 cents, by the publisher. Address

GEORGE MUNRO, MUNRO'S PUBLISHING HOUSE,

(P. O. Box 3751.)   17 to 27 Vandewater Street. New York.

Old Sleuth Library.

A Series of the Most Thrilling Detective Stories Ever Published!

ISSUED QUARTERLY.

The above books are for sale by all newsdealers, or will be sent to any address, postage prepaid, on receipt of the price, 10 cents each. Address

GEORGE MUNRO, Munro's Publishing House,

(P. O. Box 3751.)   17 to 27 Vandewater Street, New York.

The New York Fashion Bazar Book of Etiquette.

PRICE 25 CENTS.

A Guide to Good Manners and the Ways to Fashionable Society.

A COMPLETE HAND-BOOK OF BEHAVIOR

CONTAINING

All the Polite Observances of Modern Life, the Etiquette of Engagements and Marriages; the Manners and Training of Children; the Arts of Conversation and Polite Letter-writing; Invitations to Dinners, Evening Parties and Entertainments of all Descriptions; Table Manners, Etiquette of Visits and Public Places; How to Serve Breakfasts, Luncheons, Dinners and Teas; How to Dress, Travel, Shop, and Behave at Hotels and Watering-places.

This Book contains all that a lady and gentleman requires for correct behavior on all social occasions.

For sale by all newsdealers, or sent to any address on receipt of 25 cents, postage prepaid, by the publisher. Address

GEORGE MUNRO,
MUNRO'S PUBLISHING HOUSE,
P. O. Box 3751. 17 to 27 Vandewater Street, New York.

Now Ready—Beautifully Bound in Cloth—Price 50 Cents.

A NEW PEOPLE'S EDITION OF THAT MOST DELIGHTFUL OF CHILDREN'S STORIES,

ALICE'S ADVENTURES IN WONDERLAND.

By LEWIS CARROLL,
Author of "Through the Looking-Glass."

With Forty-two Beautiful Illustrations by John Tenniel.

The most delicious and taking nonsense for children ever written. A book to be read by all mothers to their little ones. It makes them dance with delight. Everybody enjoys the fun of this charming writer for the nursery.

THIS NEW PEOPLE'S EDITION, BOUND IN CLOTH, PRICE 50 CENTS. IS PRINTED IN LARGE, HANDSOME, READABLE TYPE, WITH ALL THE ORIGINAL ILLUSTRATIONS OF THE EXPENSIVE ENGLISH EDITION.

Sent by Mail on Receipt of 50 Cents.

Address GEORGE MUNRO, Munro's Publishing House,
P. O. Box 3751. 17 to 27 Vandewater Street, New York.

The Philosophy of Whist.

*AN ESSAY ON THE SCIENTIFIC AND INTELLECTUAL
ASPECTS OF THE MODERN GAME.*

IN TWO PARTS.

PART I.—THE PHILOSOPHY OF WHIST PLAY.
PART II.—THE PHILOSOPHY OF WHIST PROBABILITIES.

By *WILLIAM POLE,*

Mus. Doc. Oxon.

FELLOW OF THE ROYAL SOCIETIES OF LONDON AND EDINBURGH;
ONE OF THE EXAMINERS IN THE UNIVERSITY OF LONDON;
KNIGHT OF THE JAPANESE IMPERIAL ORDER OF THE RISING SUN.

Complete in Seaside Library (Pocket Edition), No. 669.

PRINTED IN LARGE, BOLD, HANDSOME TYPE.

PRICE 20 CENTS.

For sale by all newsdealers, or sent to any address, postage prepaid, on
receipt of the price, 20 cents. Address

GEORGE MUNRO, MUNRO'S PUBLISHING HOUSE,

P. O. Box 3751.   17 to 27 Vandewater Street, New York.

Munro's Dialogues and Speakers.

PRICE 10 CENTS EACH.

These books embrace a series of Dialogues and Speeches, all new and
original, and are just what is needed to give spice and merriment to Social
Parties, Home Entertainments, Debating Societies, School Recitations, Ama-
teur Theatricals, etc. They contain Irish, German, Negro, Yankee, and, in
fact, all kinds of Dialogues and Speeches. The following are the titles of the
books:

No. 1. The Funny Fellow's Dialogues.
No. 2. The Clemence and Donkey Dialogues.
No. 3. Mrs. Smith's Boarders' Dialogues.
No. 4. Schoolboys' Comic Dialogues.

No. 1. Vot I Know 'Bout Gruel Societies Speaker.
No. 2. The John B. Go-off Comic Speaker.
No. 3. My Boy Vilhelm's Speaker.

The above titles express, in a slight degree, the contents of the books,
which are conceded to be the best series of mirth-provoking Speeches and
Dialogues extant. Price 10 cents each. Address

GEORGE MUNRO, MUNRO'S PUBLISHING HOUSE,

P. O. Box 3751.   17 to 27 Vandewater Street, New York.

He wont be
happy
till he
gets it!